SENSUAL SURRENDER

When the kiss came, it wasn't mouth to mouth, but mouth to fingertips. Fitch kissed each and every one. "What other secrets are you hiding from me?"

Before she could answer, he lowered his head and kissed her for real, letting his tongue ease teasingly over her lips before dipping inside to taste her.

The kiss was so exquisitely beautiful it brought tears to Hilary's eyes. Her senses were thrilled with the pleasure of it, her thoughts inflamed by the blatant sensuality that came so naturally to this man. He wasn't shy about the claim he was staking, but then she hadn't expected him to be.

With a sigh of pure pleasure, Hilary relinquished herself into his care. The fear of surrendering to her own emotions, of surrendering to him, vanished as pleasure coursed through her veins. His strength folded around her as he pulled her onto his lap and against his chest. . . .

BOOK YOUR PLACE ON OUR WEBSITE
AND MAKE THE
READING CONNECTION!

We've created a customized website just for our very special readers, where you can get the inside scoop on everything that's going on with Zebra, Pinnacle and Kensington books.

When you come online, you'll have the exciting opportunity to:

- View covers of upcoming books
- Read sample chapters
- Learn about our future publishing schedule (listed by publication month *and author*)
- Find out when your favorite authors will be visiting a city near you
- Search for and order backlist books from our online catalog
- Check out author bios and background information
- Send e-mail to your favorite authors
- Meet the Kensington staff online
- Join us in weekly chats with authors, readers and other guests
- Get writing guidelines
- AND MUCH MORE!

Visit our website at
http://www.kensingtonbooks.com

HE SAID NOW

Patricia Waddell

ZEBRA BOOKS
KENSINGTON PUBLISHING CORP.
http://www.kensingtonbooks.com

ZEBRA BOOKS are published by

Kensington Publishing Corp.
850 Third Avenue
New York, NY 10022

All Kensington titles, imprints and distributed lines are available at special quantity discounts for bulk purchases for sales promotion, premiums, fund-raising, educational or institutional use.

Special book excerpts or customized printings can also be created to fit specific needs. For details, write or phone the office of the Kensington Special Sales Manager: Kensington Publishing Corp., 850 Third Avenue, New York, NY 10022. Attn. Special Sales Department. Phone: 1-800-221-2647.

First Printing: June 2004
10 9 8 7 6 5 4 3 2 1

Printed in the United States of America

*This book is dedicated to
Marianne and Frances:*

*Booksellers with a
flair for titles.*

Thank you.

Cannon to right of them,
Cannon to left of them,
Cannon behind them
Volley'd and thunder'd;
Storm'd at with shot and shell,
While horse and hero fell,
They that had fought so well
Came thro' the jaws of Death,
Back from the mouth of hell,
All that was left of them,
Left of six hundred.

—"The Charge of the Light Brigade"
Alfred, Lord Tennyson

One

William Fitch Minstead, the sixth Earl of Acker-man, assumed it was going to be an evening like most evenings. Then again, assumptions could often lead people astray.

He was in his library working when his concentration was disrupted by a female voice. His was a bachelor's residence. There were no females under his roof, or at least there shouldn't be.

Fitch left the library to stride purposefully into the foyer. Noticing the fixed smile on the face of his butler, he quickly deduced that Raskett was being poisonously polite to whomever had come calling at such a late hour.

"Please inform his lordship that it is of the utmost importance," the female said.

"Who is it?" Fitch asked. A storm was sweeping over the city. It was not the sort of evening for a woman—any woman—to be making calls.

"A young lady, milord," Raskett answered in the

stiff voice English butlers reserved for just such occasions. "A most persistent young miss who refuses to leave her card."

"It is news I wish to deliver, my good man, not a worthless scrap of paper."

Amused by the exchange, Fitch instructed Raskett to give the lady entry.

The door was opened, allowing both a spray of cold rain and the unexpected visitor to cross the threshold. A dark cloak hid the woman from Fitch's immediate appraisal. Once the hood was lowered, he was greeted by the sight of brown curls framing an ingenuous face. Gold-rimmed glasses magnified a pair of modest brown eyes. It wasn't an unpleasant face, nor was it one he had seen before.

"How may I be of service, Miss . . ."

"Miss Compton," she informed him in a precise tone. "Miss Hilary Compton of Nottinghamshire."

"You mentioned a matter of some importance."

"Yes, my lord. The utmost importance."

When Miss Compton's cloak was handed off, Fitch studied the rest of her. Slightly built, she was wearing a dark blue dress. It wasn't an expensive garment, but it was well-fitted and well-stitched, with a pleated bodice and high collar. A country lass, by her looks and stiff fashion.

The lady chose that moment to cast an implicit glance at his butler, signaling that whatever news she had come to announce was best delivered in private.

"Raskett, refreshments in the library, if you please," Fitch said. "This way, Miss Compton."

The library was the center of most bachelor residences, and the earl's library was no exception. It was a very masculine room with dark green carpet and draperies. The chairs were upholstered in

Spanish leather, worn shiny by years of use. A black horsehair sofa faced the hearth, bookended by matching giltwood tables with blue-veined marble tops. The most impressive piece of furniture was an elaborate marquetry buffet that served as a liquor cabinet.

Once they were seated, Fitch behind his desk and Miss Compton in a comfortable chair facing him, the lady wasted no time in getting to the heart of the matter.

"Forgive me for calling so late, my lord, but necessity demanded that I see you tonight."

Fitch studied her for a moment. There was no coyness in her gaze, no shadow of deception about her features. She didn't possess the frailty of the stylish young ladies he normally encountered in London, nor did she appear lacking in self-confidence. It took all of ten seconds for him to ascertain that his visitor was as pure as freshly fallen snow, and even less time to decide she was trouble.

"Whatever your business, it must be important, Miss Compton. Wretched night."

"Yes, well, the weather is often disagreeable at the most importunate times. But rain or no rain, I felt compelled to keep my promise."

"And what promise might that be?"

She pinned him with a pensive gaze, followed by a faint coloring of her cheeks. A quick exhale of breath, and the news was delivered. "I regret there can be little delicacy in a matter such as this, my lord. That being the case, I shall be forthright in telling you that you are a father."

Few things ever shook Fitch's composure, but Hilary Compton's announcement did just that. He met her gaze, his face surprisingly passive, but only for an instant. "I beg your pardon?"

"You have a daughter, my lord. An adorable little girl by the name of Lizzie. You would have known her mother as Elizabeth Bradstreet. Beth."

A memory flashed through Fitch's mind—Beth lying naked in the middle of the bed, her eyes alight with passion, her laughter filling the room.

Yes, he remembered Beth.

The daughter of a merchant, she'd been sweet and soft and full of life, all the things the misery in the Crimean had stolen from him. Their affair had been brief, but passionate, so it was possible that he had sired her child. Possible, but not very likely. He was a careful man, especially when it came to women.

"Beth told you that I'm the father?"

"Yes."

"Yet she felt no obligation to notify me of the pregnancy, or the resulting child."

"Beth was proud. You will note that I use the past tense in referring to her, my lord. I regret that I must also inform you that she is dead. Lung fever. Some five months now. She refused to tell anyone the name of the man who had fathered her child. Yours was divulged to me only when she felt the certainty of death upon her."

Fitch wasn't unmoved by the announcement of a child, or Beth Bradstreet's death; he simply didn't know how to respond to it at this particular moment. "What of her family?"

Miss Compton sat primly still in the chair, her hands folded in her lap, her gaze unwavering. Her demeanor suggested not impatience but a composed excitement that aroused Fitch's curiosity. It was a moment before she answered him.

"As expected, Beth's family disowned her. Not

sharing her family's piety, my aunt and I gave her sanctuary."

"When was this? I haven't been in Nottingham since before the war. I assume the child is of the right age for you to believe that Beth was telling the truth."

"Lizzie celebrated her ninth birthday four months ago."

Fitch took a moment to calculate the time frame. The war had begun in March of 1854. His regiment had not received orders until the fall of the same year, when it was decided the Russian naval base at Sevastopol was a direct threat to the future security of the region. He had been in Nottingham prior to leaving for the Crimean Peninsula, and he had spent several nights in Beth Bradstreet's bed.

"I'll concede that the child is the right age," he said. "But that, and my coincidental presence in Nottingham, does not confirm my parentage."

It was a reasonably tactful way to imply that he had not been Beth's only bed partner. Fitch assumed Miss Compton would understand what he meant.

She did. Her shoulders squared even more, if such a thing were possible. The gaze she set upon him was filled with righteous indignation. "Beth may not have been the virtuous daughter her family hoped for, but she was not given to falsehoods. Lizzie is your daughter."

Looking all the world like a kitten trying to be a lioness, Fitch found Miss Compton momentarily enchanting. The merest flicker of emotion crossed his face before it was mastered, then concealed.

"I admire your loyalty, Miss Compton, but admittedly, the circumstances do allow for some misgivings."

That said, Fitch moved from his desk to the window, where he stood contemplating the news that had swept into his life along with the storm.

Beyond the glass, the weather was unforgiving, as if God were striking back at the injustices of the world. But Fitch knew God had little to do with anything, but the storm. The inequalities of a man's life couldn't be laid at God's feet. They were his, and his alone.

He had been twenty-three at Balaclava. Not a child, but a young man who had thought himself ready for war. But no one had been prepared for the carnage of the Crimea.

No one.

Least of all a university-educated, second son.

He'd been a brash young man, cocky at times, who had thought himself capable of achieving great things.

Hero, indeed.

If only people knew.

One good thing had come from his suffering in the war: he had learned his limitations. It had been a humbling experience, but a beneficial one. He had also learned to bury his emotions. And bury them deep. It was only on nights like this, nights filled with thunder and lightning, that the nightmares revisited him, and only then if he was sober enough to grant them entry.

After the war, he had sold his commission and returned to England, hoping to take up life on one of his family's many estates, but fate had had other plans. His older brother had taken ill and died.

It was several days after his brother's funeral when the full weight of the situation hit him. There were those who would say that fate had played him a favorable hand, but Fitch had felt only the loneliness of being the last of his family.

Now, as the Earl of Ackerman, his life consisted of duties and obligations, and an impending sense of doom that he may never be able to escape the past.

With a deep sigh, he turned from the window to find Miss Compton staring at him. Her gaze flashed for a moment, as if something within her had quickened.

"I regret that I couldn't persuade Beth to tell you about Lizzie sooner, my lord. I did try." Her voice was pitched low, but the words were sincere.

Fitch wasn't sure how to respond. If Beth had written to him, would he have returned from the war and taken her as his wife? Perhaps. Then again, perhaps not.

The double doors solemnly opened and Raskett entered to serve the requested refreshments. While his guest was adding cream to her tea, Fitch helped himself to a stiff drink.

"Why now?" he asked, still unsure if he had fathered the child. Beth hadn't been a virgin, nor had he seduced her. They had met by chance and become lovers by choice.

"Beth and I were playmates as children. When it became apparent that her family could find no forgiveness in their hearts, she came to me. Lizzie was born several months later."

"You mentioned an aunt."

"Yes. Sadly it is my aunt's death that has brought me to London. I met with her solicitor only this morning."

"You have my sympathies."

"Thank you, my lord. However, I should tell you that I am not here to petition either funds or sympathy. I am more than willing to raise Lizzie as my own. In fact, I would relish the task. She has earned a place in my heart. My inheritance, while modest compared to your wealth, will allow me to provide her with a comfortable life."

Returning to his desk, Fitch flipped back the top of the humidor and reached for a cheroot. Etiquette demanded that he ask a lady's permission before smoking in her presence. "May I?"

"It's your library," came the dry reply.

Fitch suppressed the urge to laugh. The lady definitely had a way with words. He thought about putting the slender cigar aside, then decided she was right. It was his library, just as it was his life that was being tossed about by the news of a child.

He took his time in clipping and lighting the cigar. Only when a small ring of smoke was curling toward the ceiling did he look at her and say, "Raising a child alone is a formidable duty, Miss Compton."

"Beth entrusted Lizzie's care into my hands. I would be remiss if I did not fulfill that responsibility."

Fitch showed no reaction. Miss Hilary Compton was as irritating as she was unexpected. She was also intelligent. It showed in her spectacle-shielded eyes. The fact that she was still unmarried gave way to the suspicion that she was strongly independent, a woman capable of making her way in the world without a man's assistance.

So why was he suddenly inclined to make the lady realize that having a man in her life could be beneficial?

It was an irrelevant question, considering the business at hand. Still, Fitch found himself as curious about the messenger as he was the message.

"If you want the **child**, why seek me out, Miss Compton? If Beth divulged my name only to you, keeping the information to yourself would guarantee your continued custody."

Her chin went up an inch. Another indication that she was stubborn. "I promised Beth that I would personally tell you of Lizzie's existence, should you be interested."

The delivery of the remark made its intended impact. It was all too clear that Miss Compton considered him the ruination of one Elizabeth Bradstreet, and that she intended to right that wrong by fostering his daughter.

"I am *interested,*" Fitch replied, surprising them both. "Where is the child now?"

"In Nottingham with a trusted servant."

"You are certain that Beth named me as the father?"

"Yes, my lord." She took a moment to smile, although begrudgingly. "Beth said if you had any doubts, all you need do is look at Lizzie's left arm."

"Her left arm?"

"Again, there is little delicacy in the saying of things, my lord. Lizzie bears a birthmark on her left arm, which her mother insisted is an exact replica of one you also carry."

Fitch frowned. He did have a birthmark—on his hip. It was clover-shaped, the size of a small coin. His father had had a similar one on his forearm. If the girl shared the marking, then the odds of her being his daughter increased substantially.

Fitch wasn't an unkind man. *If* the child was his, he would do what was required: an allowance to see to her upbringing, a good education, and, in time, perhaps some recognition that she was a Minstead.

Nothing could erase her illegitimacy. Society had rules, far too many to be circumvented by compassion, but none of those rules prevented him from being an attentive father.

"I will see the child," he announced.

Fitch couldn't tell if Miss Compton was pleasantly surprised that he wanted to see Lizzie, or angry that he hadn't done the expected and denounced the child. Whatever her feelings, her expression was unreadable as she set aside her teacup.

"Before you meet Lizzie, there are some things you need to know," she said. "First of all, she believes herself to be a perfectly normal child, born to loving parents. Beth told Lizzie that her father was a man by the name of George Aimes. They were allegedly married before he was dispatched to the Crimea. Lizzie thinks her father was a war hero."

George Aimes had been a soldier in his regiment. Like Fitch, he had been worried that Her Majesty's "Crossbelt Dragoons" might be left out of the war. But the Eighth Hussars hadn't been neglected. The regiment had charged with the Light Brigade that fateful day and continued the fight until the fall of Sevastopol.

Fitch recalled Beth waltzing with George at several parties. Aimes had been too shy to do more than stumble over his own feet during their dance, then make himself scarce when another regimenteer, Lieutenant Minstead, made his interest in the lady known.

Later, George had stood with valor at Sevastopol. His death, like so many others, would forever haunt Fitch.

"I have contradicted myself," Miss Compton said, breaking into his private thoughts. "Beth did lie.

Once. But only for Lizzie's sake. Regardless of what you may think, she was a good mother."

"I'm sure she was," Fitch replied, knowing most young women would have farmed out the child within days of the birth. Others would have terminated the pregnancy, preferring the risk of abortion to the surety of social shame.

He finished off his drink before speaking again. "I admit both surprise and confusion, Miss Compton. While I can understand Beth telling the child that her father is dead, what reaction did she anticipate from me, other than financial support, which you insist you are not soliciting."

The silence that followed hung so thickly in the room every sound was magnified—the ticking of the ormolu clock on the mantelpiece, the whistle of the wind as it passed over the chimney, the pelting of rain against the windows.

Fitch knew he had the easier of the tasks that evening. He was in his own home; Miss Compton had intruded upon his privacy unannounced. He had merely to listen while she had been assigned with delivering the earth-shattering news.

"I have given the matter serious thought," she finally said. "Donald Bradstreet, Beth's father, is a man of rigid religious beliefs and unbending principles. He will never acknowledge that Lizzie is his granddaughter. Knowing that, I have to assume that Beth wanted to make sure her child would have someone else to turn to should anything happen to me."

It made sense. A child lacking a guardian or family would be placed in an orphanage. The facilities, while supported by charitable contributions, were rarely more than adolescent workhouses.

Fitch looked at his desk. It was stacked with papers and ledgers, a reminder of duties unfulfilled. There were those who saw him as too serious-minded, too absorbed in his estates and financial investments. In Parliament he carried the reputation of one whose energies were limitless if he believed the cause right and just.

"You may expect me in Nottingham by month's end," he said, true to his nature.

His guest showed no emotion, only an expression of suitable gravity, one befitting the circumstances. "Very well, my lord."

Their unorthodox conversation concluded, Fitch escorted her to the front door where Raskett was waiting to see her outside and into a hired hansom.

As the cab pulled away from the curb, Hilary prayed that the earl wouldn't take Lizzie away from her. She couldn't bear the thought of the little girl being shepherded off to some obscure estate to be raised by strangers.

The possibility had seemed unlikely when she'd first arrived at the Eaton Square town house. But now . . . The earl had seemed genuinely touched by the news of Beth's death and the fact that he had a daughter.

In addition to the unsettling thought that she might lose custody of Lizzie, Hilary had to deal with her own feelings—a tingling awareness that lacked immediate identification.

She knew very little about men, having been doorstepped after her parents' death into the care of a maiden aunt. Edwina Hoblyn had believed passionately in the education of women. She hadn't been able to abide the thought of her precious niece wasting her time with anyone not possessed of a scholarly mind.

Privately, Hilary felt a deep satisfaction that she hadn't been raised like other children. Were it not for her aunt's practicality, she might vainly believe that the earl had looked upon her with interest.

"You're brewing a tempest in a teapot," she warned herself aloud, knowing she was reacting from emotion rather than rational judgment. "The last thing you need is a man cluttering up your life."

Always a pragmatist, Hilary knew she was unlikely to receive any such attention from a man. If the occasion should arrive, it would be spawned, not by romance, but by her recent inheritance. A tidy sum, if she did say so herself.

As the hansom rolled along the rain-drenched street, turning south on King's Road, Hilary regarded her current circumstances with confusion, and a growing sense of frustration. Was it so wrong to want to be loved, to have her strengths and frailties known by another human being, and to be cherished in spite of them? To be loved so deeply, so intensely, that life could never be called *normal* again?

As a child she had spent endless hours in the library, lost to tales of adventurous men and women, stories of grand passion and sacrifice. After closing the books, she would stare out the window and dream of having a similar passion invade her own life, of having a man love her.

But she was no longer a child.

The hollow places inside her had been filled with more sensible dreams. She wanted to travel, to see the Nile flowing through the desert, to feel the hot wind caress her skin; she wanted to visit the ancient ruins of Greece, to stand upon the steps of the Parthenon and marvel at the sunset reflected in the balmy waters of the Mediterranean Sea.

Her inheritance put those dreams within reach.

Having Beth entrust Lizzie into her care had fulfilled another dream—motherhood. She could put her maternal instincts to good use without having to endure the confining fences of marriage. She could love a child and be loved in return.

The hansom rolled to a stop in front of her hotel, a modest establishment on Pimlico Road that charged reasonable rates for clean rooms. After paying the driver, Hilary gathered her cloak about her and hurried for the portico of the building. The rain showed no signs of stopping any time soon.

"Miss Compton." The clerk behind the dark oak counter acknowledged her with a smile. "Dreadful night."

"Yes, it is." She took off her cloak and gave it a hard shake, sending a spray of raindrops over the bare wooden floor. "Please see that tea is sent up to my room. And make sure the pot is steaming."

The young man immediately reached for the bell cord and gave it a hard jerk. After three days, he had learned that Miss Compton appreciated sloth even less than she appreciated lukewarm bath water and cold tea.

"Will you be needing anything else, milord?" Raskett asked as he removed the serving tray from the library table.

"No. Nothing," Fitch replied. He was standing by one of the tall, arched windows that overlooked

the street, the work on his desk forgotten. Rain
pattered against the cold glass. The stiletto sound
intensified the uncertainty of his mood. "Miss
Compton came to inform me that I have a child."

Raskett stilled on his way to the door. Tray in
hand, he turned to look at his employer. Having
jointly survived the bloodletting in the Balkans,
neither man stood on formality when they were
alone. "A child, you say?"

"A nine-year-old daughter. You remember Beth
Bradstreet. As I recall, you gave her more than a
cursory glance when we were last in Nottingham."

"The wool merchant's daughter. Aye, I remember."

Fitch told Raskett that Beth had recently died,
leaving her child, his alleged offspring, in the
keeping of Hilary Compton.

"I've decided to see the child," he told Raskett.
"Nothing is happening in Parliament that requires
my vote—Lord Mordaunt's proposal will be debated
long and loud for weeks to come. Time enough to
travel to Nottingham and back again. Make the
necessary arrangements, will you?"

"Yes, milord."

Left alone, Fitch took his brandy and cigar and
settled into his favorite chair. Since leaving the
military, he considered himself a detached, rational observer of life, devoid of the emotionalism
most people used in making decisions.

Tonight was an exception.

His head was spinning with images and thoughts:
the lighthearted Beth with her beautiful eyes and
whimsical smile; a young girl lacking both father
and mother. Then another image—Miss Hilary
Compton, confident and unadorned.

A crack of thunder rumbled over the house, like

the echo of cannon fire across a battlefield. An accompanying pain darkened Fitch's eyes, eyes that mirrored so many memories they overflowed into his sleep, fostering vivid nightmares of a war he was unable to forget.

"Damn storm."

He sat for another half an hour fighting off the fitful memories of pain and loss the storm had triggered, but despite his best efforts a familiar darkness engulfed him. He should be encouraged by the news of a child, someone else to think about, someone around whom he could center his life. A child could be an invigorating force, a reason to look to the future instead of the past, a purpose for a man who had lost his own objectives.

Could the answer be that easy? Could a new comradeship, that of father and daughter, replace the endless emotions that had accompanied him home from the Crimea? Detachment had become a survival instinct, a way to cope with the emotions of others, a way to keep from coping with the riot of emotions within himself.

It was difficult to escape the cocoon, to share the singular hours of a day with someone, and yet he longed to do just that—to open his mind and heart to another person.

As the hours progressed and the whiskey bottle emptied, Fitch once again found his thoughts drifting to the plainspoken Miss Compton. Most would see her as an unappealing spinster with no hope of making an advantageous marriage, but Fitch had seen something else. There had been passion in her eyes, and vehemence in her words. She was clever of mind and witty of tongue, not at all like the fluffy females he'd been forced to endure since gaining a title.

He took a moment to tally her physical attributes: her skin was smooth, her eyes a warm shade of brown. She had a nice mouth and an intriguing little mole just below her right ear. If she freed her hair from that appalling spinster knot and added a few curls, she could be passably pretty.

Fitch sighed. He shouldn't be thinking about the woman. He turned his attention to the hearth and studied the fire as though the battle for Balaclava were being refought by the flickering flames. Near dawn, he decided that instead of looking back over the path he had traveled, he would look to what his life could be from this day forward—to being a father, and, perhaps, if he hadn't lost his mind sometime during the night, a husband.

Two

The residence was built in the Queen Anne fashion with a hodgepodge of gables and turrets. Constructed of red brick with white latticework and a steeply pitched roof, the details were pronounced but delicate. Behind it, surrounded by an ironwork fence, lay a small garden with primrose and blackberry bushes, and beyond that a cluster of apple trees laden with new buds.

It was just the sort of house Fitch had visualized belonging to Hilary Compton. Like the lady, it was neat and efficient.

There was an anticipatory gleam in his eye as he departed the carriage. Despite the serious nature of his trip, he was looking forward to seeing Miss Compton again.

He took a moment to appreciate the day. It was brisk and clear. The sun was shining with the promise of the season and the air, translucent compared to that of London, was sweet with the smell of new grass and hearty wildflowers.

It was spring, a time of new beginnings.

Inside the house, Hilary briefly considered asking Annie, the maid, to take Lizzie into the village and away from the upcoming encounter. Since leaving London, she'd been plagued by consistent thoughts of the Earl of Ackerman. Thoughts that had nothing to do with Lizzie, and everything to do with what Hilary now realized was a strange fascination with the man himself.

Their first meeting had left a lasting impression. Looking into his dark eyes, she'd felt temporarily lost. The potency of the moment, the depth of it, the disturbing awareness, and the fact that she'd been unable to forget it, held an alarming significance. One that Hilary preferred not to analyze at the moment.

Tucking her glasses in her pocket, she answered the door. "Good day, my lord. Please, do come in."

"Miss Compton," he said, removing his hat to reveal wavy black hair, much like that atop Lizzie's own head. He stepped into the foyer with intimidating ease, then turned to face her once again. "I hope to find you well."

"Yes, thank you." Hilary managed to hide her nervousness as she took his hat and gloves. "Before I bring Lizzie into the parlor to meet you, I would like a moment of your time. There are some things we have yet to discuss."

"Of course," he agreed, giving her a cordial smile as she turned to deposit his hat and gloves on a side table.

A Venetian mirror offered Hilary a clear view of the man as he looked her over with evident curiosity. Unsure what the Earl of Ackerman might find interesting about her and unaccustomed to male scrutiny of any kind, she caught herself short of blushing. "This way," she said, turning toward the parlor.

Fitch followed, thinking she looked very presentable in a skirt of dove-gray wool and a blue silk blouse with a high collar. Her hair was secured in that same unforgiving knot at the base of her neck. She was very prim and proper, he thought, and not all that excited about seeing him again.

Having a man's usual experience with women, and not one whit of understanding as to how their minds worked, Fitch decided to focus on the young girl he was about to meet. Surely, a child would be free of the prejudices and precautions time bestowed on the adults of her gender.

The parlor was a cozy room. A small Georgian table held a white bowl filled with flowers. The curtains were blue, sprigged with a vague flowery design, the seat beneath the largest window covered with cushions in the same fabric. There were two glass-front satinwood bookcases, filled to capacity, and a small revolving bookstand next to the sofa.

It was a room in which Fitch felt immediately at ease.

"Would you care for tea?" Hilary asked before sitting down.

"No, thank you."

Fitch had spent a good portion of the last two weeks deciding how he would approach Beth's daughter and her guardian, but now that he was actually in Nottingham, in the parlor of the house where they lived, he realized his preparation had been in vain. He didn't have the slightest idea how to get on with things.

Fortunately, the clear-thinking Miss Compton did.

Once she was seated on the sofa, hands folded in the perfect pose of a lady of good breeding, she informed him, "I told Lizzie that while I was in London, I happened upon a man who had known her father. That man, being a gentleman and a fellow comrade in arms, wanted to make her acquaintance. I thought it the best explanation for your visit."

"As good an explanation as any, and close to the truth. I do know her father, if I am he, and I did serve with George Aimes during the war."

Fitch told himself it didn't matter that another man had taken his place as Lizzie's official father. It wasn't as if he could publicly claim the child now. Doing so would cause more harm than good. And there was still the doubt of her parentage to be satisfied.

Unaware of the earl's specific thoughts, Hilary continued by saying, "I should also tell you that Lizzie doesn't resemble her mother as much as you may expect. Her hair is dark, like yours, and curly. She has dark brown eyes—again, very much like yours. Since there is no picture of her father, she has no way of knowing what George Aimes looked like."

A faint smile lifted one corner of Fitch's mouth. "George had red hair and light eyes. Blue, I think."

"Beth's eyes were blue," Hilary said. "She was very beautiful."

"Yes, she was," Fitch remarked, ending it at that. Though he appeared relaxed, there was an attentiveness and purpose about him that couldn't be ignored, even by a woman who had vainly tucked her glasses away. "Forgive my bluntness, Miss Compton, but I didn't come to Nottingham to discuss Beth Bradstreet. Words can't change the past, and

I have no intention of doing penance for a sin that has no absolution. I am here because of the child."

So there'd be no discussing Beth. Hilary wasn't surprised, and in many ways, she was relieved. All young ladies knew the rules, and broke them at their peril. If caught they became outcasts, their reputations forever tarnished, their families shamed.

Unfairly, gentlemen were not subject to the same scrutiny. A man was free to enjoy himself. The disparity required questioning, but until women were educated beyond embroidery and piano, the inequity would remain.

The earl directed the conversation by inquiring, "May I ask how we happened to meet? In case it becomes relevant, of course."

"At one of the London lending libraries," she told him. "Lizzie knows I love books."

Fitch lifted a dark brow, looking oddly amused. "I haven't walked into a real library since leaving Cambridge. Tell me, was I looking for a particular volume, or merely browsing the shelves? What do you prefer, Miss Compton, novels or poetry or something more philosophical? And how would I know you, or that the child you are harboring belonged to a former comrade in arms, had we not struck up a conversation? Such introductions are usually accomplished at parties or soirées. Informative chatter is then engaged in during a leisurely stroll through the park. A man boasts modestly of his accomplishments while the lady clings to his arm."

Hilary felt a prickle of irritation. Determined not to let any man get the best of her, she took a calming breath to ward off her temper. She couldn't allow her personal feelings to get in the way of

Lizzie's future, but that didn't keep her from applying her usual candor.

"While I appreciate your sentiments, my lord, you must remember that Lizzie is only nine. She has no idea how things are accomplished in London. Truthfully, I have never danced a step in my life. Nor do I have illusions about myself. I am the daughter of a country squire of little means and no particular social note. I also know that my age labels me a spinster, a woman who has failed at the most feminine of goals, that of gaining a husband. Do not think to flatter me by suggesting that the explanation I gave Lizzie is not a plausible one. Were I to say that I met you at a ball, she would exhaust both of us with questions."

Fitch flinched inwardly. They had crossed the bridge into personal matters, and he had crossed it rather badly.

"Forgive me. It was not my intention to cause you distress."

"The truth often brings distress, my lord, but I believe it the best path," she said with assurance. "While society may see me as a woman on the threshold of failure, I do not share their view. My unmarried state offers me protection against the mockery of that same society. London's gilt and coquetry hold no charm for me, nor do I wish to pretend to be something I am not."

He gave her a wolfish smile that unconsciously increased his handsomeness. "Are you always so plainspoken?"

"Yes." That said, she surprised him even more by adding, "This is far more awkward than I first imagined, my lord. I traveled to London with the assumption—"

"That I'd want no part of the child."

A nervous moment followed the remark, an uneasy silence not unlike the lull before a storm, but Hilary refused to let the awkwardness daunt her. The situation demanded clarification.

"One must admit that a man of your rank and privilege could be expected to react differently."

The earl showed no sign of surprise at her assumption, though Hilary noted that his eyes darkened. He studied her dispassionately for several long moments, and she felt her cheeks grow warm. His inescapable gaze had her nerve endings electrified. Finally, he spoke.

"I cannot account for other men of rank and privilege," he said stiffly. "As you mentioned before, delicacy is lacking in matters such as this. Beth and I were intimate, lovers for a short while, but essentially strangers. I do not wish to be a stranger to my daughter."

Hilary had anticipated several reactions—his wanting to get to know Lizzie had been one of them. Still, she was slightly disoriented by the announcement. It meant she would be seeing the earl from time to time, and she wasn't entirely sure how she would like having him coming and going—in, then out—of her life. As for Lizzie, she could foresee the earl spoiling his daughter with presents and an occasional visit. Or did he have something more permanent in mind?

"There are varying degrees of familiarity, my lord. My only concern is that Lizzie not be hurt by your acquaintance."

It was a short statement, but an important one.

The light from the window settled across the earl's face, and the brooding quality of his eyes—eyes that held Hilary's in a silent duel of wills.

"Your reluctance is understandable, Miss Compton. I know you had feelings for Beth. She was your friend. And now you have feelings for her child. I did not come here to belittle the generous role you have played in their lives. On the contrary, I applaud it. Friendship is to be valued."

Damn the man! He was saying all the right things, doing all the right things. It would be so much easier to deal with him were he the seducing scoundrel she'd expected.

"Beth told me that your family estate is in Winslow in Buckinghamshire," she said calmly. "Do you reside there when not in London?"

"Yes, for the most part," Fitch said, realizing a temporary truce was being announced by the change in topic, though he wasn't sure how or why. "I have smaller estates in Norfolk and Cambridgeshire, and another in Conwy in Wales, inherited from my great-grandmother."

Despite her polite manner, Fitch could sense the depth of Hilary's disappointment. It was obvious that she cared deeply for Beth's child, *his* child, and was reluctant to let anyone step into Lizzie's life. Of course, the lady had no notion of his plans.

Standing, he said, "I would like to meet Lizzie now."

"Yes, of course. I will bring her to you."

Fitch watched as she exited the room. A true gentleman never lacked for social pleasantries, but somehow he felt unsure of himself with Hilary Compton. Perhaps it was her honesty, or the way she looked directly into a man's eyes when she spoke to him. Or perhaps it was the daydream he'd carried from London, the image of her standing in front of a fire, her skin warm and glowing, her hair unbound and falling about her naked shoulders. Whatever the reason, he found himself smiling.

The smile faded at the sound of footsteps.

A short second later, the parlor door opened and a child appeared, a little girl with brownish-black hair and wide eyes with long, dark lashes. She was wearing a blue-striped pinafore. She smiled as she stepped into the room, closed the distance that separated them, then bobbed into a perfect little curtsy that set her curls to bouncing.

Fitch couldn't take his eyes off the child. She was undoubtedly a Minstead. The resemblance to his family, especially his mother, was uncanny.

"Good day, my lord. I'm Lizzie Aimes, and I'm ever so pleased to make your acquaintance."

Looking down at his daughter, Fitch felt a sudden surge of gratitude; his relationship with Beth hadn't been an honorable one, yet he was being rewarded with an opportunity to right that wrong. He marveled at how calm he felt. The tide of turmoil that had come with the London announcement had subsided the moment Lizzie had stepped into the room. Beyond the calm, there was a new goal at hand: being all his daughter needed him to be.

"Hello, Lizzie," he said, looking down into a pair of inquisitive brown eyes. "I'm your . . . I was a friend of your father's. A very close friend."

"Aunt Hilary told me." She turned to where her aunt was standing, just inside the doorway. "Annie's right. He's very handsome."

Fitch laughed. "And you're very pretty. The prettiest girl in all of Nottingham, I would wager."

"Oh, you mustn't gamble," Lizzie said seriously. "It's a sin, I think."

Somewhere outside, a dog barked. The explosive sound sent a covey of birds flying by the window.

"That's Sylvester," Lizzie told him. "It's time for our walk. He's a very smart dog."

"May I come along?" Fitch asked.

Lizzie looked to Hilary for approval. A nod from her aunt sent her scampering from the room, calling out to Annie that she needed her bonnet. She and his lordship were going to take Sylvester for a romp in the woods.

Hilary smiled. "I should warn you that Lizzie has a restless intellect. She will plague you with questions."

"You will join us?" Fitch asked, hoping that she might surprise him again and say yes.

"Thank you, but I think not. You came for Lizzie."

"Yes. But, having done so, I'm not sure how one goes about making the acquaintance of a nine-year-old."

Hilary remained silent. She would be a long time forgetting the expression on the earl's face when Lizzie had stepped into the room. For a second, his eyes had sparkled with delight.

She took a moment to study him now. There was a touch of gray at his temples, though she doubted he was more than two or three years past his thirtieth birthday. Despite his immaculate clothing, there was something volatile about him—an aura of danger, a masculine mystique that made him far more tempting than he should be. The thought brought an uneasiness with it. The last thing she needed was to become enamored of the man, and yet, if she hoped to remain a part of Lizzie's life, she had to accept the fact that the earl would be there with her.

Sylvester was a silky-haired spaniel that leapt about Fitch's ankles, then ran off into the woods the second the gate was unlatched. **The** earl and Lizzie followed at a more leisurely pace, the little girl chatting away as she walked by his side.

"Do you like apple tarts?" she asked him. "Annie is baking them for supper. I was helping her in the kitchen, but she wouldn't let me peel the apples. I'm too small to handle a knife, but she let me stir the cinnamon and sugar into the dough."

"I do like apple tarts," Fitch replied. "And plum duffs and bread pudding with lots of raisins."

His confession earned him an accepting smile. A second later, his newfound daughter stopped to investigate a bird, chirping away on a branch over her head. "Do you like music? Aunt Hilary plays the piano. She's teaching me to play it, too." Then, without taking a breath, she asked Fitch a question that put him back on his heels. "Do you think my father loved me? Samantha Cheadle—she's my friend—said fathers only love their sons. She said daughters aren't important."

Regret coiled deep inside Fitch's chest. He lowered himself to one knee; then, looking into eyes that mirrored his own, he explained. "I've been told that fathers love their little girls in a very special way. I know if I were fortunate to have a daughter such as you, I'd be ever so thankful."

"Are you certain?" she asked, her eyes full of hope.

"Absolutely certain."

His answer earned him a big smile and a tight hug around the neck. Fitch held his daughter close as tears dampened his eyes. His instantaneous love went unquestioned as he stood up and offered her his hand.

"Sylvester is barking. Let's go see what he's found." The spaniel's discovery was a baby hedgehog.

The tiny animal had curled itself into a prickly brown ball while the dog pranced and barked in a circle around it.

"What is it?" Lizzie asked.

"A hedgehog. They curl up to protect themselves."

"It's so tiny. I can't tell its head from its tail," she said, bending down to examine the animal more thoroughly. "I wonder if its mama died." She looked up at Fitch. "My mama died. I cried until I got sick and had to throw up. Aunt Hilary cried, too. Now when we miss Mama, we talk about all the wonderful days before the angels took her away."

Fitch didn't know what to say. There had been no angels on the battlefield, only corpses and the cries of maimed men as Russian cannon fire cut through the ranks. How could he offer Lizzie comfort when he couldn't comfort himself?

"Do you think the hedgehog would like to live in the garden?" she asked. "It's a lovely garden, and I promise to take very good care of it."

"I don't see why not."

She clapped her hands together as if he'd just given her the world. They returned to the house with the hedgehog nestled inside Fitch's upside-down hat.

Hilary smiled indulgently when Lizzie and the earl appeared at the door with the new resident.

"It isn't much of a pet," Lizzie informed her. "It spends all its time rolled into a ball. I haven't seen its face yet."

"We had a hedgehog in the garden when I was a boy at Winslow," Fitch said. "A saucer of milk was guaranteed to make it come out of hiding."

A few minutes later all conversation ceased as a saucer of milk was placed on the floor. Ever so slowly the tight, furry ball relaxed and a pair of dark eyes appeared, followed by an equally dark nose. Soon the small animal was standing on four tiny feet and turning toward the milk.

Not until the saucer was empty, and the hedgehog was curled into a contented ball in the corner of the room, did Fitch ask, "What will you name it?"

"Is it a boy or a girl?"

"A girl, I think." He held his breath, half expecting his inquisitive daughter to ask how he could tell the difference.

Lizzie pondered the question long and hard, then smiled. "Hattie. You carried her here in your hat."

"Hattie the hedgehog," he chuckled. "Very well. But she isn't the sort of pet one keeps in the kitchen."

"It's frightfully cold in the garden," Lizzie said much too seriously. "Especially at night."

It was Hilary's turn to say something. "Oh, no, you don't, young lady. I will tolerate Sylvester sleeping under your bed, but not a hedgehog."

Reluctantly, Lizzie agreed and Hattie was carried into the garden. Fitch and Hilary stood at a distance while Lizzie arranged dried leaves and grass to her satisfaction, insisting that if the poor wee animal had to sleep outside, it needed a nice, snug bed.

Slowly, Fitch turned his gaze from his daughter to the woman standing a few feet away. "With your permission, I would like to visit again tomorrow."

"Of course, my lord."

Fitch watched her, knowing she was embarrassed by the boldness of his stare. The delicate, heightened color in her cheeks reminded him of the porcelain skin of a Dresden figurine he'd recently admired in a Bond Street window. But unlike the statuette, Hilary Compton was a flesh-and-blood woman. A woman struggling to control her emotions.

He had made an important decision today, but it wasn't solely his decision to make. He was bound to Lizzie by blood, but Hilary was bound by devotion. One was no less important than the other. Not wanting to upset the delicate balance of things, Fitch chose his words carefully.

"I think children are astute enough to know when something is amiss in their lives. I would not want to cause my daughter additional heartache by stealing her away from the only home she has known."

"Thank you, my lord."

"I am the one who should be thanking you. Were it not for your dedication to Beth and her child, things could have turned out much differently. I can think of no reason why I should want to take Lizzie away from someone she loves, someone who obviously loves her. However, I do plan on taking an active role in her life. I want to give her whatever happiness I can."

"You already have," she said, pointing to the hedgehog that was being put to bed. "Lizzie loves animals."

Smiling, Fitch joined his daughter.

Lizzie was disappointed that the earl wouldn't be staying for supper, but delighted when he vowed to visit the very next day. "I'll save an apple tart for you," she promised.

"And I'll bring a box and some fresh straw so Hattie can have a proper bed."

Fitch knelt down and held out his arms. Lizzie was more than happy to give him a hug and a kiss on the cheek.

Hilary watched the exchange between daughter and estranged father with mixed feelings. Closely observed, it was impossible not to see the family resemblance. She wondered how those who knew the earl personally would react should they see him with Lizzie in one of the London parks he had mentioned. Knowing people's enthusiasm for chit-chat, she was certain some would jump to the correct conclusion.

The ensuing gossip would do little damage to the earl. Men were expected to have indiscretions in their lives. But malice-filled words could affect an impressionable child like Lizzie. Her father knew that, too. It was one of the reasons he'd agreed to leave Lizzie in her care. Neither guardian nor child had any social connections, and everyone in Nottingham believed as Lizzie did, that Beth Bradstreet had been legally married to George Aimes.

Hilary allowed herself to indulge in a moment of speculation. Would the earl have married Beth? Or would he have pacified her with flowery words and a monthly allowance, or perhaps a nice cottage where he would be welcomed when no one was looking. Beth had been beautiful, and she had felt something for Lieutenant Minstead or she wouldn't have become his lover.

Lover.

Speculation turned into something else as Hilary tried to imagine what it would be like to feel the earl's strong hands moving over her body. Would he be gentle or masterful with a woman? She stared at him, silently evaluating his strength. He was tall and broad of shoulders. His movements were graceful for a man his size, his speech filled with authority, and those dark, soulful eyes ... One glance could set a woman's heart aflutter.

Masterful, she decided.

Fitch said one last word of good-bye to Lizzie, then turned to take his leave of Hilary. He made a point of holding her gaze for several seconds before lifting her bare hand to his mouth and kissing it.

"Until tomorrow, Miss Compton."

Speechless, Hilary stared after him. A casual kiss on the hand, a very proper, very acceptable kiss, and she suddenly felt as if her whole life had undergone some magical metamorphosis.

She tried reminding herself that there were a dozen reasons why she shouldn't look forward to the following day and the earl's return; then, glancing down at the hand he had just kissed, she promptly forgot each and every one.

Three

By the time Fitch finished tucking Lizzie in for the night, the drizzle that had dampened the afternoon had turned into a full-fledged storm. A galelike wind whined and moaned as rain fell in thick gray sheets. His driver, a crusty old man by the name of Wyton, had settled the horse and carriage into the small mews behind the house. Wyton was in the kitchen now, having a late supper and staying dry until his lordship had need of him.

Finding Hilary in the parlor, Fitch decided this particular storm might be a blessing in disguise. He'd been trying to arrange a few minutes alone with the lady for the last several days, but circumstances, and a very active daughter, hadn't allowed the opportunity.

"May I join you?" he asked, stepping into the parlor where the polished furniture reflected the firelight.

"Of course, my lord. The storm makes for a nasty night."

"Lizzie doesn't seem to mind. She fell asleep as soon as her head hit the pillow." He crossed to the table where Annie had left a decanter of brandy. Over the course of the last ten days, he'd become comfortable with the household. Enough to pour himself a drink and take a seat without being formally invited to do either.

"I'll be returning to London tomorrow," he said.

After what seemed like an unconscionably long time, Hilary replied, "Did you tell Lizzie?"

"Yes. She asked me not to leave."

"Of course she did. Since your arrival she's acquired a hedgehog named Hattie, twin kittens christened Twiddle Dee and Twiddle Dum, three new bonnets, a red velvet coat that will be the envy of every girl in St. Mary's parish, a music box, and the promise of her very own pony come spring."

"You think I'm spoiling her."

"I think you're overly enthusiastic," Hilary said. "You've become a father without warning and in a manner guaranteed to upset anyone's equilibrium."

She was seated on the sofa while the earl sat in a comfortable Biedermeier armchair. Firelight streamed from the hearth, creating a sea of flickering shadows between them. Hilary hadn't responded directly to Fitch's announcement that he would be leaving Nottingham because she feared if she said anything, it would be to ask him to stay.

The last few days had been a revelation. Before meeting the Earl of Ackerman, she had thought herself content. Now, she was struggling against the powerful effect he was having on her emotions and on her body.

She thought about him constantly. The compelling angles of his profile, the thick black hair

that seemed forever in disarray, and his smile . . .
While it started in his eyes and slowly softened his
face, Hilary sensed it never reached his heart.

Fitch sat quietly for some time. The prevailing
weather put him in a strange mood. It was a wind-
swept night with a bleakly colored sky. Seated in
the snug little parlor, he contemplated how easily
his life had changed course. He thought of the
people he had loved—his parents and his brother.
He thought of old passions and youthful dreams,
of longings and the melancholy that had settled
over him since leaving the military.

He watched as Hilary left the sofa and moved to
the window. The firelight illuminated her profile
and Fitch noticed that the twisted knot of hair resting on her slim neck had been artistically done.
She was attractive in a simple, unassuming way that
she chose to conceal with dull colors and stiff-necked
blouses.

A sliver of lightning arced through the sky, and
she smiled as if it had danced just for her.

"You like storms?"

"Yes. I think them beautiful," she answered.
"When I was a little girl, not much younger than
Lizzie, I saw lightning strike a tree. The wood splintered as if struck by Thor's hammer, and I watched
in awe as the tree began to burn. Truthfully, it was
that day that I started believing in God. Until then,
he had been little more than a puzzling character
in a leather bound book on my father's night
table."

Fitch frowned as he lifted the brandy snifter to
his mouth. He had celebrated his thirtieth birthday and two more, but so much of his life seemed
over. He thought of the war, of the men he had

commanded, of the ones who had been buried in the cold soil of the Balkans. As for God . . .

"I'm not sure I believe in God."

That snippet of news earned him a reproachful look.

"If you don't believe in God, then what do you believe in, my lord?"

Another pause. Another sip of brandy. More thoughts before he replied, "The order of things, I suppose. Day and night. Summer followed by winter. Life followed by death."

Hilary could see the complex mix of anguish and remorse on his face. It was at times like this that she sensed the depths of the earl's loneliness the most. During the course of the last week, she had learned that he was a complicated man. His eyes could glow with compassion or mystery, depending upon his mood. He was intelligent without being boastful, generous without being foolhardy, but most of all, he was sad.

Lizzie could make the sadness disappear, but only for a short while. When Fitch wasn't with his daughter, his eyes had a bleak desperation about them. It was then that Hilary longed most to reach out and touch him, to tell him that should he need a friend, she would gladly become one.

Not wanting to lose the intimacy of the conversation—it was the first time they had spoken of personal things—Hilary told him her own thoughts.

"I would feel hopelessly forlorn should I believe that life is but a path to the grave," she said, delivering the retort gracefully. "I prefer to think of it as a perpetual portrait, a work of art that cannot be fully appreciated until the last brush stroke is put to canvas."

A boom of thunder followed her definition, as if God were putting his stamp of approval on the eloquent phrasing.

"A romantic bluestocking," Fitch said, raising his glass high. "I never thought to meet one."

"You mock me, sir."

"No. On the contrary, I salute you, Miss Compton. It isn't every day a man makes the acquaintance of a woman who possesses both a scholar's mind *and* a poet's heart."

Hilary mutely admitted it was the most flattering thing anyone had ever said to her. She'd long since turned a deaf ear to the people who thought her a hopeless spinster, focusing instead on the people she did care about: her aunt and Beth and Lizzie. Now she had only Lizzie, and a growing suspicion that she was falling in love with the Earl of Ackerman.

With each passing day, more and more of her thoughts centered around the man. With each passing night, she grew more restless.

It was a scandalous thing to admit that the agitation was due to physical desire. The earl had awakened something within her, something wicked and wonderful, and Hilary longed to have it become a reality. The fact that she dared to think such outrageous thoughts was proof that love addled a woman's brain. But beneath the concern a current of newfound joy rippled and danced through her.

"I have a question to ask of you, or rather, a request," Fitch said, lowering his glass without tasting its contents. "I would like you to bring Lizzie to London."

It was the beginning of the plan that had come to mind that gray morning in London.

"The city can be daunting to an adult, my lord. I

fear what impression it might leave on a child so used to country life. Are you certain it wouldn't be better to wait until Lizzie knows you better, perhaps in a year or two?"

Fitch left the chair and crossed the room to where she was standing, his strides long and lithe. The width of his shoulders had suited a uniform well, suggesting the agile strength new recruits needed to see in a commanding officer.

A half smile curved his mouth. "Have you no urge to visit the library again, Miss Compton? No desire to spend a leisurely afternoon browsing through an art gallery or museum? What of the theater or opera? Surely a woman with the heart of a poet would find such pastimes entertaining?"

Hilary wasn't sure how to respond.

"Come to London," he said. "You know Lizzie will enjoy it."

His voice had a hypnotic quality and Hilary knew she wasn't going to be able to refuse him. Her face felt warm, as if she was blushing, though she had no reason to do so. The earl couldn't read her mind. He had no way of knowing that she longed to wrap her arms around him, to offer him comfort from whatever sadness burdened him. "Very well, if you wish it."

She looked away from his face then, down to where the lapels of his jacket formed a vee, to where she could see the rich linen of his shirt and the embroidered emerald silk of his waistcoat. Somewhere beneath his finely tailored clothes, beneath flesh and bone, lay his heart.

Slowly, her gaze returned to his face, only to discover that he was surveying her with equal intensity. He regarded her for another moment before speaking.

"Have you ever been kissed?"

"No." If she was anything, it was honest. "Why should it matter?"

"It matters a great deal. In fact, at this moment, I can't think of anything more important."

He cased his hand around the nape of her neck.

Hilary's eyes went wide.

He lowered his head.

Her lips parted and a small sound escaped.

He kissed her tentatively at first, brushing his mouth lightly over hers, allowing her time to get used to being touched. Another light caress, followed by a sensual glide of his tongue over the trembling surface of her lower lip, told Fitch she was shocked but curious.

He reached around and spread his hand wide across her lower back to keep her in his arms. The kiss went on, his mouth molding to hers, his tongue lightly teasing, silently asking hers to do the same. When it didn't, Fitch realized just how innocent she was, and how jaded his own life had become since the war.

"I think we've finally found something upon which we can agree," he said softly.

The second kiss came more naturally. When he lowered his head this time, her face lifted to meet him halfway. His hand pressed lightly against her back, telling her that he wanted her closer. She complied, bringing her hands up to rest hesitantly against his chest. Fitch sensed her fear, and the passion she was keeping locked inside.

Wanting to taste that passion, to prove that it did indeed exist, he made the kiss a lingering one, a lazy play of lips and tongue. Gradually her tongue joined his, hesitantly exploring.

Hilary felt as if she'd discovered her own private

corner of heaven. Never in her wildest imagination had she thought being kissed—kissing a man in return—could be so wonderful. The arousing warmth of his mouth, the flavor of brandy on his tongue, the heat of his hand pressed against her back, the scent of his cologne—everything about him was intoxicating. Her senses were overwhelmed, wanting to absorb it all. Her mind raced to record every detail, every nuance, so it could be remembered later. Remembered and cherished.

It was her first encounter with passion.

When it ended, Hilary rested her forehead against his chest and took a deep breath.

Fitch held her close, listening to the sound of her breathing, feeling the soft tremors that shook her body. He hadn't been unaffected by the kiss. It had been weeks since he'd had a woman, and he'd had days to think about what it would be like to taste the prim little spinster. It had been nice.

Very nice.

Hilary backed away from him, then moved across the room to stand behind the settee. Her face was flushed and her gaze downcast. It was obvious that she was embarrassed. "I think it's time for you to leave, my lord."

"It was a very nice kiss, Miss Compton. Neither of us should regret it."

Hilary refused to meet his gaze, but when he didn't leave the room, she had little choice. Though her voice remained calm, her emotions were in turmoil. "I have always prided myself on being a practical woman. I forgot that practicality tonight."

"Kissing isn't meant to be practical, it's meant to be pleasurable. You did enjoy the kiss, didn't you?"

Angry at herself for submitting to the man's advances far too readily, Hilary wrestled with a host of emotions. She had enjoyed the kiss. That wasn't the issue. The issue was, *why?*

Instead of puzzling over the question, she put it to the only person who could answer it. "Why did you kiss me? If I were pretty, I might assume that you were attracted to me, but I'm not pretty. If I were the daughter of a peer, I might assume that you had honorable intentions toward me, but my parents held no rank above that of father and mother. Another explanation could be boredom. Nottingham is a quiet town compared to London. We have few diversities here."

Fitch let out a frustrated breath. "Must you analyze everything, Miss Compton? Can't a man kiss a woman for the simple pleasure of it?"

As much as Hilary longed to believe that the earl had kissed her for all the right reasons, she couldn't convince herself that he was truly attracted to her. Chin up and eyes wide, she turned to look at him. "Am I a diversity, my lord? Do you see me as a lonely spinster who will allow herself to be used for a man's amusement?"

Fitch located his brandy glass and took a quick drink.

"Are you intentionally trying to test my temper, Miss Compton, or are you so certain of your lack of appeal you can't imagine a man *wanting* to kiss you?"

She smiled without humor. "And what do you find appealing about me, my lord?

He held out his hand. "Come here."

Hilary didn't move. She couldn't. Her knees were mush. It was preposterous, since she'd never been a weak-willed ninny. But the earl's kiss had changed all that. Tonight, he had made her feel very much like a woman, and it frightened her.

"Come here," he repeated. "I dislike having to shout across the room."

Hilary felt her confidence draining away. Why was he looking as if he knew something she didn't? There was the barest hint of a smile in his eyes. It confused her. She confused herself, feeling things she'd never felt before, thinking things that normally wouldn't enter her mind, wanting things that were as unlikely as the church granting sainthood to Lucifer.

"You are a stubborn woman," Fitch mumbled as he moved to where she was standing. "Did my kiss truly offend you?"

"You confuse me," Hilary said, avoiding a direct answer. "When I first saw you that night in London, I didn't expect you to care a whit about Lizzie. What I did expect was to be shown the door after I told you she existed."

"And when you weren't?"

"I wasn't sure what to make of you. I'm still not sure."

He reached out and touched her cheek. "If it's any consolation, I'm just as unsure what to make of you."

They stood there for a moment, both silent, both staring into each other's eyes. A log rolled in the grate, popping and cracking, sending a cloud of sparks up the chimney. Neither noticed.

"You didn't answer my question," Hilary prompted, knowing her voice was as shaky as the rest of her.

He took her by the hand and led her to the sofa. Once they were seated, he continued to hold her hand. "What do I find appealing about you? Hmmm, let me see . . . You have nice eyes, when they aren't hidden behind your glasses. You're intelligent, kind-hearted, extremely quick-witted, and you move like a ballerina. You may not know how to dance, but I'll wager it wouldn't take you long to learn. You have a natural grace."

"You think me graceful?"

"Yes."

He tipped her chin up and kissed her. It was a quick kiss, and totally unexpected. Hilary was just recovering from it when he surprised her even more.

"Marry me."

"What!"

He stood and swept her an eloquent bow. "Miss Compton, will you do me the honor of becoming my wife?"

"Marriage? You and I?"

Lizzie was the reason, of course, but knowing the motive didn't lessen the shock of his proposal. For a brief moment, Hilary was tempted to say yes.

"I know what you're thinking, my lord. You can't admit to being Lizzie's father without making her mother out a liar. On the other hand, if you marry her guardian, you can reclaim the jurisdiction Beth took from you. Your relationship will be legitimized. Lizzie will live under your roof, and I'm sure that within a matter of days she'll be calling you Papa. That's what you want, isn't it?"

"You're a very perceptive woman, Miss Compton. And yes, I want my daughter. But I also find myself wanting a wife. It's time I took my obligations seriously. What better solution than for us to marry? We both love Lizzie, and I can think of no reason why we wouldn't suit."

It was an honest answer, one Hilary had to respect even if it did put a dent in her heart. She disengaged her hand from his and came to her feet.

Moving away, she didn't stop until she'd reached the opposite side of the room, where she stared out the window.

The storm was easing. Rain still dampened the windows, but it was a lazy drizzle, not the fierce lashing that had rattled the panes earlier in the evening.

"I suppose I should be flattered," she said. "It isn't every day that an earl proposes to a spinster."

Fitch refused to be baited by the remark. He'd spent too much time on the battlefield to be outflanked by a novice.

"The idea has occurred to you, hasn't it? We both love Lizzie. She needs a mother and a father. What better way to share her than to become her legal parents? Once we're married, I can arrange a formal adoption. She can take my name, be accepted by society, lay claim to everything that is rightfully hers."

He was right on both counts. Hilary *had* thought about marriage. She'd thought of little else these last few days. To do otherwise had seemed impossible with the man sitting at the head of the dinner table six nights out of seven. And the evenings spent in the parlor, Lizzie surrounded by an assortment of pets while her father looked on, occasional smiles sent across the room to where she sat embroidering or reading. Anyone looking through the window would have seen them as the perfect family.

Hilary was too innately practical not to expound on the proposal he'd offered. "Marriage is more than legalities, my lord. Your solution will undoubtedly benefit your daughter, but what of yourself? What of me?"

Fitch had considered all the possibilities. In fact,

he'd spent the better part of the week imagining himself married to Hilary Compton. None of the thoughts had been intolerable.

"I like you, Miss Compton. I enjoy your candor and your wit. To that regard, our marriage can be whatever we wish it to be. If you prefer living in the country, there is Winslow. If, on the other hand, you wish to accompany me to London during those times when Parliament demands my attention, I will be glad of the company. You can have parties, if you like. Fill the library with books floor to ceiling, if you like. My only requirements are your fidelity and an heir."

Hilary addressed the first and ignored the second. "I have never been given to deception, my lord. In return, I would require honesty and respect from whomever I marry."

"There has been nothing but honesty between us since that first night in London. And I do respect you. If I didn't, I wouldn't have stopped with a few kisses. I would have plied my expertise, and come morning you'd have found yourself bound by conscience and morals to marry me."

Hilary's temper began to simmer. "The last few days should have alerted you to the fact that I'm used to speaking my mind."

"Most eloquently," Fitch countered.

"I am no child, my lord. Nor am I foolish enough to think that the marriage of convenience you are proposing will offer any convenience to me, except that of having Lizzie at my side."

Fitch refilled his glass. Somewhere in the house a door opened and closed, letting a whistle of wind invade the downstairs corridor—Wyton on his way to the carriage house. It was getting late and they had a full day's travel ahead of them tomorrow.

His expression turned pensive. "What sort of *conveniences* are we talking about?"

"Freedom to do what I think is best for me," Hilary replied. "While I cannot deny that your offer is tempting, I refuse to sacrifice my personal dignity for a wedding ring. You are asking me to put myself, everything I am or hope to be, under your authority."

"And that worries you?"

"Yes."

As usual, Hilary's candor impressed him. Fitch gave the matter another moment's thought. There was no point calling her to task; her independent attitudes ran too deep to be dissuaded in one day's time. Once they were married, he could guide her with a firmer hand.

"I am not beyond allowing you certain freedoms, but I will not be castrated to satisfy some free-thinking idealism. If you accept my proposal, Miss Compton, then I expect you to *be* a wife."

Nothing in the earl's dark eyes gave Hilary the impression that he didn't mean what he was saying. No doubt they could debate the advantages and disadvantages of marriage well into the night. Needing time to unravel and examine her emotions, she looked at him with a vestige of calm.

"I will consider your proposal, my lord, and give you my answer in the morning."

Fitch smiled. He and the obstinate Miss Compton had been playing a game of stalk and retreat for the last hour. It was time to take control of the situation.

Sensing what he had planned, Hilary skirted around the end of the settee, but Fitch outflanked her. She thought to dissuade him with a polite word or two, but before she could get them said, a hand eased around the nape of her neck and pulled her close.

"While you're contemplating my marriage proposal, Miss Compton, think about this."

It wasn't the gentlemanly kiss he had bestowed upon her earlier—a leisurely, soft, patient kiss. This kiss was deep and demanding. He held her close, his thighs pressed hard against her, his hands firm on her back, though Hilary didn't struggle to get away from him. She had no desire to escape. She relented to the wonder of it all, the turbulent passion, the slow, sensual probing of his tongue. She was still clinging to him when he nuzzled his nose against her hair and whispered, "Marry me, and I'll kiss you like that every night."

The next minute he was gone, and Hilary found herself staring at an empty room.

Four

Hilary willed her mind to blankness the next morning. The patchwork of events leading up to the earl's proposal had kept her thoughts racing most of the night. She'd reached her decision. There was no more thinking to be done.

She began the day as she did every day with a vigorous brushing of her thick, wavy hair. After braiding it, she twisted it into a respectable knot, not having the patience for anything more fashionable. After that came the selection of her wardrobe. She looked over the array of sensible clothing—dark skirts and high-necked blouses, and the occasional day dress.

After a brief moment in which she wished she'd spent less time at lending libraries and more in some of London's stylish shops, she selected a nutmeg-brown skirt matched with a cream-colored blouse with small pearl buttons and a minimum of lace. The only addition to her attire was a cameo brooch, a family heirloom that had belonged to her maternal grandmother.

Giving herself one last glance in the mirror, she uttered a resolute sigh and made her way downstairs to leave the house by the parlor door that opened onto the garden.

It was the beginning of a beautiful spring day. The morning sky was a transparent blue, the sunlight more silver than gold. The wind shook the low-hanging branches of the weeping willow at the corner of the garden and a residue of raindrops fell to the ground.

Hilary's heart contracted a little at the perfection of the day. She loved the softness that came with spring: the tender shoots of grass, the perfume of wildflowers, the gentle fingering of the wind against her face and hair.

She often visited the garden in the early morning, seeking the solace of the season. Generally at such times she did not think of anything in particular, choosing instead to give her mind free rein to settle where it would—but not this morning.

Today her sense of well-being was dampened by the possibility that the decision she'd made could easily turn into the biggest mistake of her life.

She would marry the Earl of Ackerman.

Her choice was based on a collage of logic and emotion, the most important item being Lizzie's well-being, or so she'd told herself last night. In the light of day, Hilary knew she was going to marry the earl as much for herself as for anyone. All that had happened within the last few weeks had stirred her to the depths of her being. She had become absorbingly interested in the man Lizzie called Uncle Fitch, and everything she did was now centered around him.

Since leaving childhood and entering the vulnerable realm of womanhood, she had kept to herself, contemptuously aloof from other young women who seemed concerned only with the snaring of a husband. Admittedly, she had often envied those same young women their sentimental preoccupation. Now she knew the meaning of that fixation—to be taken over by the mere thought of a man was enough to muddle any woman's brain.

During his ten-day sojourn in Nottingham, the earl had not spoken a single word of love to her. There had been nothing in the outward course of events to raise her hopes that he might one day return her feelings. The depths of his affection for her could be measured by a few kisses, and yet there had been an undercurrent as potent as springtime upon the land when he had taken her into his arms.

"Aunt Edwina would think me mad," she said as she passed the box where the hedgehog lay sleeping within a blanket of yellow straw. "She would say I am allowing my heart to rule my head, that I'm settling for second best. And I suppose I am, but my heart feels compelled to follow this path. I can only hope that the earl can learn to love me, if not passionately, then with contented reverence. It is better than dying a lonely old woman with nothing but books and unfulfilled dreams."

Hattie didn't so much as uncurl at the ostentatious announcement that Hilary was about to forsake her last ounce of common sense. The hedgehog, which now shared a saucer of milk each morning with Twiddle Dee and Twiddle Dum, continued sleeping as if the most important decision in Hilary's life had no significance whatsoever.

Realizing that she'd lost track of time, Hilary returned to the house and the meal Annie served precisely at eight each morning. In her exalted mood, she wasn't particularly hungry, but a cup of tea would be nice.

Fitch walked up the flagstone path to Hilary's front door with a sense of anticipation mixed with resolute determination. His mood was not unlike that of a soldier going to war, though he loathed the comparison.

The war had taught him that strategy and preparation could win or lose a battle, and he was determined to win Hilary's hand in marriage. The fact that he had proposed had surprised him as much as the lady in question. His intentions had been only to offer an invitation to visit London, where he could woo her properly, but once he'd kissed her, felt her unmistakable capacity for passion, he hadn't hesitated to ask the question.

Having said the words, they had settled nicely into his mind. The latter half of the night, spent alone in his room at the Nottingham Inn, had given him time for additional thought. Fitch hadn't changed his mind. He and Hilary were well suited, discounting several of her unconventional attitudes, which he was confident he could temper once she was his legal wife.

Her lack of what society would call "fashionable beauty" didn't overly concern him, either. She wasn't ugly by any stretch of the imagination, simply unadorned in her manner of dress. He had learned long ago not to judge a person by appearance alone.

Hilary was exactly what she appeared to be—a levelheaded, well-educated woman with an innate abundance of obstinacy. She was also loyal and courageous, qualities he admired in both men and women, though they were oftentimes harder to discern in the fairer sex.

Fitch was only a few feet away from the front door when it opened and Lizzie came bubbling out. She squealed with delight when he swooped her up into his arms and swung her high in the air.

"Hilary said I shouldn't call you Papa until after the wedding," Lizzie exclaimed. "I've wanted a father for so long—please say the wedding will be soon."

Fitch looked toward the door to find Hilary standing there. The slight nod of her head answered last night's question.

"As soon as possible," he told Lizzie, whose dark curls were tied back with a blue ribbon. Her cherub face had been scrubbed clean, and she was all smiles. "Is next month soon enough?"

"A whole month," she pouted. "But that's forever."

"You'll have plenty to keep you busy, and as soon as you get to London, I'll take you for a ride in Hyde Park."

"What about Sylvester and Hattie and the kittens? Can I bring them to London?"

"I think your pets should remain here in Nottingham for the time being. As soon as I can, I'll have someone take them to Winslow. It's a big estate with more than enough room for a few more residents."

Lizzie's smile faded. "What shall I do in London without them?"

Fitch gave her a kiss on the nose. "There are always things to do in the city," he told her, though he wasn't entirely sure how a child's time would be occupied. His would be taken up with duties in

Parliament, finding a suitable house for Hilary and Lizzie to occupy until the wedding, and, of course, the procurement of a license and a church.

"Can't we go now?" his inquisitive daughter asked, tugging him toward the front door because he wasn't moving fast enough to satisfy her impatience.

"Not just yet," Hilary said, stepping outside to join them. "Weddings are complicated things. One does not run to the altar without making sure everything is in order."

Her expression told Fitch that she'd deliberately chosen her words to convey a message. Before he dashed off to London, there were things still to be settled between them.

Lizzie reluctantly accepted Hilary's explanation, but not without asking, "How soon, then?"

"Next week. I'll send a coach for you and your aunt, and Annie, if she wants to join you," Fitch answered, not giving his bride-to-be time to plot a delay. Having decided to marry, he was just as impatient as his daughter to get things done.

Once Lizzie's enthusiasm for the upcoming wedding had been quieted, she went off to the garden to see to her pets. Fitch invited Hilary to take a short stroll.

Placing her hand on his offered arm, they took the same path he and Lizzie had walked that first day. There was silence except for the humming of insects. Sylvester darted ahead, his silky tail fanning wildly as he snooped about the trees and greenery that lined the path.

"I detect the need for conversation," Fitch said, once they were beyond hearing distance. "But first, may I say that I'm pleased you've decided to become my wife."

"Perhaps you should wait before making that remark, my lord. You may not be so pleased with my terms."

Fitch stopped under the sprawling boughs of an ancient oak. His gaze was intensely serious when he addressed her. "The only *terms* to our marriage will be the wedding vows we speak. If you think to restrict my rights as a husband, think again. My title requires an heir, and since meeting Lizzie I've discovered that I'm more fond of children than I had first supposed. That means this marriage will be real in every sense of the word."

"You made that abundantly clear last night," Hilary replied, doing her best to act as if they were exchanging words about the weather rather than the most intimate of acts. She looked away, but only for a second, before meeting his gaze. When she did, her heart stopped, then began again with a slow, hard beat that warned her to proceed cautiously. "I am prepared to be a wife, my lord. Were I not, I would decline your proposal."

Fitch concealed his relief, his gaze never wavering. "Do you have some doubt about our union being an amicable one?"

"No."

When she didn't clarify the statement, he prompted her. "I have never known you to be short of words. Say whatever you think needs saying. I won't take offense."

"There is no offense in my thoughts, my lord, only an awareness of what most men expect of marriage."

"And what is that, besides the obvious?"

The obvious was enough to make Hilary's stomach flutter as the earl tightened his hand possessively over hers. For a moment she feared that he'd kiss her again, thereby ending their conversation, for she knew she'd be incapable of intelligent speech afterwards.

When he didn't pull her into his arms, Hilary gave a light shrug of her shoulders. "It seems to me that men measure the success or failure of a marriage by their own contentment. They want an agreeable wife, one who is courteous and well-spoken, a woman who doesn't disagree in public and only rarely in private. Unfortunately, they show little interest in what makes the woman content."

"I would have you happy," Fitch said with all sincerity. "As for the rest, you are undoubtedly correct. A man does not like having his life disturbed by domestic upsets. We are not the daring, adventurous creatures females so often think us to be. But being a practical woman, you already know that."

"I also know that few women are as content in marriage as they publicly profess. I should not care to be among them, if there is a way to avoid it."

Fitch toyed with the idea of kissing her, but decided it was best to get things—whatever those things might be—said and out of the way.

"Do you have a remedy for discontentment in mind?"

"I suppose you could call it that," Hilary said, her mouth curving into the faintest of smiles. "I do have personal pursuits, things that interest me, things that have intrigued me for years."

"Intellectual pursuits?"

"Of a nature. I've always possessed a desire for travel. I want to see all the wonderful places I have read about for years. My aunt's inheritance has finally put that goal within reach, but marriage would restrict it somewhat."

"Somewhat," Fitch agreed. "To where do you propose traveling?"

"Egypt would be my first choice," she told him. "The Pyramids. I've longed for years to see them. And Greece. History has always fascinated me. And Rome, of course. One's intellectual pursuits could not be satisfied without seeing that grand city. Oh, and the canals of Venice."

"Rome is a grand city," Fitch assured her. "As for Venice, it's beyond description."

Her eyes brightened with interest. "Tell me about Rome. Did you see the Vatican, the ceiling so diligently and lovingly painted by Michelangelo? Do the figures really speak to you in a silence so awe inspiring one is left with a neck ache from staring up at them?"

"Yes," Fitch confessed, thinking Hilary much more idealistic than she wanted people to believe. Each and every site she had named was known for its romantic nature. "What else interests you?"

"My interests are boundless, my lord."

Fitch laughed. "Do you think you can manage a few months of marriage without getting too bored? Parliament is not easily ignored, and an extensive tour of the Continent takes time. As for Egypt . . . perhaps a trip to reward you for giving me an heir."

"Reward," Hilary scoffed. "Leave it to a man to choose that particular word."

To her consternation, Fitch laughed again. "I can see that marriage to you is going to be complicated, Miss Compton."

Hilary wished she could disagree, but the earl

had her dead to rights. A slow smile curved her mouth. "I do enjoy being argumentative when it suits my purpose."

"It's just as I suspected. Underneath that prim and proper exterior beats the heart of a mutineer."

He waited for her to argue that there wasn't a rebellious bone in her body, but she didn't.

Her attitude, style of dress, and forthrightness proclaimed her as a free-thinking woman. More importantly, her manner lacked that quality—elusive in definition—that he'd come to associate with women in general: a compound of self-absorption, and beneath it, a frightening innocence about the true nature of life. Unlike most aristocratic young ladies, who were born only to breathe the stagnant air of the upper classes, Hilary was comfortable with herself and her surroundings.

"There are a few other issues," she announced. There was a question in her manner, and a short pause, as if she were mentally preparing a list.

"Such as?"

"My personal rights," she said. "I have no intentions of becoming a comfortable wife—by that I mean a woman who allows her husband to do her thinking for her. I will choose my own friends, and manage whatever property and funds are now mine. Regardless of the current laws, I am not incapable of thinking or acting in a sensible, responsible manner. I have not been raised from the cradle, as have some females, to think myself inferior in any way. While ours will be a marriage of convenience, I would also have it be one of mutual respect. I will not endeavor to impose my will on you, expecting the same courtesy in return. If you can agree to those terms, my lord, then you may consider us engaged."

Fitch listened, amused by her extreme ideas. The little lady was proving to be quite a strategist. She wasn't leaving anything to chance. But it didn't keep him from saying, "We will marry one month from today."

"I would prefer more time," she said, noting that he had neither agreed nor disagreed with her conditions. "And I would have your agreement that you will honor my individuality once we are married."

"I prefer marrying as soon as possible," he countered. "There's no point in waiting. Neither of us has family who require consulting, and Lizzie is in full agreement that we should marry as quickly as possible. A month is more than enough time to make the preparations, unless you want the pageantry of a larger affair."

Hilary hesitated just long enough for Fitch to know she was still having second thoughts.

"Pageantry doesn't interest me, my lord. But need I remind you that we are essentially strangers? Two people who plan on spending the remainder of their mortal days together should know more about each other than a few inconsequential facts."

It wasn't that she didn't want to marry him, it was that she *sensed* more about him than she knew for certain. She recalled the previous night of tossing and turning and pacing the floor while she struggled with whether or not to accept the first, and only, marriage proposal of her life. Even the small amount of sleep she'd gotten had been filled with dreams of him.

"Surely there is more to you than meets the eye," she added, knowing he had no intention of volunteering any information. "How do you occupy your time when you aren't in the House of Lords? Do you have any interests beyond those of the normal gentleman?"

"Nothing out of the ordinary. I occasionally gamble, but never too deep. I attend the races whenever possible. I enjoy managing my estates, though I employ stewards for the day-to-day operations. My vote in Parliament is more conservative than liberal—"

"Having met you, that's understandable," Hilary remarked. She stood motionless on the path. "I was thinking along more *personal* lines."

"Marriage will see to our acquaintance," Fitch replied. "Though there is something to be said for engagements."

Before Hilary could protest, he was kissing her, ignoring the sum of things that they did not have in common to concentrate on the passion they shared.

It was a gentle kiss at first, before becoming something else: the lips that had brushed hers ever so lightly fastened over her mouth hungrily, and Hilary was swept into a passionate embrace. She decided—with what sense she could salvage—that being kissed by the Earl of Ackerman was akin to having one's soul shot into the heavens like a well-aimed arrow. The sensation was exhilarating.

Never relinquishing her lips, Fitch backed Hilary against the trunk of a large tree. He held her in place with the full length of his body, letting her feel the differences between them, but controlling his passion. It was time the lady realized she wasn't dealing with an amateur. He'd learned how to kiss when he was fourteen, and the ensuing years had honed his skill to that of a master. The truth was, he liked kissing. He liked the feel of a woman in his arms, the softness and the scent and the taste of her.

Sliding his arm around her waist, he brought her into more direct contact with his body. His fingers moved to the buttons on her blouse. They were small, but he was well experienced, and they came undone easily. He peeled back the collar, exposing the pale skin beneath it. She shivered at his touch, but she didn't push him away.

"Do you like to be touched?" He trailed a finger across the ridge of her collarbone.

"I'm not sure." She shivered as she said the words, unable to control the confusion that came with the touch of his hand.

"Then it's time you found out." He lowered his head and pressed his lips to her throat. Even though she'd made up her mind, Fitch didn't consider it wasteful to do a little more persuading.

Hilary couldn't stop the soft gasp of surprise his touch created. Cast into the unknown, she had no logical way to deal with the sensations he was arousing, so she simply enjoyed them.

"Your skin is soft and warm," Fitch said, breathing the words against the point where her pulse was beating. The fragrance of scented soap rose from her body, and his control teetered on the edge for a moment. "I'm tempted to postpone my return to London. I'd very much like to find out if the rest of you is as sweet."

He shifted his hold, placing his hands on her hips while his lower body fitted snuggly against her. A glance told him her nipples were already hard, pouting for his mouth. He wanted to bare them to his sight, to taste them, to feel her reaction as he made love to her.

He forgot they were in the woods, forgot his carriage was waiting, forgot his manners as he kissed her lips, her eyes, her hair, her neck, letting his hands roam more intimately over her.

Hilary trembled beneath his kisses, responding despite her common sense, turning her head breathlessly as he kissed her face and neck with increasing passion. He was taking her places she'd never imagined, to heights so intolerable she wanted to weep with the joy of the journey. An extraordinary, inexplicable sensation raced through her heart as he continued kissing her.

Knowing he had to stop after the next kiss, Fitch seized her face in his hands and pressed his mouth down on hers in a fierce show of passion. Hilary returned the kiss with a burst of enthusiasm that left them both shaken, clinging to each other.

A few seconds later, Fitch shook his head in wonder and touched her sun-burnished hair with the tips of his fingers. When Hilary looked up at him he was smiling, a lazy, confident smile that made his eyes gleam. She smiled in return. For a moment, for one breathless moment, it seemed as if love was within her grasp.

The moment came to a startling halt as Sylvester came bounding out of the woods in hot pursuit of a rabbit that darted across the path in a flash of grayish-brown fur.

Fitch laughed, then stepped back. "London is waiting. Pity. I'd rather stay here."

With another smile, he reached out and began to fasten the small pearl buttons he had so deftly undone a few minutes earlier. "You're a very distracting female, Miss Compton."

Unsure what to say, Hilary pushed his hands away and finished righting her blouse. Her face grew warm with embarrassment, but there was no undoing what had caused it. "You're the one who is distracting, my lord. And I have yet to receive your answer. I will not marry a man who thinks to dissuade me with kisses."

He laughed. "Your individuality is in no danger, since I have no desire to turn you into another woman. I rather like you just the way you are." A quick kiss was added for emphasis. "Are we in agreement?"

"Lizzie and I will be packed and ready in one week's time, my lord."

Hilary's tone was deferential, but beneath it lay a deep determination to make her marriage to the earl more than convenient. The earl—this man and their upcoming marriage—was her one chance for happiness, and she had no intention of taking them casually, or of letting her life become long years of silence and solitude as a docile, obedient wife.

She had made her decision last night, and she reaffirmed it now, looking at him, watching the play of sunlight and shadow over his face. Marriage would merge their lives—two people sharing the same house, the same meals, the same bed. But her most fervent wish was to share more, much more.

"You're looking very serious," Fitch said as they returned to the house, walking slowly and side by side.

"I want a church wedding," she told him.

"I'm not a heathen, despite what I may have said last night."

"Not a large wedding. I don't know anyone in London."

"A small ceremony suits me as well," Fitch agreed. He could see the house through the trees and he wanted to stop and kiss her again, to linger indefinitely over her mouth, to take the taste of her to London with him, but he didn't. Lizzie was playing in the garden and soon she'd see them and come running.

He stopped anyway, not for a kiss, but for a last moment alone with her. What should a man say at a time like this? There was too much honesty between them for him to spout a lie, were he given to falsehoods, which he wasn't. If he complimented her, she'd rebuke him with a reminder that there were far prettier women he could marry. So he spoke the truth and said what was on his mind.

"Thank you. For Lizzie, and for agreeing to marry me."

"You're welcome," Hilary replied, remembering all the dreams she had set aside years ago. Did she dare to dream them again?

Five

Fitch woke up with a start. Sweat ran in tiny rivulets down his bare torso. He panted, unable to get enough air into his lungs. After a few minutes, he slumped against the pillows, still trembling.

Time passed—he had no idea how much—while he took slow, deep breaths to ease the anxiety that always followed the nightmares. He closed his eyes and tried to think of something pleasant—how Hilary had tasted the last time he'd kissed her—but sleep came intermittently, then disappeared completely.

He lay quietly then, time slipping away, agonizingly slow in its passage. Now and again a random thought came to mind, cloaked in wishes and dreams of what might have been if he hadn't gone to war, hadn't left Beth carrying his child. Then, letting go of what might have been, he thought of what was yet to be, of his marriage to Hilary and the children they would share.

It caused him to ponder momentarily, but he

was too restless to give the future the contemplation it deserved.

There was a storm, brief but disturbing; the rain always brought back the smell of decay and death. Despite his best efforts, he couldn't abandon the nightmare that had torn him awake. He had been standing in the hospital ward after the battle for Inkermann.

Hundreds had been killed, three times that number wounded. No one had been spared in helping the surgeons gather those who might be saved. By day's end he had been soaked through with blood from carrying amputated limbs from the surgery tent to where a pit had been dug to bury them.

He looked down at his now clean hands and shuddered, seeing them the way they had been that day—stained with blood.

Tossing back the coverlet, he walked naked to the window. The emptiness of the night swallowed all but the sound of the rain. So much darkness. So much loss.

The storm undermined his confidence, as only a storm could do. Walking across the room to where Raskett had left a decanter of whiskey, he poured himself a drink. During the war he had faced death's dramatic conflict countless times, and survived. But the ghosts had refused to fade with victory. There had been no new dawning of light, as with each new day, but a continual sense of unrest.

How he longed to put it behind him, and yet there seemed no end to the nightmares, no end to the memories. They visited him regularly, and with each appearance the reality of war returned full force—mangled corpses and maimed bodies, blood-stained uniforms and the soulful moans of the dying, the false pride of victory, and the ugliness of it all that had followed him around the Crimean like a foul smell carried by a persistent wind.

The emptiness of the room suddenly became intolerable. Fitch dressed, pulling on his trousers and a shirt, then went downstairs.

Night was speeding away, and dawn's pale light shone dimly against the eastern sky. Within the city, life began to stir. Glancing out the library window, he could make out the misty, shrouded shapes of vendors' wagons, delivering milk and other produce, while the gentry of Eaton Square—all but one—lay sleeping in their beds.

Crossing to his desk, Fitch glanced at the liquor cabinet. He was tempted to pour himself another drink. He was prevented from giving in to the temptation by the library door opening and Raskett coming in, carrying a tray upon which sat a Sheffield plated coffeepot.

"I thought you might be in need of this, milord," the servant said, placing the tray on the Georgian satinwood side table near the window. "Damp morning."

"Yes, it is," Fitch replied, wondering if Raskett was also plagued by dreams.

The two men had served together for two wretched years in the Crimea, Raskett as an ensign, Fitch as a lieutenant, then a colonel—field promotions in the deadly Balkan Peninsula had been an everyday occurrence.

Though they had never spoken of it, Fitch was certain the butler knew all too well how little sleep his employer got on a stormy night.

"I'll bring a breakfast tray when you're ready," Raskett said, turning up the gasolier and filling the room with light. The furnishings lost their ghostly outline and took on the warmth of burnished wood and soft-grained leather.

It was Sunday, a day unlike the other days of the week throughout the whole of England. Church would be attended by most, master and servant alike. Fitch rarely graced the pews, unless invited to a wedding, or called by the necessity of a funeral it would be inappropriate not to attend.

Since leaving the Crimea, he'd lost his appetite for biblical duty. War had not allowed Sunday to be observed as a day of prayer and dedication. The fighting had continued, heedless of man's faithfulness to God. The whole affair had seemed a mockery, since the pretext had been a quarrel between Russia and France over guardianship of the holy places in Palestine.

"Will you be attending services?" Raskett asked, heedless of Fitch's personal thoughts, or perhaps because of them.

"No. I will spend the day working. I've decided to implement a new irrigation project at Winslow. The work will begin this summer." He accepted the cup of coffee Raskett handed his way. Steam floated over the rim of the porcelain mug, warming the air around it. "You might as well know that I've asked Miss Compton to marry me."

"Congratulations, sir." There was a curious set to his chin as he looked at Fitch. "The staff at Winslow will be pleased. Mrs. Ellerbeck most of all. She has long thought it time for you to marry and begin a family."

Fitch smiled, knowing Mrs. Ellerbeck, a staunch but well-meaning housekeeper who ruled Winslow Manor single-handedly, had dropped more than one or two comments about his lack of a wife and heir. "Then Mrs. Ellerbeck will be pleased to know that I will gain a family along with a wife. My daughter, Lizzie—though time will delegate when and if she ever learns her true identity—is the primary reason I proposed to Hilary."

"Then you acknowledge that the child is yours," Raskett said, helping himself to a cup of coffee. It wasn't unusual for him to join his employer in either a morning or evening refreshment, especially when Fitch was in need of airing his thoughts on one matter or another. "I was curious."

"My very reason for traveling to Nottingham," Fitch admitted. "My curiosity was satisfied. Within a month's time, this house will cease being a bachelor residence. I expect you will tolerate the change well enough."

"I'll manage," Raskett said, harboring a faint smile. "It should prove interesting."

"Interesting indeed," Fitch said, his mood improving as the gray light of dawn washed over the windows. The rain was easing. Hansoms for hire joined the parade of market wagons moving up and down the cobblestone streets, their harnesses jingling in a metallic song that was commonplace to the city. "Miss Compton is far from docile. In fact, I fear she may prove totally unmanageable as a wife. She is a most opinionated woman, my friend. Dogmatic in her views and dedicated to her independence. Our arguments will be lively ones. She expects me to yield the authority of a husband without the blink of an eye."

"Will you?"

"No," Fitch said, setting down his coffee cup and reaching for a cigar. In his mind he could see

Hilary's sensitive, stubborn face. "I will tolerate more than most men, but not as much as she would like."

"A man should rule his own household."

Fitch looked past the end of his glowing cigar to see a slight smile curving the butler's mouth. A spontaneous smile found its way to his own mouth. "I suppose it is amusing for any man to think he can *manage* a female. They're such erratic creatures."

"That they are, milord."

"Come," Fitch said, setting his cigar in a brass ashtray. He unrolled a sheet that showed crisscrossed lines, with neat notations off to the side. "You helped the engineering corps during the war. I'll have your opinion on these plans. Do you think the ditches deep enough?"

Raskett joined him at the desk and talk of women and their unpredictable ways was postponed.

It was evening when Fitch set out for his club in St. James. The sun had dried the last evidence of the storm away, leaving the streets shimmering in the light haze of the setting sun. Carriages and omnibuses rolled along the streets, taking people home after their day's business.

Fitch sat back in his carriage, his mind occupied with the responsibilities of taking a wife. He expected things to be awkward at first. Until now, his life had been centered around the freedom of a bachelor, a man who answered to no one but himself. The taking of a wife would require some changes, but not, as he had indicated to Raskett that morning, nearly as many changes as Hilary might like to impose.

There would be alterations, of course. No more lonely dinners eaten in the library, no more quiet evenings spent in the library, reading or simply gazing into the fire, and no more solitary nights. The bedchamber adjoining his would finally serve a useful purpose.

He stepped down in front of his club, nodding cordially to the liveried footman who met him at the door. The mammoth clock in the foyer chimed eight as he handed his cloak to yet another footman, this one a young man serving his apprenticeship under the stern eye of the club's majordomo.

Fitch strolled across the tiled floor, up the steps, and into the main saloon. Seeing the Marquis of Waltham enjoying a glass of port while browsing the *Evening Chronicle*, Fitch joined him, making himself comfortable in a high-backed leather chair with wide arms and a matching ottoman.

The marquis immediately lowered his newspaper. "Wondered if you'd show yourself tonight. Sent a man around to your place last week. That militarized butler of yours told him you'd gone off for some business in Nottingham. Buying another estate?"

"Not this time. The business was personal."

Waltham's expression changed, his eyes taking on an inquisitive gleam, but when Fitch offered no more details, the discussion turned to the debate of several reform laws currently before Parliament. A few minutes later, the men were joined by yet another of the night's players. The Earl of Granby, dressed in an impeccably cut gray coat with a black velvet collar, strolled into the club looking as content as his friends knew him to be.

"Nottingham, Fitch, and for two weeks," he said in greeting. "It must have been important, not to have sent a note by Morland's place. The old gent will expect an accounting. Can't have his 'lads' dashing off without so much as a by-your-leave. Discipline, and all that."

"He'll get one," Fitch said, intentionally saving his announcement until all the players were in the gaming room. The duke would appear precisely at eight-thirty, followed shortly thereafter by the Viscount Rathbone, who insisted on being late just to goad the old man. "How is Catherine?"

"As lovely as ever, and just as feisty," Granby grumbled, without losing his smile. "Had a roaring argument just before leaving the house. She refuses to return to the country. Insists pregnancy doesn't make a woman an invalid."

"It doesn't," Waltham said. "Evelyn didn't have a complaint until the night of the birth. Then she had plenty to say—mostly about me."

Granby visibly shuddered. "I for one do not intend to be within hearing distance. I'm going to take solace in my library until I can greet my first-born properly."

The briefest of smiles flickered across Waltham's face. "Very courageous of you."

"Fitch is the hero, not me," Granby said.

Neither man noticed the slight stiffening of Fitch's mouth as the remark was passed. The praise that was often heaped on him for his bravery in battle only served to remind him that he had fallen short of the mark. Admittedly, he had been a good officer, standing firm under fire, but courageous acts came easily when a man expected to be killed. There was little heroism in surviving, only a dull pain that came with knowing so many others hadn't.

The evening progressed as expected with the duke striding into the club as the clock chimed the half hour. He was a stately man with silver-white hair and a zeal for life. In his late sixties, he still possessed the charm and wit to capture a lady's attention. Since the death of their fathers, he had taken to overseeing, and occasionally meddling in, the lives of the younger men who played cards with him each Wednesday night.

"Ackerman," he said, formally referring to Fitch, which meant the earl had fallen out of grace with His Grace. "Heard you found your way back to the city."

"I was in Nottingham," Fitch said. "A matter of some importance, Your Grace."

"Yes, well, a man should see to his affairs," the duke replied. He glanced around the room. "Speaking of affairs, I suppose Rathbone has yet to be seen. Good thing I asked Sterling to drop by—can't play a decent game of cards when one of you lads goes missing."

Fitch accepted the reprimand wordlessly, giving the duke his due.

A few minutes later, both Sterling and Rathbone showed themselves. Sterling was the oldest of the duke's "lads," Rathbone the youngest. The Viscount Sterling had married for a second time and, like Granby, appeared to enjoy having a wife. Rathbone vowed never to marry. The two were complete opposites, but as frequently happened with good friends, their differing personalities complemented each other rather than causing dissention.

It was an hour into the play, after Sterling had won the first hand, that Fitch casually asked Waltham if he might be interested in renting the house he owned on Lambeth Road.

"Any particular reason?" the marquis asked.

"My fiancée is in need of a residence," Fitch said as he fanned out his cards to study them. He didn't have to look up to know that everyone at the table was staring at him. "Three weeks should be sufficient. We're to marry the last week in May."

A short silence lasted until a fusillade of words broke out, indicating what the youngest player at the table thought of the announcement.

"Marry!" Rathbone slapped his cards facedown on the green baize top. "Bullocks, you say. You can't get married."

"Why not? It's inevitable if you carry a title, which we all do."

"Bloody hell!" Rathbone pushed back his chair and came to his feet. He marched to the sideboard and poured himself a drink, then turned to glare at Fitch. "So that's what you were doing in Nottingham. Wooing a woman."

"Sit down, Rathbone," the duke said sharply. "As Fitch said, marriage is inevitable, unless you wish to forfeit your title to the crown."

Rathbone sat down, but he wasn't finished voicing his displeasure. "Who is the chit? And why go to Nottingham? Every young lady of marriageable age is on her way to London. The Season is upon us."

"Not every young lady," Fitch replied. "And I wouldn't have met Miss Compton at one of the balls. She isn't gentry."

"This is getting more interesting by the moment," Granby said, reaching for his drink. "Marriage. I must say, Catherine will be pleased. She remarked only last week that you needed a wife. Thinks you're getting too set in your ways."

"I'm pleased that her mind will be put to rest."

"Miss Compton of Nottingham," Morland said, casting a hard glare across the table at Rathbone. "I look forward to meeting the young lady."

"Yes, well, she isn't all that young," Fitch admitted, putting down his cards. There would be no more play until he came clean with the details. "Eight-and-twenty, and quite independent. She has a ward. An impish little girl by the name of Lizzie. I'm thinking to adopt the child. Her father served with me in the Crimea."

"Admirable," Sterling announced, making his first comment since the news hit the room. "A wife and a child. You're undertaking a major change in your life, my friend. I hope it proves to be a happy one."

"I don't foresee any complications. And there is the matter of an heir. Might as well get the duty done."

Granby laughed. "It's not as much of a duty as one might think, if the lady suits you."

"She suits," Fitch said, unable to hide his smile.

"Then the house on Lambeth Road is yours," Waltham said. "But no rent. Won't hear of it. When should Mrs. Grunne have the house readied?"

"Week's end," Fitch told him. "And, thank you. I disliked the idea of putting them up in a hotel or an inn. Lizzie likes the out of doors, and as I recall, there is a park nearby."

"Complete with birds to feed and squirrels to steal the bread crumbs," Waltham said laughingly.

"I thought to pay a call on Lady Forbes-Hammond," Fitch said. "She seems to have a talent when it comes to weddings."

"Arranged mine nicely enough," Viscount Sterling agreed. "But then, I married her niece."

It had been a nice wedding, Fitch thought. And his friend was certainly happier for having married the blue-eyed Rebecca.

"That only leaves one thing unsettled." He looked toward Rathbone.

The silent message got the expected results.

"No. I won't do it. Attending Sterling's and Waltham's weddings was bad enough. Then Granby," he glared across the table. "I let him out of my sight for one summer and he's married faster than a Tower Hill pickpocket can pilfer a watch. Mother has been singing the praises of marriage ever since. Bloody hell, do you know what she'll say once she hears you're to take the dreaded leap? I'll be the only 'lad' left without a wife. There's to be no peace for me, I tell you, no peace at all. The very thought of marriage gives me a rash."

"I'll have Raskett mix up an ointment," Fitch chuckled.

"Why not ask Morland?" Rathbone suggested, grabbing at the last available straw.

"Because, if he agrees, he will be busy escorting my bride down the aisle. Hilary has no immediate family."

"I'd be honored," Morland said. "As will Rathbone."

The ducal dictate put an end to the viscount's argument and play was resumed. Fitch won the next hand.

At the close of the evening, Sterling, Waltham, and Granby each returned to their wives. Rathbone, still doubting Fitch's sanity, was out the door and off to do more damage to his reputation. He was often referred to by the admiring soubriquet of "Viscount Virile." The volume of his sexual exploits had earned him the title, one he claimed without regret or reservation.

Fitch walked the duke to his carriage. It was a balmy night, but not a brilliant one. The moon was low over the rooftops, its illumination lessened by a bank of thick clouds.

The two men walked casually, the duke with an elegant stride aided only slightly by his cane, Fitch with the gait of a man who had once worn a uniform. They were silent, as was the street in front of the prestigious club, except for the occasional sound drifting out as a door was opened, then closed. There were no falling stars, no thunder-on-the-left, no presage in the air, and yet Fitch felt tense, as if he were about to go into battle.

"Good night, lad," the duke said once he was seated in the black-and-gold-lacquered carriage with its ducal crest emblazoned on the doors. "And congratulations. I hope your marriage lessens the burden you carry so solitarily."

"I have no burdens, Your Grace," Fitch lied, doing a fine job of it, or so he thought.

The duke looked at him, his gaze so like that of a father it was unnerving. "You always were the most stubborn of the lot. Rathbone thinks himself to be, but you've caused me the most worry over the years."

"I have no burden, at least none that weigh any heavier on me than they would any other man," Fitch said, thinking Morland's insight into his character too clear for comfort.

"Say what you will, but you buried your father before the war, and your only brother three years later. You've changed. No man could be called upon to do what you've done and not feel the impact of the experience. It's time you married and got on with your life. If Miss Compton can bring you happiness, then this marriage has my blessing. Good night, lad."

"Good night, Your Grace."

All the way back to Eaton Square, Fitch thought of what the duke had said, about the joy of not being alone, of having someone with whom he could share the events of everyday life. If only it could be that easy. If only his mind wasn't constantly filled with memories of a tragic, destructive war that had gained nothing tangible in the long run but the death of too many men.

Perhaps the duke was right. Perhaps Hilary and Lizzie would help him regain the zest for life he had had as a young man. As the carriage turned into the respectable square where his residence was located, Fitch hoped the exhilaration he had felt the moment he'd seen Lizzie would be enough to balance and eventually outweigh the desolate feelings he had carried back from the Crimea.

Fitch handed his card to the butler, a starchy old man with a longish nose and dull eyes.

"The Earl of Ackerman to see Lady Forbes-Hammond."

The butler peered down at the card. "I will ask if her ladyship is receiving, milord."

Fitch took off his hat and gloves, passing them to the servant as if there were no question as to whether or not he would be received by the lady of the house. The butler accepted them without comment.

He was then shown into the withdrawing room. Outside, the weather was bright and mild, but there were clouds gathering to the east of the city, over the Channel. Fitch was too well experienced with the changeable weather of England not to know that rain could turn the day into an uncomfortable one quickly enough to catch a man without a proper coat to shed the water.

With some trepidation, he had made his deci-

sion to call on Lady Forbes-Hammond and begin
the arrangements for his upcoming marriage. As
he stood in the middle of the heavily decorated
room, Fitch hoped Hilary hadn't changed her mind.
There had been notable reluctance on her part
that last day in Nottingham, though he was certain
she had enjoyed his kisses.

If Miss Compton didn't arrive in London as
scheduled, he would not hesitate to return to Nottingham and fetch her himself, though he loathed
the idea of their marriage beginning on such an
aggressive foot. It would serve their future much
better were Hilary to surrender herself into his
keeping without a major confrontation.

While he was not of the opinion that a female
shouldn't exercise her mind, he did believe that it
was a husband's place to protect and care for the
woman to whom he gave his name. In that regard,
he meant to be the best husband he could be, giving Hilary no remorse for accepting his proposal.

The door opened as he finished the thought
and Lady Felicity Forbes-Hammond made a grand
entrance in a morning gown of mulberry silk and
black lace. She was a wealthy woman, widowed for
most of her adult life, who continued to keep an
active hand in Society. Her silver hair gleamed to
match the jewels around her neck and on her
hands as she greeted her visitor with an enthusiastic smile.

Fitch bowed over her hand. "I hope my calling
isn't an intrusion," he said. "But after a conversation at my club last night, I thought to seek you out
and ask a favor."

"A favor?" Felicity replied, making the word sound
mysterious. She motioned toward a chair, while seating herself on the settee. "I must say I'm intrigued

by your unexpected visit. You say you had a conversation last night at your club. With whom, may I ask?"

"The Duke of Morland, though it wasn't he who brought you to mind, but the Viscount Sterling. You are an aunt to his wife."

"Yes." Felicity smiled with pride. "And greataunt to his son and daughter. They've only just arrived in London. Rebecca is sure to call soon."

"Then perhaps you can commission her help as well."

"With what do you require help, my lord?"

"A wedding," Fitch told her. "I'm to marry at the end of May. Knowing your talent in such manners, and having a personal recommendation from Lord Sterling, I thought to seek your advice in the matter."

"A wedding!"

Her pale eyes began to sparkle and for a brief moment Fitch thought she might clap her hands the way Lizzie did whenever he gave her a gift.

"Oh my, but this is a surprise. From your reputation, I had assumed you to be as steadfast in your bachelor ways as that young scamp Rathbone. I daresay getting him to the altar will take some doing."

Fitch's smile was agreement enough. The details of his upcoming nuptials were delayed while a maid served tea. The moment the door closed behind the servant, Felicity inched to the edge of her seat and demanded to know everything there was to know about the bride.

"Her name is Miss Hilary Compton. Her aunt, with whom she has lived most of her life, recently died. Hilary is from Nottingham, and a woman of strong individual ideas."

"How interesting," Felicity said. "A woman of individual ideas, is she? Oh, this is intriguing. And how did you come to propose marriage to such a lady?"

"Totally unexpectedly, I assure you," Fitch laughed. "But having asked, I find myself eager for the wedding. It will be a small affair attended by close friends. Can you recommend a chapel?"

Felicity sipped her tea while she gave the matter some thought. "There is a small church in Knightsbridge, not far from Kensington Gardens. I attended a thoroughly enjoyable wedding there last Season. Nothing so grandiose as St. Paul's or Westminster, of course, but well kept by a devoted minister and suitable for a small affair. I will send a man this afternoon with a note, inquiring if the chapel can be made available." She frowned a bit before pinning Fitch with an inquisitive stare. "I hope you are not rushing the lady to the altar. One could arouse a good deal of gossip, were that the case."

"I assure you the haste has nothing to do with necessity. Miss Compton is the most virtuous of women. I am simply eager to marry now that I have found her."

"Is she in the city?"

"Not at the moment. I expect her at week's end. She will be residing on Lambeth Road. Lord Waltham has been generous enough to donate a small residence which he purchased a few years ago."

"I know the house. He and Lady Waltham escape to it when the social swirl becomes too demanding. A delightful couple, don't you agree? Nothing wrong with that union, I tell you. Firm as the walls of Buckingham Palace. Very well, my lord. I shall keep my calendar open."

"Thank you. If I may impose even more, Hilary

will also require the services of a seamstress. While adequate for the country and a quiet lifestyle, her wardrobe will be lacking for the Season."

"Shopping is hardly an imposition. Once the news is out—and rest assured, it will get out—you're certain to be delivered more invitations than you can possibly accept. You're considered quite a catch, young man. Any man who served in the military has a certain mystique the ladies find irresistible. Everyone will want to meet the young woman who managed to convince you that marriage has its advantages."

Fitch smiled, knowing all too well the curiosity that accompanied the Season. Hilary was a woman of feminine simplicity that was contradicted when she spoke her mind. It would be interesting to see how his friends reacted to her.

"I should also tell you that there is a child. Her name is Lizzie and she is nine years old. Miss Compton is her guardian."

"Then Miss Compton is no young chit."

"No, madame, she is not. She is a woman of independent means with attitudes to match."

"How delightful," Felicity said. "Well, my lord, you have certainly brightened my day. Just imagine, I had started out the morning thinking it rather dull. Now I have a wedding to plan and a bride to clothe. I shall begin immediately."

Six

"Annie, take care, or you'll fall out the window," Hilary said, reaching out to give the wide-eyed maid's skirt a tug.

"But I've never seen London before." She slumped back in her seat as the traveling coach turned onto yet another cobblestone thoroughfare. "So much crammed into such a small space. And the people! Look at them, too many to count, lords and ladies, crowding the streets like villagers on market day."

"Not everyone is London is a lord or a lady," Hilary told her. "In fact, the aristocracy is in the minority. They stand out because they dress so flamboyantly."

"You'll be dressing that way," Annie said with pride. "You're marrying an earl."

Hilary made no comment. Lizzie was asleep, her head resting in her aunt's lap. It had been a long day and she was amazed that the child had tolerated the journey as well as she had. Lizzie was far too active to keep confined for long periods at a time. Fortunately, she had fallen asleep shortly after they had stopped for lunch.

"Look!" Annie exclaimed as they rolled past Hyde Park's eastern half. The greenery was in sharp contrast to the prestigious architecture that surrounded it, buildings of gray-white English limestone neighbored by those of red brick.

It was late in the afternoon, and as was the custom, the park was full of riders and carriages. *Being seen* was as important an event as any during the Season that would have its official beginnings in a few days' time. The Derby was attended by the elite as well as the common. They flooded to the race like a river flowed to the sea.

Hilary sat quietly in the carriage. She'd have to find a shop and purchase a suitable dress before the race. Nothing in her wardrobe even hinted at the sophistication into which she was about to step.

"Oh, my!" Annie said, popping her head out the window again. "Is that where the queen lives?"

Hilary leaned forward, being careful not to disturb Lizzie. The carriage was moving briskly along, past the gates to Buckingham Palace. The opulence of the royal residence was easy to see, even from a distance. Hilary had been just as impressed as Annie when she'd first viewed the majestic structure.

Had it been only a few weeks ago that she'd made that first eventful journey to London? Looking down at Lizzie's sleeping face, framed by thick, dark curls that had come loose of their ribbon, Hilary knew there was little point deliberating the issue now. She was on her way to becoming a wife.

It took another hour for the coach to make its

way across the Thames, using the Lambeth Bridge. The earl had sent a letter with the driver, informing her that he had procured a small house on Lambeth Road for her and Lizzie to live in until the wedding.

As expected, it was a nice neighborhood, the lane lined with trees and the houses neatly tended. In the distance, dogs barked and the sound of children's laughter could be heard. A street sweeper tipped his hat as the coach rolled by. Annie waved in reply, then took Lizzie from Hilary's lap as the child began to stir.

"She'll give us fits come bedtime," Annie said.

"Perhaps not. Sleeping in a coach isn't nearly as comfortable as being tucked into a feather bed."

"I don't want to go to bed," Lizzie said drowsily. She rubbed her eyes. "I just woke up."

"Not for hours," Hilary promised. "Now, let Annie straighten your ribbons. You don't want Uncle Fitch seeing you looking all wrinkled."

"Are we there yet?" Lizzie asked, wiggling off Annie's lap so she could peer out the window. "Where's the park?"

"We will find it tomorrow morning," Hilary said. "Now, sit still, and let Annie make some order of you."

By the time the coach rolled to a stop, Lizzie was as presentable as possible. She let out a squeal when the door was opened, not by the footman who had accompanied the coachman and who had sat atop with him, but by the earl himself.

"Hello, pumpkin," he said, holding Lizzie in his arms to give her a quick kiss on the nose before setting her feet on the ground. "Did you have a nice trip?"

"Oh, yes," Lizzie told him. "But the best part is finally getting here. London's a very long way from Nottingham."

"So it is," Fitch said. "Stay here while I help Hilary down. Then we'll have a look at the house."

Lizzie was already looking, running to the wrought-iron fence and peeking over it to see what, if anything, might be hiding in the neatly trimmed bushes that bordered the walkway and front steps.

Hilary's heart did a somersault as she gathered her skirts and descended from the coach, with Fitch's helpful hand. A short second later she was standing on the walk, looking into those mystifying eyes. He looked resplendent in a fawn-colored topcoat and trousers with his dark hair falling over his forehead in an unruly manner that made him seem younger than his years.

"Miss Compton," he said with all formality. "Welcome to London. I trust the trip was tolerable."

"As well as can be expected," she said, feeling frumpy as she stood next to the well-dressed man.

The ladies they had seen riding in the park had been dressed in the latest of style, with flowing flounces and billowy skirts spread out around them like silky flower gardens, their bonnets placed with perfection over their coiffures, their parasols twirling. She, on the other hand, was wearing a green traveling suit that was at least three years out of fashion. A very wrinkled traveling suit. Hilary didn't want to think about her hair. She was sure it was creeping out of its pins by now.

"Come inside," he said, offering his arm. "Mr. and Mrs. Grunne keep the house. They're an affable couple. I'm sure you'll be made to feel at home."

Hilary was too bedazzled by the earl's charming smile and gleaming, dark eyes to notice much about the house, but she forced herself to look. She studied it according to her own standards of architecture and found it more than acceptable. The roof was dark slate, gliding down and over a porte cochere and a side veranda. The tower windows of the second and third floors each boasted a small balcony of wrought iron. The front door was inset within a vestibule and approached by wide stone steps.

It was a pleasant house, not ostentatious, but well constructed and pleasing to the eye.

The door was opened by a congenial man in a footman's uniform. His wife, a robust woman with taffy-colored hair and brown eyes, wearing a starched apron over a dark blue dress, was waiting in the foyer.

"Welcome," she said. "And this be the little one?"

"This is Lizzie," the earl said, letting go of his daughter's hand. "And this is Miss Compton."

Mrs. Grunne smiled. "I've some shortcake and jam in the kitchen, Miss Lizzie. How about a taste and a glass of milk?"

Lizzie didn't need to be asked twice. She followed Mrs. Grunne toward the back of the house, her curls bouncing with every step, her hair ribbons slightly crooked but still tied.

"I've missed her," Fitch said.

"She's missed you," Hilary replied as she untied her bonnet. Like her traveling suit, it was several years out of fashion, a dull creation of brown felt and black netting with a few small feathers. She placed it on the table, before peeling off her gloves. "So have I."

"Have you?" He turned to study her. "How much?"

"I've been quite bored, if you must know. Annie rarely argues with me."

Fitch laughed. "Were I not an honorable man, I would kiss you here and now with Mr. Grunne looking on," he said, lowering his voice to a silky smoothness.

"How improper." Hilary astonished herself by using a teasing tone. She'd never flirted in her life.

Fitch accepted the challenge. Taking her by the arm, he led her into a cheery parlor decorated in bold green-and-gold stripes. Yellow chintz curtains framed French windows and a door that opened onto a small walled garden at the back of the house.

He released his hold on her, then leaned against the door. "A kiss between an engaged couple is hardly improper."

"Then why close the door?"

"Because I'm thinking about more than one kiss," he said, taking a step toward her. "What about you, my very practical bride-to-be. Have you thought about kissing me?"

"Once or twice." She was flirting again, and having fun doing it. "The house is lovely," she remarked, changing the subject so he wouldn't think her too dazzled by his charms. "It belongs to a marquis?"

"The Marquis of Waltham and his wife, Lady Evelyn. You'll meet them at the dinner party they're hosting in three days."

"A party in three days," she said, stunned by the idea of being thrust into a group of strange aristocrats with only three days in which to prepare herself.

"A very small dinner party—the night before the Derby."

She turned away from him and concentrated on the room. Studying the play of light over the furnishings gave her a moment to focus her thoughts.

It was a delightful room. The tall windows allowed the sunlight to fill every corner. Beyond the door, long briars of wild roses trailed pink against a carpet of green grass.

"The Derby is a terrible crush, but an entertaining one," Fitch said, moving closer to where she stood clutching her hands together. He'd never seen a woman frightened by the mere mention of a party. He reminded himself that Hilary was new to the social swirl of London. "I shall be at your side the entire evening," he assured her.

When she continued staring at a vase filled with fresh flowers, Fitch realized she was far more ill at ease than he'd expected her to be. He studied her and saw the intelligence, as well as the vulnerability. He even caught a glimpse of the wife she would make. Everything about her pleased him at that moment.

"Feeling like a fish out of water, love?"

Hilary swirled around at the sound of the endearment. It was the first time he'd addressed her in such a way, and like so many things about him, it took her by surprise.

"Somewhat," she admitted. "While I am eager to meet your friends and to make a good impression, I cannot promise that I won't disappoint you. My manners are not lacking, but social grace is something else. Were your companions those of an intellectual society, I would feel more at ease. I've never been very good at making idle chatter."

"You will not disappoint," he said, close enough now to reach out and touch her, which he did. A light caress to her cheek. "My friends are nice people, despite their privileged lifestyle. You will be accepted, because you are to be my wife."

Hilary stepped back at the same time she managed a small smile. "It's as easy as that, is it? I agree to marry an earl, and without a single inquiry into my true nature, I am greeted with open arms. I would think Society more selective."

"Your nature is honest and sincere," Fitch said. "You need no further recommendation."

The compliment pleased her, but it did little to ease the worry of a party—and at the home of a marquis. Whatever would she wear?

"Don't be frightened."

"I'm not frightened," she said, denying the charge. "It is only that I had hoped for more time in which to acclimate myself to the demands of the city."

"There's nothing wrong with being apprehensive about meeting new people. Or is it being alone with me that has you wringing your hands?"

Hilary untangled her fingers, giving him a sharp glare as she did so. "I have been alone with you before, my lord."

"Yes, you have."

His tone alerted Hilary to his intentions, but too late. She paused in her breathing for a moment, her eyes fixed on his face as he stepped even closer. The scent of his cologne assaulted her—not forcefully, but with the same subtlety as his smile, like a lazy sunset that had to be admired or lost forever.

Hilary tried averting her gaze to stop the trembling within, but it did no good. She was tired and the trip from Nottingham had afforded her too many hours in which to think. At the moment her confidence was wavering. How had she ever thought herself adequate to the task of being an earl's wife? She disliked Society and its stiff rules and wagging tongues. The malignant influence of social gossip could be felt for months—nay, years—if one were not careful. What would they say when they saw her?

"Hilary."

She opened her eyes, unaware that she'd closed them. Her heart raced as she met Fitch's gaze. Still, she hesitated. What was there to say? She knew so little about this man and next to nothing about the world he inhabited.

"I'm about to kiss you," Fitch said. "A gentleman's ego is more easily appeased when he believes the kiss to be wanted. You're looking at me as if I just sprouted horns and a forked tail."

"I'm sorry. I was just thinking about all that has to be done before the wedding."

"It will all sort itself out," he assured her. "In fact, you can expect visitors tomorrow morning. The wives of my closest friends, Ladies Waltham, Granby, and Sterling, and Lady Forbes-Hammond, a widow, and an expert on the Season. They plan to offer their assistance."

"Their assistance?"

"Shopping for your trousseau," he said, waving aside the subject to show how little it mattered to him. "Waltham's wife has an eye for fashion. Knows all the right shops."

Hilary looked down at her wrinkled skirt. "Fashion has never been one of my major considerations."

"Nor mine. Whatever you need, buy it. I'm a wealthy man."

Hilary frowned. "I will accept this house because of Lizzie, but until we are married I will make use of my own funds."

"A trousseau can be expensive."

"I'm not a pauper. My decision to marry you had nothing to do with money."

Fitch wasn't in the mood to argue. He had instructed Lady Forbes-Hammond that any and all vouchers were to be sent to him for payment. That being the case, it was time to take Hilary's mind off matters of finance.

"Wet your lips," he instructed her in that silky tone that heated the very marrow of her bones

"Why?"

"Because I'm going to kiss you."

With her hair creeping out of its pins, creating a mass of tiny brown curls around her face, she moistened her lips with the tip of her tongue, then frowned suspiciously.

"Say my name."

Hilary hesitated again.

"It's William. William Fitch Minstead, but I prefer Fitch. It's the name I've known since Eton."

"Fitch," she said, disliking the way it came out in a shaky whisper that revealed her nervousness.

Closing one hand around the nape of her neck, Fitch watched her maple-brown eyes flash with emotion, and her soft little mouth open as if she were about to speak. An unexpected urge of desire infused his blood. More than just the need to kiss her, it flamed until his groin grew hot and heavy.

They stood, only vaguely aware of the sunlight warming the room and the sound of Lizzie's laughter from the kitchen. Looking deeply into her eyes, Fitch was once again amazed by the honesty he saw there. He'd never known a woman who wore her feelings so openly. Or did she?

What did she expect from him? Not now—the kiss was inevitable—but in the future, years down the road? What dreams did she harbor deep in her heart and mind? And could he fulfill those dreams? It was the first time the question had surfaced so clearly in his mind, and he wondered if by asking her to marry him he'd done her an injustice.

A certain nervousness went hand in hand with seeing her again. When he'd reflected upon their last meeting, he'd wondered if they would be able to recapture the same quality of rapport they had shared in Nottingham. Seeing her again, the sparkle in her eyes and the gladness of her smile when she'd stepped down from the carriage, lessened his concerns.

All thought faded as his mouth pressed against hers. "You taste good," he said. He kissed her lightly, his mouth lingering until he felt her shudder in response.

Then, wrapping his arms around her and bringing her tight against his body, he kissed her more fully. He hadn't thought of taking another woman since meeting her, and his abstinence was evident in the hardness that pressed against her lower belly.

Hilary returned the kiss feverishly, unable to control her response, opening her mouth to receive his tongue as he rocked his body gently against her, then more forcefully.

A deep stirring of passion began in the very center of her, moving outward like ripples on a pond, consuming her. His hands felt wonderfully warm where they pressed against her back. Then they moved up and around to cradle her breasts. There was an urgent gentleness to his touch as he molded her against the open palm of his hand, then squeezed, sending a shock wave of pleasure through her.

She felt the buttons on the front of her military-style jacket coming undone, felt his hands exploring under the fabric, smoothing over the fine muslin of her camisole. Hilary shivered when he unlaced the undergarment. She hadn't bothered with a corset. The confines of the coach had been stifling enough, and her jacket had covered her completely.

But it was gone now, lying on the floor and his mouth was on her skin. He feathered kisses across the ridge of her collarbone, blew his breath over the swell of her breasts, then lowered his head and kissed the shadowy valley he'd exposed.

Her senses reeled when he sipped at her nipples through the muslin as though he were sampling a fine wine.

Hilary closed her eyes, thinking nothing had ever felt this good, never wanting the hot, damp pressure of his mouth to leave her. Dazed by the new sensation, she gave herself over to it. Soon she was clutching at his shoulders, her legs limps, unable to support her weight.

The delicious kisses went on and on, the exquisite sensations building and building.

Finally, Fitch forced himself to stop. He looked down at her pert little breasts, the crowns hard and as red as rosebuds. He hadn't meant to do more than kiss her, but once his hands had found their way to her breasts . . .

"You *are* distracting. And delicious," he said. He brushed several curls away from her shocked face with fingertips that trembled. "Much too distracting. One more kiss and I'm certain to forget my manners."

Hilary was tempted to ask him to forget—to beg him to keep kissing her. She vowed it was the most wonderful thing.

"You must be tired from traveling, and the door is unlocked," he said as his hands lowered to her waist, then completely away. "Were it not, I'd find out if that sofa feels as comfortable as it looks."

Hilary blushed in spite of herself. She began righting her clothing, thinking of the day she'd agreed to marry him. He'd unfastened her blouse then, and she'd thought him bold. What he'd just done to her was more than bold—it was amazing. She prayed a strong cup of tea would cure the affliction.

He kissed her again, an affectionate kiss.

Hilary lifted her hands and cupped his face between her palms. "I have missed you, my lord."

"And my kisses?"

"And your kisses."

Like a cool, refreshing breeze, her words eased the tension that had been abiding within him since his return to London. His mood was no longer anxious, but filled with anticipation.

Soon, he thought, *but not today.* He was a tolerant man when patience was necessary. It wasn't the time or place to rush her into something she wasn't ready for yet. She was a woman of character, and she was to be his wife. He wanted her content in all aspects of their marriage, especially the bedchamber.

"You need to rest. I'll return later tonight and we shall have dinner. No, stay here. I'll say my good-byes to Lizzie."

Hilary sat down as soon as the door closed, surprised that she hadn't collapsed the moment he'd released her. Her breasts were aching, and there was a notable dampness between her legs. So these were the physical ramifications of passion. But, oh, sweet Lord, the other—the wanting and needing and not knowing what to do about it—that was even worse.

A few minutes later she heard Mr. Grunne bid his lordship a good day, followed by the closing of the front door.

Hilary remained in the library for another ten minutes, sitting in a small Hepplewhite shield-back chair and staring out at the garden. Slowly her thoughts cleared.

Buttoning her jacket snugly over her still-tingling breasts, she went in search of Annie. She needed a bath and a nap, and then she needed the strength to resist the earl until they were legally husband and wife. The first two were easy, the last extremely questionable.

Seven

Hilary stared at her reflection in the mirror. She was wearing an emerald-green gown with a polonaise, tight above the waist, then full and long over a perfectly proportioned crinoline. The silky confection was trimmed with tiny ruffles and pleated ruching. The color suited her, as did the French-cut diamond pendant shining gloriously at her throat.

The necklace was a gift from the earl. She had returned from shopping to find that he had called to take Lizzie for an outing in the park. He had left the gift with a short note asking that she wear it to the party tonight. The note had been signed with the words, *fondest regards.*

They weren't the words Hilary longed to hear, but the gift was a beautiful one, and she couldn't help but smile once the necklace completed her new ensemble.

Her current transformation, from country lass to fashionable lady of London, was entirely due to Lady Evelyn Waltham's keen eye for style. Evelyn was a woman of impeccable taste, whose clothing could inspire jealousy with a mere glance. Hilary had been amazed to learn that before marrying the marquis, Evelyn had once been employed as a shop girl on Bond Street as well as a seamstress to the theater.

Fitch had been right about one thing. The wives of his closest friends were wonderful women. The apprehension she'd brought with her to London was quickly fading under the light of their new-found friendship.

"I can't believe it," Hilary said in an awed whisper as she turned around. "It's really me."

"The key is color and texture. Never wear pastels. Your skin is too fair. And promise me, no more browns."

"I promise," Hilary said, feeling like the fairytale princesses she had read about as a young girl. She'd come to Mayfair, at Lady Waltham's insistence, to dress for the party that would begin in less than an hour.

"Now for the finale." Evelyn walked to the vanity table and reached for a small gold-and-tortoise-shell box.

"What's that?"

"A rouge pot," Evelyn said. "Sewing for the theater means you spend a lot of time with actors and actresses. Only a touch, to put some color in your cheeks."

"Do you use it?" Hilary asked suspiciously.

"Sometimes. Of course, Marshall doesn't know."

Hilary allowed a minuscule amount of rouge to be applied, followed by a dab of French perfume.

"I'll leave you alone to catch your breath," Evelyn said. "And remember, you're among friends."

Hilary nodded, but unfortunately, no amount

of reassurance could chase the butterflies from her stomach. She moved to the bedroom window and willfully tried to close her mind to anything more disturbing than the trivialities of the evening. Only the evening wasn't all that trivial.

The last three days had been so full of activity there had been little time for sober reflection of her future with the Earl of Ackerman. Three hectic, exhausting days of shopping for everything from slippers to a satin robe for her wedding night. And it wasn't over yet. Madame Montaigne was to make her wedding gown. Evelyn had helped to select the fabric, just as she'd guided the couturier's hand in everything else Hilary would need to complete her wardrobe.

Lady Granby, another new friend, had suggested something to brighten Hilary's hair. The recipe was a rinse of lemon juice, cider vinegar, and chamomile to bring out the shine.

Now, instead of a dull brown knot at the nape of her neck, Hilary's face was framed by soft curls that gleamed under the light of the bedroom gasoliers. The rest of her hair was curled and pinned chignon-fashion on the top of her head, accentuating her slender neck and the diamond solitaire.

In spite of the satisfaction she gained from looking prettier than she'd ever looked before, Hilary would not have anyone know that her confidence was shaken by fright—the fear that she might never know the happiness she saw in the faces of her new friends. Their marriages were blessed with love, the kind that shone in their eyes and brightened their faces. A deep, abiding love that would last throughout the years.

Hilary thought of Lizzie and knew the reason for her marriage to the earl had substance, but the fear remained as she saw the first carriage roll up to the curb.

She went downstairs to find Lady Forbes-Hammond just arriving. Felicity reminded Hilary of her Aunt Edwina. Like her aunt, Felicity was possessed of eyes that could be judgmental and, upon occasion, disapproving; that those same eyes could be, and were, kind and friendly when they glanced Hilary's way meant a great deal to the young woman who had been taken under Felicity's social wing.

Dressed in royal blue bombazine with a black lace overskirt, Lady Forbes-Hammond was escorted into the Mayfair residence on the arm of a tall, stately gentleman whom Hilary knew to be the Duke of Morland.

"Your Grace," Hilary said, dipping into a graceful curtsy that spread her silk skirts over the Carrara marble tile of the foyer in a gentle wave of color.

"My pleasure, Miss Compton," the duke said with an approving smile. "Seeing you, it's easy to understand how Ackerman became so enchanted in such a short time. May I congratulate you on your engagement?"

"You may, Your Grace."

It was Fitch who replied. He strolled into the parlor, looking dangerously handsome in black evening attire. With little ceremony he came to stand beside Hilary, his gaze even more approving than the duke's. "You are right. I am enchanted."

The words were spoken as a reply to the duke's comment, but Fitch didn't take his eyes off Hilary when he said them. "You look lovely, my dear."

"Yes, she does," Evelyn agreed. She was wearing a gown of corded silk. The deep-plum-colored dress shimmered in the light as she stood next to her husband, the Marquis of Waltham.

It was evening and the French windows of the main drawing room had been opened to the night, allowing the breeze to drift throughout the lower level of the house. A sumptuous supper would soon be laid out in the formal dining room, which could comfortably seat twenty people. There would be imported French champagne and tasty beef.

But first there would be conversation, and the customary mixing and mingling of people that was expected at such an affair.

The drawing room was ablaze with light that spilled out and onto the nearby street and garden. Fitch seated Hilary in an ebonized chair with classical figures painted on the arms and back railing. He assumed a place beside her, then lifted two glasses from the passing tray held aloft by a liveried footman.

"Thank you," Hilary whispered, "though I'm so nervous I fear drinking anything until I've eaten."

"Honest to a fault, my dear. I like that about you, but not as much as I like seeing you tonight. You do look lovely. Whatever the dress cost, it was worth it."

He studied her again, his gaze moving possessively over her. The announcement of their engagement, which had appeared in the papers two days ago, had all but made her his property; the wedding was a formality.

Fitch was content to lay claim to her.

Hilary was still battling her doubts. There were so many things about the man that perplexed her— and pleased her. He could dazzle any woman with his charm; equally, he could captivate his male friends with an incisive discussion on politics, a ribald joke, or a humorous story. He could be hardheaded, or unselfishly generous. He seemed at ease and yet there was an aura of tension about him, of something barely contained, so that when he moved or spoke, she half expected the air to crackle.

Yet for all that he puzzled her, she couldn't prevent the odd feeling that marrying him was the only thing to do. Still nervous about what lay ahead, Hilary pressed a cool fingertip to the diamond solitaire at her throat.

"Thank you for the present, my lord. It's the most beautiful of gifts. As to the cost of my gown, that is another matter. One I would like to discuss with you when privacy permits."

"I'm to be scolded, am I? Very well, but be forewarned, I shan't change my mind. Spend your money on books, if you must. Everything else you require will be paid for by me."

"Those were not the terms of our agreement," she reminded him.

Before Fitch could respond, they were joined by Lady Forbes-Hammond. "Miss Compton has been a delight these last few days. You were right in describing her as a woman of independent thought. We've had several enlightening conversations."

"I'm sure," Fitch replied, wondering what they'd discussed that had put the mischievous gleam in Felicity's blue eyes.

"Charming," Felicity said, looking at Hilary. "And sure to make you an excellent wife."

"My sentiments exactly," Fitch agreed.

When Felicity moved on to speak to the other guests, Fitch turned his attention back to Hilary. "You were scolding me, my dear."

"Oh, stop being so charming about it," she said in an undertone that reached only his ears. "I expressly asked you to allow me the right to pay for my own purchases. You ignored my request."

"Guilty as charged."

"The matter is not closed," she told him firmly. "My coming to London does not change the terms of our agreement."

"You agreed to become my wife," Fitch said without a change of pace or attitude. "Sooner or later I will be responsible for putting the clothes on your back, among other things. Delaying the inevitable hardly makes sense."

"It is not a matter of time, it is a matter of principle, my lord. I will not allow you to dictate every facet of my life."

They were prevented from continuing the discussion by the ringing of the dinner bell.

It was a brilliant assemblage that made their way into the dining room. The light from the foyer chandelier reflected and gleamed upon a fortune in jewels as the female guests passed beneath it, each on the arm of an immaculately dressed man.

The Duke of Morland was listening with apparent fascination to whatever the middle-aged woman clinging to his arm was saying. He seemed absorbed in her words as if she were the most charming woman on earth. But of course he would have looked the same if she were a monumental bore; it was the gentlemanly thing to do.

The house was filled with just such gentlemen. Despite the reception she had been given by those close to him, Hilary knew there were others who would see her more critically. Society prided itself on a watchful eye.

"Stop worrying," Fitch said, managing to know

her thoughts. "Before the night is over, you will have enchanted everyone as thoroughly as you've enchanted me."

Hilary acknowledged the compliment with a smile, but her emotional response went much deeper. No amount of practicality would allow her to set aside the need for love, romantic or passionate, the need for the same harmonious elation that her new friends enjoyed in their marriages. She wanted Fitch to be more than enchanted—she wanted him to fall in love with her.

"Relax and enjoy the evening," Fitch said as he helped to seat her. "I'll only be a table's breadth away."

The huge, oblong table was covered with a white damask cloth. In the center was a five-branched candelabrum. Each place setting held an array of different crystal goblets, elaborate silverware, and small silver bowls filled with fresh fruit. The first course was a simple choice of soups, followed by more sophisticated fare of boiled salmon, turbot, and lobster rissoles. The beef was sliced as thin as paper, the gravy spooned over it laced with rum. Hilary knew dessert was to be plum sorbet served with chopped nuts and small blocks of vanilla cake, but her mind wasn't on the menu.

The excitement of the party had yet to superimpose itself over her initial concerns—that of her future as Lady Ackerman. Her mind had been temporarily turned aside from the worry, but now that the evening was under way, and appearing successful, the anxiety returned to plague her.

"So this is Miss Compton?" Lord Granby said, addressing Fitch from across the table but looking at Hilary, who was seated between him and the

Duke of Morland. "Catherine has told me how interesting it has been to make her acquaintance."

Fitch smiled. "Don't encourage her. I can never say what is going on in that *interesting* mind of hers."

"At least you admit that she *has* a mind," Catherine said, glaring at her husband. "Norton wants to forbid me the Derby tomorrow. He thinks my condition too delicate to withstand the excitement of a simple horse race."

While Catherine was definitely pregnant and undoubtedly one of the most beautiful women Fitch had ever seen, there was nothing delicate about her. She had the body and inner strength of a woman who could bear a dozen children and still remain young at heart.

"I am not forbidding you," Granby said. "I merely suggested that you may wish to forego the excitement of the day." He looked pointedly at the roundness of his wife's figure. "That is *my* heir, madame."

Catherine smiled as only a woman who knew she was well loved could smile. "I will not spoil Hilary's first party by commenting on how dreadfully autocratic men can be. She may well change her mind about marrying Fitch, and I shan't have that happen."

Fitch smiled to himself. Being seated next to Granby's pregnant wife, and seeing his friend's pride and contentment, aroused a new desire in him—the desire to father another child, a child he could share with its mother from its very conception. He wanted to watch Hilary's figure bloom with pregnancy, to see his son suckling at her bared breast.

During the last few weeks, he had come to terms

with Beth's decision to keep Lizzie's existence from him. Not knowing how he would have reacted to the news, he was able to admit that providence may have known best in taking nine years to bring him and his daughter together. But he had missed so much, things that could never be recovered, things he now had an opportunity to enjoy with the children Hilary would give him.

He looked across the table at her. She was smiling at something Morland had just said. Fitch knew the seating cards had not been placed haphazardly. Hilary had been put next to His Grace to indicate to the other guests, those who were not a part of Fitch's inner circle, that Miss Compton had been duly accepted as the upcoming Lady Ackerman.

"I understand you play the piano with exceptional talent, Miss Compton," someone at the table said.

Fitch recognized the woman as Lady Agnes Gruesby, a friend of Lady Forbes-Hammond's and a patron of the classical arts.

"I play, though the exceptionality of my talent is questionable," Hilary replied.

"Then you must play for us after dinner," Morland requested. "A sampling of your skill will allow us to be the judges."

"If you like," Hilary agreed.

From across the table, Fitch gave her a reassuring nod, and she smiled. It really was silly to allow the man to have such an influence over her every word or deed, but it did help to know he was close by. She drew a strength from him that, until recently, she hadn't known she'd lacked.

* * *

It was later, when the male guests had returned
to the drawing room to rejoin their counterparts
after a brief interlude for brandy and cigars, that
Hilary found herself being escorted into the music
room.

"The duke insists," Fitch told her.

"I've never played in front of people before,"
she whispered. She'd been expanding her friendship with Evelyn, Catherine, and Rebecca, and
making the acquaintance of the other female guests,
all of whom had wished her congratulations on
her upcoming marriage to the earl, when Fitch
had taken possession of her.

He smiled as he led her to the piano, a grand
rosewood instrument that was the centerpiece of
the parlor. The remainder of the room was furnished with a long settee, comfortable chairs, and
shawl-draped tables. The chairs were low to the
floor, allowing the ladies to sit gracefully in spite of
the large hoops and crinoline skirts fashion demanded.

Light was provided by a Waterford chandelier.
The wall behind the piano displayed a gilt mirror
that allowed the player to see his or her audience.
The adjoining wall was adorned with small, classical paintings and Chinese fans.

Releasing Hilary's hand, Fitch pulled out the
tapestry-covered piano bench. "What shall you
play?"

"I haven't the foggiest," she said, seating herself.
Her hands felt cold and stiff. She flexed her fingers.

She glanced up and into the mirror to find the
room filled to capacity. Closing her eyes, she took
a calming breath, then laid her fingers gently upon
the keys and willed the music to flow, not from her

skill as a musician but from her heart, the way Edwina had taught her that all good music should be played.

A few seconds later the air swelled with the vibrant, defining notes of Beethoven's *Moonlight Sonata*. The music rose like a tide, then floated like a cloud, filling the room and pushing at the ceiling, mingled with the thoughts of those seated and listening.

As she played, Fitch realized that Hilary's talent surpassed that of most people. She wasn't giving a simple recital of memorized notes, but was miraculously expressing something beyond the music itself, something from within her very soul.

He looked around the room to find everyone equally enthralled by her fervent style. As her fingers moved over the keys, touching, then releasing, the magic, his body began to vibrate with each note she played, as if she were making love to him with a fierce, yet soothing, passion unlike any he'd ever known.

When the music stopped, reaching a crescendo, then softening to delicate tones before dying completely, the room remained still, silently awed by the wonder of what they'd just heard. It took Fitch a moment to regain his own composure. He stood, then walked to the piano and offered Hilary his hand.

"That was beautiful," he whispered.

She blushed as he turned her to face her audience, and the applause began. It started, one single pair of hands clapping, then swept through the room. At Lady Gruesby's request, she played another selection, then another.

"My child, you play as though heaven were at your fingertips," the duke decreed when the music softened to silence a third time. "Yours is not a talent, but a gift."

Everyone agreed, but it was Fitch's arm around her waist, the surety of his presence, that gave Hilary the most pleasure.

"You're a woman of surprising passion," Fitch said later. "I had never thought to be aroused by the sound of a piano, but I was tonight. Morland is right. You have a gift."

They were in his carriage, on the way back to Lambeth Road, and finally alone. Beyond the closed curtains, the night was imponderably soft and black, the moonlight shimmering.

"I've always enjoyed music. Next to books, it's my favorite thing."

"Come, sit next to me," he said, patting the cushioned seat. "I've waited all evening to kiss you properly."

Recalling his recent remark about becoming aroused by her playing, Hilary hesitated. He patted the seat again, and she relented. It had been three days since they'd had more than a moment alone.

When the kiss came, it wasn't mouth to mouth, but mouth to fingertips. Fitch kissed each and every one. "What other secrets are you hiding from me?"

Before she could answer, he lowered his head and kissed her for real, letting his tongue ease teasingly over her lips before dipping inside to taste her.

The kiss was so exquisitely beautiful it brought tears to Hilary's eyes. Her senses soared with the pleasure of it, inflamed by the blatant sensuality that came so naturally to this man. He wasn't shy about the claim he was staking, but then, she hadn't expected him to be.

With a sigh of pure pleasure, Hilary relinquished herself into his care. The fear of surrendering to her own emotions, of surrendering to him, vanished as pleasure coursed through her. His strength encased her as he pulled her onto his lap and against his chest.

He whispered to her, his tone gentle, the words soothing. Large, strong hands stroked her back repeatedly, easing her more fully against him.

Hilary clung to him, feeling disoriented yet content to be where she was. Her mind quickly blocked out everything but the wonder of him, the fascination of having a tiny part of her dreams come true. She felt completely alive. Fitch was everything she wanted—captivating, intriguing, brazenly appealing to all her senses. Suddenly, all the sharp, painful edges of reality were transformed into something warm and welcoming.

She gave herself to the kiss the same way she knew she was going to give herself to the man—completely.

Fitch made no attempt to fight the hunger waiting to be satisfied. He pulled her forcefully against him, his mouth wild and brutally demanding. The kiss turned deeper—hotter, then hotter still.

The satisfaction that swirled through Hilary was mind-boggling. She marveled at the penetration of his tongue, at the way he tasted, at the heat building up inside her, becoming a part of her. She arched in his arms, straining to get closer to the fire. All the hollow places inside her were filled now—overflowing with sensation.

Fitch pulled away just enough to set his hands to work, baring her breasts. She was small but perfectly made, with soft, pink nipples that grew hard the moment the air touched them. The dim light created alluring shadows, emphasizing the soft mounds. He buried his face in the valley between her breasts and breathed in the scent of her skin. Her body was pale cream and dusky rose, soft and elegantly feminine.

He put his mouth to her breast. She tangled her fingers in his hair. His tongue laved a nipple. Her muscles clenched in reaction. His hands molded and lifted. She moaned, punctuating each beat of pleasure with a responding gasp. It had never been like this for her; she'd never felt such hot arrows of desire, never thought to experience such pure pleasure.

Hilary felt no embarrassment as he worshipped at her breast, at the way he ran his tongue around the pearled tip before taking it into his mouth. There was a tingling sensation, just short of pain, as he drew on her. The feeling built, liquidizing her insides and warming her blood until time faded, until seconds and minutes and hours ceased to exist, until the night melted into feelings and needs and thoughts wordlessly expressed between a man and a woman.

It was Fitch who first realized that the carriage had stopped. He mumbled a short profanity, then chuckled softly. "Too distracting," he said. "And all your fault."

Velvet brown eyes stared up at him. Hilary lay in his arms divided into two people, one lost in sensual delight, the other struggling to remain civilized.

"My fault?" she said teasingly. "I did naught but play the piano."

"Like a witch casting a spell." He was finding it

difficult to regain his composure. He was aroused and aching, and her breasts were still bare. "I'm mesmerized," he whispered before lowering his head for one last taste of her.

His mouth was warm as it journeyed from the swell of her breast to her mouth. It was then—during that kiss—that Hilary realized just how strong love could be, betraying even the most diligent mind. Love was fear and ecstasy, surrender and hope, pain and pleasure. For even the most chaste of Fitch's kisses could arouse those feelings within her.

Her arms found their way around his neck, and the pleasure became more intense, the love almost unbearable, until she was once again sinking into a warm, swirling mist with no thought to time or place.

The only prudent thought that crossed her mind was that they were still in the carriage. But his kisses were so sweet, his caressing hands so gentle, nothing else mattered but the compelling need to give and receive. This was what she wanted—his loving, gentle and fierce.

He pulled her arms from around his neck and crossed them over her bared breasts. "Enough. Inside with you while I still have some control."

Fitch leaned his head back against the cushioned seat and sighed heavily as passion continued to surge through him. He willed it away and slowly his body began to obey. He would see her to the door but no farther, or their wedding night would happen here and now without the benefit of ceremony. Nobility for its own sake spoke to him, and he was able to smile.

"Aren't you coming in?" She righted her clothing as best she could, then draped a white shawl, one of the day's many purchases, around her shoulders. "Lizzie is sleeping, but you could look in on her."

"Not tonight. There'll be no leaving if I do."

Hilary smiled as he opened the carriage door, then handed her down. She supposed she could credit tonight's passion to the new gown or Beethoven's *Moonlight Sonata,* but it didn't seem likely that Fitch would allow such things to arouse him, which meant she was responsible for his passion.

His body was hard with desire because he wanted *her.* He'd enjoyed kissing her as much as she'd enjoyed being kissed. It wasn't seduction, but a mutual wanting.

The revelation was both exhilarating and encouraging. If two people could share one strong emotion, why not another?

For the first time in days, she dared to dream that the earl's heart was waiting to be found. That one day soon she might fall asleep in his arms and wake up to find him beside her, to look across the breakfast table and see him smiling, and know with certainty that she was loved.

The night encircled them in its dark embrace as Hilary reached into her reticule and withdrew the key to the front door. Unsure when the party might end, she'd instructed Mr. Grunne that he need not wait up for her.

She handed the key to Fitch, then smiled. "Passion is a tempting thing, is it not, my lord?"

"Ask me not to go," he said in a throaty voice. "And I'll show you just how *tempting* it really is."

Hilary wanted to—oh, how she wanted. But she didn't. Not because her conscience chose that moment to rear its prickly head, but because Mr. Grunne had not followed her instructions to retire

at his normal hour. He opened the door before
Fitch could put the key to the lock.

The spell was broken, washed away by the foyer
lights.

Rallying his manners, Fitch smiled briefly. "Good
night," he said. "I shall call for you in the morning.
The Derby is best enjoyed when seen from the beginning of the day."

"Good night, my lord." She watched as he walked
to the curb. A few moments later, the sleek black
carriage was under way, disappearing into the night.

Eight

The Derby Day crowd consisted of gentlemen and ladies, their clothing imprinted by the expensive cut and fabric found only in the establishments of Oxford and Regent Streets, joined by soldiers strutting about in scarlet coats with bright brass buttons. There were butchers and bakers, bootmakers and grocers, clerks and chimney sweeps, pastry cooks and parlor maids. Everyone enjoyed a day at Epsom Downs.

Hilary was all eyes as she sat in the Grand Stand and looked at the betting-ring situated under the noses of an elite class of Londoners. The course had been shoveled and racked and smoothed earlier in the morning, soon to be trampled anew under the hooves of sleek thoroughbreds racing for the laurels.

"It's all so exciting," she said, leaning close to Fitch, who had not left her side since exiting the carriage. She was wearing a peacock-blue frock with a short jacket adorned with gold military braiding on the lapel and sleeves and a matching hat that was little more than a pouf of satin ribbons and silk flowers.

She was, as were all the ladies present, very properly fluted and puffed, bonneted and gloved. A white lace parasol was nearby should she need it to shield her from the sun. "I didn't expect it to be so colorful."

Fitch smiled. "It is a bit like attending a fair."

The magic of the day began shortly after dawn when people started migrating up the hill; by noon the road and pavement were overrun by a ravening host of Londoners, all anticipating a grand day, bent on devouring every steamed sausage roll the vendors could supply while they drank the Spread Eagle Tavern dry of ale.

The betting would range from half-crowns and shillings to thousand-pound notes, wagered by gentlemen and apprentices alike. The area around the Epsom-Tower clock was filled with booths and Gypsy-tents, with coffee vendors and bakers selling pastries for a penny. Most would not see the race. Hadn't come to see it, but rather to hawk their wares and be a part of the speculation that filled the air until the "great event" was run and the Grand Stand emptied of its elite, who would hurry home to prepare themselves for tonight's parties.

"Oh, look there," she said, pointing to where the Grand Stand steps began. "Doesn't Evelyn look beautiful? She's been so nice to me. Everyone has."

"I expected no less," Fitch replied, knowing Hilary had surprised a few of them in return, especially last night when she'd played the piano so beautifully.

If he closed his eyes, he could still hear the music, had heard it in his dreams. But there was little time to reflect on how he had spent the night after leaving Hilary on the doorstep of a rented house. Rathbone had arrived.

Fitch made the necessary instructions, knowing full well that the viscount had already gleaned as much information as he could from their other friends. Rathbone left little to chance when it came to women, his or anyone else's.

Today he was dressed as a gentleman and performing the part to perfection. He leaned over Hilary's hand, covered by a white lace fingerless mitten, with just the right air of cordiality and interest. At twenty-nine, there was a dazzle to the young viscount that sprang not so much from his remarkable good looks as from his charismatic character and personality. He could entertain a woman with a smile, whether he was rendering a polite compliment or the brawniest whisper. Even his enemies, mostly jealous husbands, couldn't deny the potency of his magnetism. It was both enviable and worrisome.

"Congratulations on your upcoming marriage, Miss Compton," Rathbone said, smiling as he inspected her from head to toe and back again. "Fitch is the best of us, you know. He's always been Morland's favorite, while I, on the other hand, find myself consistently flayed by His Grace's eloquent tongue."

"A consistency you encourage, or so I'm told," Hilary replied. She'd been warned about the viscount by Lady Forbes-Hammond, who had referred to him as a charming but lovable rascal.

Rathbone laughed, realizing that his invincible charm was being wasted. "I can see that you are well smitten with Lord Fitch. Pity. Rumor has it that I'm the best of all companions on Derby Day."

"Then, by all means, join us," she said, indicating an empty seat. "The race is soon to start."

Fitch accepted Rathbone's nod of approval. Hilary had passed muster, and while the viscount was still of the mind that marriage had little to offer a sane man, it was evident he had resigned himself to his friend's fate.

Hilary gave little thought to the horse that took the finish line or the money that was won or lost, depending upon its speed. She was too caught up in the excitement of the day. It wasn't until later that evening, after the initial excitement of the Derby had faded and most of London's elite had taken to their carriages for a night of parties, that she realized just how much she had enjoyed the day.

She was sitting in the garden while Fitch saw Lizzie put to bed. Nightfall had drifted across the city in gossamer sheets of gray twilight. Now, the sky was ablaze with stars, the moon a waning sliver of light surrounded by wispy clouds. All was still. Even the wind had ceased to sing.

The first solitude of the day sent her thoughts tumbling like an autumn leaf caught by a November wind. She stared up at the stars, wondering how best to gauge Fitch's regard for her. Was he beginning to see her as a wife rather than a mother for Lizzie, as a person rather than one of hundreds of women who could supply him with an heir?

"Here you are," the object of her thoughts said as he joined her. His jacket had been shed, his vest unbuttoned, and his shirtsleeves rolled up. He held a glass of brandy in one hand and a glowing cheroot in the other.

"Yes, here I am."

"Now, that's a pensive answer if ever I've heard

one." A glance toward the sky fostered a question. "Wishing upon a star?"

"It does seem the perfect night. But no, I was merely reflecting upon the day."

"You enjoyed yourself?"

"Yes. It was wonderful."

"I'm glad."

Silence reigned for several minutes and a vile doubt crept into Hilary's mind. Was this to be the pattern of her future life, hours spent in the company of others, only to have all conversation cease when she found herself alone with her husband?

"Lizzie wants to take a balloon ride," Fitch said. He leaned against the garden wall, one knee bent as his booted foot rested against the red bricks.

"A balloon ride?"

"A Hyde Park vendor sells them. A few pence will get you a magnificent view of London's rooftops."

"And Lizzie has convinced you that she must see each and every rooftop or perish."

"Something like that. Will you join us?"

"Tomorrow?"

"It was my plan, weather permitting. Do you have another engagement? More shopping?"

"Dancing lessons."

"Dancing lessons? And when did this come about?"

"Lady Forbes-Hammond arranged them, my lord. You did accept an invitation to Lady Wakesmyth's ball, did you not? And it is on Friday, only six days away."

"I can rearrange my schedule," he said, not admitting to the fact that he'd completely forgotten she'd told him that she'd never danced a step in her life. He smiled, a very sweet smile, but his eyes remained dark. "Raskett plays a rather good piano. Nothing like you, of course, but adequate. And I can think of nothing more enjoyable than holding you in my arms while you learn the waltz."

"I'm sure I'd find the instruction just as enjoyable, but Felicity has already made the arrangements. Monsieur Cavaignac is expecting me tomorrow afternoon. I'm told he is often employed by the aspiring parents of young ladies here for the Season. I suspect he's kept busy polishing their ballroom skills."

Ballroom skills. Fitch smiled at the diplomatic way Hilary had phrased it. As a titled bachelor with considerable wealth, he was all too familiar with the skills used by wide-eyed innocents and their ambitious mothers during the Season. However, his opinion of Society, neither good nor bad depending upon his mood, did not stop him from circulating among his peers. He found parties and soirees as enlightening as he found them humorous.

"I do look forward to waltzing with you," she said. "Let us hope that Monsieur Cavaignac is an excellent teacher."

"He is getting an excellent pupil," Fitch said. He tossed his cheroot into the dew-dampened grass and stepped away from the wall.

Hilary recognized the look on his face. He planned on ending this evening the same way he'd ended the previous one—with her in his arms. But tonight there'd be no footman at the front door. Mr. and Mrs. Grunne had taken themselves off to the local pub for a bit of relaxation. With Lizzie tucked in for the night, and Annie upstairs where she was likely to stay unless called upon, there was little chance they'd be interrupted.

"Tell me about your brother," she said, always eager for one of the earl's kisses but wanting to know more about the man.

The question caught Fitch completely off guard. "My brother's name was Christian."

"Yes, Lady Forbes-Hammond told me. What was he like?"

Fitch wondered what else Felicity had said about his brother. That Christian had been handsome and charming and agreeable with life, that he'd been well educated and able to assume their father's title? That he'd died too young?

Talking about Christian should have been a singularly appealing offer, but each word Fitch spoke of his brother always brought him back to those final words, those final moments when he'd been forced to sit by and watch death leech the life from Christian's body. There had been no one else in the room, only him and the brother he had loved without envy or hesitation.

"He was three years my senior," Fitch told her, "the eldest son. The title came to me upon his passing."

"You had already left the military by then?"

"Yes."

She waited, hoping Fitch would take it upon himself to be more descriptive, more revealing of the relationship he had had with his family. When nothing more was said, she asked another question. "Do you resent your earldom?"

"At times."

"Is there something else you'd rather be doing? Some boyhood dream still unfulfilled?"

"No." A chuckle lightened his voice. "There was a time when I was very young that I'd thought of taking to the sea, but my first Channel crossing purged me of the idea. I got seasick."

"So you became a soldier instead."

"It *is* considered an honorable profession."

Hilary noted the change in his tone. Gone was the lighthearted reference to childhood dreams. In its place was a dull, dry answer that was no answer at all.

"I would like to kiss you," he announced, disposing of his brandy glass by setting it on the ground.

"I'd prefer conversation," she said candidly. "Two people who are engaged to be married should be able to approach whatever topic they wish without prevarication. We know so little of each other."

"The past is not a topic that interests me."

His face was in shadow but his words carried no such vagueness. Hilary tried to hide her disappointment.

"Very well. I heard you and Lord Granby discussing an irrigation project at Winslow. Are you planning to expand the crops?"

"Next summer, if the ditches can be prepared properly this year."

"And what will you grow?"

"What difference does it make?"

"I am simply trying to learn something about the man I am about to marry," Hilary countered indignantly. "I will be your wife. Is my curiosity about our future home incomprehensible, or do you believe that I should restrain my interest to the interior of the house?"

"Beets," Fitch said succinctly. "I'm going to grow sugar beets."

The moonlit garden was not turning into the romantic venue he had anticipated. He'd promised himself, after the episode in the carriage last night, that he'd keep his control, allow Hilary to come to their marriage bed a virgin. But that didn't mean they couldn't enjoy themselves in other ways.

"Sugar beets is a worthwhile crop," she replied, thinking the man the most stubborn she'd ever met, but resolute in getting more than a few mundane facts out of him. "You have stables there. Another assumption I drew from your conversations today."

"Yes."

"Then I must learn to ride as well as waltz."

"You've never ridden?"

"No. Aunt Edwina drove the brougham into the village every week. I became quite proficient at harassing the horse, but we had no sidesaddle."

"I will teach you to ride," Fitch said, thinking of several ways, none of which involved a horse or a saddle.

"Thank you."

"So proper," he teased. He brought her hand from her lap to his lips, kissing it softly. She'd changed from her Derby Day ensemble into a dress of deep blue and soft gray. The colors accented her pale skin and drew attention to her dark eyes.

He held her gaze for a long moment before moving to take her mouth. Her lips were warm and soft and they parted slightly, welcoming him. Their tongues grazed, caressed, stilled only to caress again. His left hand raised to her neck. She breathed a small sigh, and he smiled deep within himself. Then he kissed her as he'd wanted to kiss her all day, with passion and force, his mouth hard and demanding upon hers, his tongue probing deeper.

Hilary felt her resolve melting, felt her body surrendering to each kiss, each touch. He was so very good at kissing. Why couldn't he be as good with words? Why couldn't he open his heart and mind and share more than his body?

The thought spoiled the moment the same way Mr. Grunne had spoiled it last night. A door opened, shining light on the simple truth that Fitch had proposed marriage not out of love for her but because it was the most convenient way to claim his daughter.

"Please," she said, turning her head before he could capture her mouth again.

Fitch heard the rejection in her voice and felt it in the stiffening of her body. He controlled his temper. The war had taught him that unleashed emotions begot only more disaster.

"My apologies," he said, releasing her.

She knew she'd wounded his pride. "It isn't that I don't enjoy being with you. I do. The day was long, wonderfully so, and I'm very tired."

"Then you must rest." There was no anger in his voice, no expression of wounded pride in his eyes. He'd already masked them. "Go upstairs. I'll see the door locked as I leave."

"Good night, my lord." She gave him a reconciliatory kiss on the cheek, then walked past him and into the house.

"Good night," Fitch said after her. Admittedly, she should be tired. It had been a long day. Still, she had responded to his kisses. He'd felt her response, sensed her arousal as only a man could.

Shrugging off his disappointment, he set about seeing the doors locked before exiting the house.

Four days after being dismissed with a chaste kiss on the cheek, Fitch stepped from his carriage south of Regent's Park. The address he sought was No. 24 Baker Street, the dance studio of Monsieur Cavaignac. He had obtained the address from Lady Forbes-Hammond earlier in the day, after accidentally coming upon her when departing his tailor's shop. Learning that Hilary's lesson ended at three o'clock, he had decided to surprise her with an invitation to join him for afternoon refreshments.

It was a nice day, the sky blue, though not entirely free of clouds, the wind brisk but not chilling. A cup of chocolate might suit, or coffee in one of the many stalls that could be found throughout the city. Either way, they could spend some time together before he was called back to Westminster and a meeting with the Under Secretary that was sure to go well into the evening.

No. 24 was a building like many others in Marylebone. Monsieur Cavaignac's studio was a simple, white-painted brick house of three stories with a hip roof, double-hung windows, and a chimney on one side. A plaque with raised lettering was displayed on the wrought-iron fence, giving Monsieur's name and the information that lessons were conducted *By Appointment Only.*

A few minutes after knocking on the door and presenting his card to the footman, Fitch was told that Miss Compton was still in the ballroom with Monsieur.

He was led into an elegant room filled with aqueous sunlight filtered through louvered shutters. The very leanness of the room gave it the illusion of space. The colors, pale gold and light blue, lent a romantic atmosphere, conducive to dancing. A grand piano sat mute in the far corner.

Hilary was standing near the windows, talking to her instructor. So intent were they, in what appeared to Fitch as an engaging conversation, neither noticed their visitor.

Monsieur Cavaignac was much younger than Fitch had expected. His features were serious and well defined, his eyes exceptionally dark. A very handsome man in his early thirties, tall and thin with black hair and impeccable posture, he was oblivious to the visitor standing in the doorway. His words, to which Hilary was listening intently, were describing the wonders of Paris and the reasons why she must be sure to visit the French capital one day.

It wasn't the conversation that bothered Fitch. It was the way Hilary was hanging on to every word, as oblivious to his presence as the instructor. Her smile was radiant and her eyes were gleaming. The sunlight streaming through the windows poured onto her hair, giving it a golden sheen. Dressed in a gown of dark blue silk with a full crinoline and a small draping of ruffles at the back, she caught Fitch's eye and held it the same way she was holding the attention of Monsieur Cavaignac.

A feeling very much like jealousy, no doubt unrecognizable because he'd never felt it before, rushed through Fitch. Hilary belonged to him. Their marriage had yet to take place, but an engagement was just as binding in the eyes of most.

"Have you traveled beyond France and England?" Hilary asked of Monsieur Cavaignac, unaware that her fiancé was listening. "I would so love to see more than England's green countryside—not that I don't think it beautiful."

"England does have a certain beauty," Cavaignac agreed, "but one cannot envision the beauty of the Continent without seeing it with one's own eyes. I am very well traveled. My father was an ambassador of the French court for many years. His last posting was in New Zealand, a rich island that makes one think of Eden."

"New Zealand! Oh, I can't imagine traveling that far. It would seem like another world."

"It does. A breathtaking world. But I have also lived in Constantinople, St. Petersburg, and Amsterdam. The world is a place of marvels, Miss Compton. I shall have to tell you about them when you return tomorrow for your next lesson."

Two heads turned toward the door when Fitch discreetly cleared his throat.

"My lord," Hilary said, smiling. "You've surprised me."

"I hope it's a pleasant surprise," Fitch said, strolling into the room. His steps rang out as he crossed the smooth hardwood floor. "I thought to escort you home after an afternoon of dancing."

"May I present Monsieur Cavaignac," Hilary said, indicating the handsome Frenchman standing at her side. "He's been very patient with my lack of experience in the ballroom. Monsieur, this is the Earl of Ackerman, my fiancé."

"A fortunate man, monsieur," Cavaignac said, nodding to Fitch as he gave a small click of his heels. "Mademoiselle is an apt pupil. As graceful as a butterfly in a spring garden."

Hilary blushed.

Fitch gritted his teeth.

"She will be dancing as though she were born to the ballroom," Cavaignac assured him. "Music is in her blood. The sound brings her to life."

"I would like to test the theory," Fitch said. "Do you play, Monsieur?"

"But, of course."

"Then a waltz," Fitch commanded.

Hilary shook her head.

Fitch ignored her as the Frenchman walked to the piano and sat down. Hilary was still shaking her head when Fitch held out his hand.

"I'd rather wait," she whispered.

"I wouldn't." He took her by the hand and led her into the middle of the room.

The music followed, and they began to dance. Hilary tried to concentrate, to remember what Monsieur had told her, that the waltz wasn't a chore but a way of expressing oneself. She wanted to communicate that she was happy to see Fitch, but her delight was diminished by the solemn expression on his face. Why was he looking so sour?

Nothing was said as Fitch shared the rhythm of the music with her, turning and swirling and making it seem all so natural, as if they'd been born to dance together.

She seemed to know instinctively what he was going to do, following his lead with ease. Amazed again that a man his size could move with such elegance, Hilary felt as if the music was transforming her, turning her from an awkward country bumpkin into a graceful princess.

She stumbled, but only once. Fitch tightened his hold around her waist, making the mishap seem like nothing. Hilary smiled up at him. He smiled in return, but as she'd noted so often in the past, the smile did not reach his eyes.

She was just beginning to relax and enjoy the intimacy of the dance when the music stopped.

"I'm sorry," she said, keeping her voice low. "I'll try not to step on your toes the next time."

"Nonsense. You dance very well. Much too well to be in need of more lessons," Fitch announced.

"But—"

"I was retained for six lessons—Mademoiselle has had but four," Cavaignac said, intervening for her. "The last two will give her polish and confidence."

"She requires neither," Fitch said. His voice carried a finality that the Frenchman understood all too well. "As for your fee, it will be paid in full."

The epitome of a gentleman, since his craft required it, Monsieur Cavaignac accepted his dismissal with a graceful bow.

"Mademoiselle." He swept Hilary another bow. He brought his heels together, then bent and neatly kissed her hand. "The earl is correct. You waltz divinely."

"Thank you," she said. "I've enjoyed the lessons. And the conversation. I do hope to see Paris one day."

Hilary left the house on Fitch's arm. It wasn't until they were outside, standing on the walk between the wrought-iron fence with its neatly lettered sign and the carriage waiting to take them wherever the earl wished to go, that she removed her hand from his arm.

"We will talk," she said, broaching no argument.

"I thought to take you for an afternoon outing. My schedule is free this afternoon, though duty will recall me to Westminster this evening. What would you like to do? A walk in the park? A cup of coffee while we converse?"

"What I have to say doesn't require refreshments," Hilary told him. She allowed herself to be helped into the carriage. Once seated, she smoothed out her skirts, waiting for Fitch to take his own seat and for the carriage door to be closed.

"Your recent rudeness is inexcusable," she said once they were on their way. "How dare you dismiss Monsieur Cavaignac so boldly, and without cause."

"If you require additional instruction, I will give it," Fitch said, knowing his behavior had been questionable, but not willing to explain why.

"I would need no instruction were I not attending a ball, and I would not be attending the ball if I hadn't agreed to marry you," she told him in no uncertain terms. "Your behavior today gives me pause, my lord. I find your conduct more than arrogant and unnaturally willful. I would like an explanation."

A flash of emotion crossed Fitch's face, then vanished, leaving his expression grave. "The explanation has already been given. You are as graceful as the butterfly to which Monsieur Cavaignac so eloquently referred. I have been dancing the waltz for years and can find no fault in your partnering. Thus more lessons are unnecessary."

"And that is that," Hilary scoffed. "*You* have decided. *You* have dismissed my dance instructor, and *you* are satisfied. Well, my lord, I am not."

"I apologize if my actions upset you. As for my arrogance, I'm sure this will not be the first time we disagree on such things. However, it will be my place as your husband to make similar decisions."

"And my place as your wife to accept them. How precarious," Hilary replied with a calculated edge to her voice. "Being the fiancée, then the wife of an earl. One day I am wooed, the next, dictated to as if I were a child. Tell me, my lord, should I expect to be sent to my room without supper if I don't abide by your decision?"

The first shadow of anger began to show on Fitch's face. "Only if you deliberately provoke me, as you're doing now."

Hilary did not reply to the jibe. Fitch's conduct had robbed her of the satisfaction she'd gained from her lesson. She was angry, and there was little she could do to hide it.

Nothing more was said until they arrived at the Winged Goose, a small eatery known for its rum coffee in the winter and cold lemonade in the summer.

Fitch handed her down from the carriage, then across the street, dodging a hansom cab and a sweeper's cart along the way. The entrance to the eatery was a common door, used by an adjacent inn. The inside was beautifully appointed, with pastoral pictures and pewter plates lining one wall.

They were welcomed by the waiter as soon as they walked through the door, and offered a small table advantageously placed before being advised of the day's menu.

Fitch consulted Hilary as to her preference, then ordered two coffees and a plate of salmon and pickle sandwiches.

"What shall we talk about?" he asked, hoping to leave their previous disagreement behind them.

"Nothing, if you plan to pacify me with platitudes. The status of our relationship, if you wish to discuss a subject of substance." She said the words, feeling an uncontrollable need to spark the temper Fitch had allowed to show in the carriage. If he could get angry, then perhaps he'd finally say something she wanted to hear, something more revealing than common chitchat.

"The status of our relationship is that of an engaged couple who will be married in less than two weeks," he replied. There was no conciliation in his voice, and no anger. "If you think to change your mind, think again."

Hilary was disappointed at the same time she began to wonder if she'd ever get past the man's defenses. One might think there was nothing beneath his polished surface, but she knew better. She'd felt the warmth of his arms, the taste of his kisses, but most of all she'd seen him with Lizzie— seen his capacity for love. There had to be a way to tap into those feelings, to expand them to include his wife.

"I have no intention of changing my mind and breaking Lizzie's heart," she told him, "but that doesn't make me any less angry with you."

The waiter returned to the table with their meal, which was neither lunch nor dinner, but something in between. Fitch used the interruption to change the course of their conversation, telling Hilary about the current goings-on in Parliament and the numerous reform bills being debated.

She realized that he was reacting, not to today's event, but to the night following the Derby when she'd accused him of being distant and reclusive. While the current discussion revealed his political attitudes and the fact that he was a man given to thought before action, it did little to show more than the smooth surface of a very complicated man.

Still, he was trying. It was a small victory, and a step in the right direction that she willingly embraced.

Taking a bit of advice Felicity had offered her the previous day, Hilary refused to let the earl get her off balance.

It does nothing, my child, but increase a man's attitude that he can get you at a disadvantage with the slightest word, Felicity had said. *Patience, not passion, is the key to a man's heart. The earl is used to keeping his own counsel. Give him time to get used to the idea of a wife who is willing to listen, and he'll soon be speaking freely.*

Hilary sipped her coffee, hoping Lady Forbes-Hammond was right. By the time they exited the eatery, she felt somewhat better, but not entirely confident that she could burrow into the earl's heart as easily as his kisses suggested.

His mood had lightened in tune with hers, and she dared not ruin it by asking that her lessons be reinstated. Instead, she decided to take matters into her own hands. She would pen Monsieur Cavaignac a note, asking that her instruction resume, and insisting that he allow her to pay a double fee for the last two lessons.

She disliked subterfuge, but the idea of stumbling over her own two feet in the middle of Lady Wakesmyth's ballroom suited her even less.

Nine

The evening of Lady Wakesmyth's ball was as near to a perfect night as London could remember. A breeze from the east drove wispy clouds across a twilight sky while a faint haze on the horizon promised that fog would soon be stealing up the Thames to blanket the city.

The street outside the Wakesmyth residence was alive with carriages and livery. Footmen bustled importantly to and fro, while inside a small army of servants scampered like mice in a maze to make sure the night was a success.

The gown Hilary had chosen for the evening was amethyst in color, stylish but not seductive, with a neckline of gold lace. The hem was gathered, revealing a matching gold lace underskirt. Her hair was pulled up and away from her face and secured with mother-of-pearl combs. She was surprised to discover that she was looking forward to the ball.

Actually, it was the thought of waltzing with Fitch that had her excited. He sat across from her now, looking dashingly handsome in evening black. The overwhelming nature of his presence served to remind Hilary that when he wasn't with her he left an empty space in her life. The trouble was, even when he was there, filling the space, he wasn't filling it completely. If only he would offer her feelings instead of polite words and expensive presents.

The mother-of-pearl combs had been a present, delivered that morning with a note that he looked forward to seeing them in her hair. In the gold-dappled light of the carriage lamps, their sheen complemented her gown.

Soon they were departing the carriage, stepping down onto a red carpet that wove its way up marble steps and into a house ablaze with light. The interior was equally amazing, a harmonious blend of crimson, white, and gold. The foyer, a rectangular entryway beneath a balcony supported by white Roman-style columns, was the least ostentatious of the rooms.

"Ready?" Fitch asked. "You've met most of the people," he added as the footmen opened the double doors. "Relax and enjoy yourself."

Hilary took a deep breath. So many thoughts were tumbling through her mind, she was almost incoherent. The ballroom was a rainbow of people. The music enveloped her, while the overhead chandelier, the largest exhibit of cut glass she'd ever seen, cast pinpoints of light over the guests.

"Breathe," Fitch whispered as he tucked her arm in his and moved into the room. "It's only a party."

"It's frightening," she whispered back.

He smiled, making her fears melt away. "You look lovely."

And she did.

Others thought so, too. Fitch could tell by the looks she drew as he led her into the crush of people. A number of men would make it their business to see that she was captured for a dance before the evening came to an end. After endless ribbons, silk flowers, and white gauze dresses, Hilary's simplicity was refreshing. There was an intense femininity about her that contradicted her lack of exposure to Society, a vital sensuality that Evelyn had uncovered and Hilary seemed completely unaware of—and that made her appealing.

Fitch was torn between watching the excitement in her eyes and an attempt not to stare at her mouth. A mouth he hadn't kissed for an entire week.

Lord and Lady Waltham had arrived earlier. As always, Evelyn looked breathtaking in a gown of deep blue silk cut to accentuate her slender figure. Rathbone soon joined them. The conversation was light and cheerful. The viscount smiled. He was enjoying himself as he inspected the room, evaluating all the pretty ladies, deciding which ones he could seduce and which ones were to be avoided at all cost.

One young lady's expression dissolved into complete adoration after receiving one of the viscount's smiles. Lady Waltham laughed, insisting that it was disgusting to see one man have so strong an effect on so many women.

"I'm cursed with charm," Rathbone defended himself. He bowed, then excused himself. Another lady had entered the room. Her face, as finely proportioned as a cameo with a light flush of color, was the sort that aroused a man's immediate interest.

Hilary stood by Fitch's side, content to be an observer and listener. After a few minutes, she decided the crowd was harmless enough, lords and ladies in grand style, a throng of Londoners participating vicariously in the splendor of the Season.

"Dance with me?" Fitch asked as the melodious notes of a waltz filled the room.

The crowd seethed as if someone had stirred them with a spoon. There were nods of acknowledgment, an inspection of her attire, and several appreciative murmurs as he led her through the glittering crowd and onto the dance floor.

"People are staring," she said. In comparison to most of the women in the room, Hilary's gown was modest. Still, the color suited her, and the fabric was soft and flowing as she moved. She didn't feel inadequate, only nervous.

"A most unpleasant necessity, to be sure, but one that cannot be avoided," Fitch said, assuming an apologetic expression. "We are to be married, and they're curious."

Hilary was immediately grateful that Monsieur Cavaignac had agreed to the clandestine lessons. Fitch danced the way he did everything else, with a male grace that was impressively powerful. Hilary suspected that it was the mystique of that power, a strength that transcended the physical, that so intrigued her.

Her future husband was a man of will; it was written in the way he moved and spoke, in the determined lines of his face. He was inclined to think that success was a simple matter of deciding what he wanted, then getting it.

After all, he had gotten what he wanted from her—an agreement to marry, and Lizzie. Most of all, Lizzie. She shouldn't let herself forget that, no matter the glitter of the evening. This was perfunctory, just as the Derby had been, a rite of passage into *his* world. A world that offered security and wealth but no guarantee of happiness.

"Monsieur Cavaignac taught you well," Fitch said, executing a daring turn on the crowded floor.

Hilary had already decided to tell him that she had returned to Baker Street. This seemed as good a moment as any.

"Today's lesson was the most instructive of all. I learned how to converse with my partner while I keep my feet to myself."

The remark was meant to be humorous, but Fitch didn't smile. "Today's lesson? You returned to Cavaignac's studio even though I requested the lessons be terminated?"

"Yes."

His hand tightened on hers, but his face remained a diplomatic mask, revealing nothing to those who might be watching. "You risk much, my dear, if you think to flaunt your disobedience."

"I have spoken no vows of *obedience*," she reminded him. "Until I do, I will make my own decisions. I told you as much the day I agreed to marry you. Just as I'm telling you tonight that I completed the six lessons for which Monsieur Cavaignac was originally commissioned. Secrets are for people who have something to hide."

The music ended, but instead of leading her back to the group which now included Lord and Lady Sterling, Fitch took her in the opposite direction, toward the glass doors that opened onto the terrace.

It was a warm night. The stars shone bright against the blackness of the sky, and the air was heavy with the scents the wind carried from the surrounding city. Grecian urns dripped with greenery, decorating the steps that led down to the garden.

Hilary received Fitch's firm grasp on her hand with no complaint. He led her into a shadowy corner, away from the main walk. When they stopped, she smiled up at him.

"If you think to dissuade me with charm, it will not work," Fitch announced. "I will know why you disobeyed me." He held up a hand to prevent her interruption. "Married or not, as my fiancée, you have an obligation."

"Do not speak to me of obligations, my lord. I have carried more than my share these last few years."

"We speak of a different kind of obligation, as well you know." He saw her expression harden and moved on before she could scold him the way she'd done in the eatery. "We agreed to be honest with each other."

"For heaven's sake, my lord, use your wits. If I were inclined to be dishonest, we'd still be inside, and you'd have no knowledge that I attended two more dance lessons. And stop being so ill-tempered. I have done nothing to deserve it. One would think I spent the time rolling around in a hayloft with some bootman instead of dancing with a perfectly talented instructor who felt guilty because I coerced him into taking double pay for his services."

"I am unsure which to do first," Fitch said. "Kiss you, or thrash you."

"I'd prefer the kissing," she told him, fully aware that he was angry because he'd hauled her outside to receive a scathing lecture, only to receive one himself. "There is moonlight and music."

"And madness," Fitch said. "For I must be mad to think you hold one ounce of regret about evading my request."

"The only regret I have, my lord, is that you suffer from the same prejudice that afflicts most men—you think a woman cannot think for herself, and therefore strenuously object when she does. Still, it seems only fair to give you a chance to reconsider."

Fitch had to laugh—what else could he do? "I suppose that's what I deserve for proposing to a woman with a vibrant mind and a willful nature."

"The very least."

"Then, the very least I am due is some recompense."

A bank of clouds momentarily covered the moon, leaving them in a darkness the starlight could not penetrate. In the obscurity Hilary felt her chin being raised, and Fitch's lips pressing down on her own. The sudden vehemence with which he wound his arms around her caused Hilary to catch her breath. The passion with which he kissed her made her heart beat erratically.

The force of the kiss revealed that Fitch meant to dominate her, and yet Hilary couldn't help but feel possessed of her own feminine power over him.

The cloth of his coat was smooth against her hands, the muscle beneath it hard and unyielding. She could feel the beating of his heart as her own echoed in her ears. With a brush of her fingertips over his face, his arms tightened, and her lips parted under the sweet, drowning sensations. His body trembled against hers, her hands dug into the cloth at his shoulders. She could scarcely breathe, but it didn't matter.

There was a desperation in his touch, as if he

were trying frantically to hold on to something of great value, something that might slip away. She was shaking with exultation when he finally ended the kiss.

The grip of his hands eased, but he still held her close.

"I fear I may not be able to wait until you are my wife."

He looked into her eyes so long, so searchingly, that Hilary knew every cranny of her mind, every secret thought had to be revealed to him, for there was no hiding the love she felt for this man.

"The wedding is in two weeks," she said, understanding how he felt because she felt the same way. "You have the power to beguile me, my lord. Were we alone, I would not refuse you."

He drew back and smiled at her, then pulled her close again and held her in a quiet, comforting embrace, resting his chin on her hair. Inside Hilary, the last knot of doubt unraveled. She could not see his eyes now, but she knew they were thoughtful, faintly sad, clouded with past pain.

With the same gravity she invested in all her thoughts, she gave herself to the task of realizing just how much she had come to love the Earl of Ackerman. That being the case, she would find the path to his heart. There was no other way. To live without him now would be to die a little each and every day.

"So much for lecturing you," Fitch whispered a moment later.

Hilary didn't bother with prevarication. "I'm certain another opportunity will present itself. We seem destined to disagree on the attitude of a good and proper wife."

"You're a minx," he laughed. "One determined to give me more trouble than she is worth."

"Me?" She looked dutifully startled by the prediction.

"You," he said with emphasis.

She smiled, wanting to cherish the moment, to take the time to absorb its sweetness—the shadows of the trees swaying overhead, the roses kissed by glittering drops of dew, the smile on his face, the warmth of his arms. Everything around her was tranquil, as faint as the remembrance of a sweet dream.

The only reality was the love within her heart. Funny, but she had always thought of love as something pleasant, as bright and clear as a summer day. She knew now that that type of love was meant for a member of one's family, for her Aunt Edwina, and Beth, and Lizzie. The kind of love she felt for Fitch was confusing and furtive, invigorating and exciting. It was so much richer than anything one could imagine in a dream.

Even more puzzling was the fact that she'd fallen so completely in love in such a short time. That the deep stirring within her when he was near, the desire to touch and be touched, the scorching passion that he knew so well how to rouse, was her, the woman she'd been hiding for years.

Her body was still tight with anticipation from his kisses, and yet there was an unexpected security in being with a man whose touch could magnify every nuance of her being. There were times when she wanted to make him angry, to tempt him beyond the steadfast control he wore the same way he'd once worn a uniform, but he never bored her, and she never found him trivial. Just the opposite.

"One more kiss," he said, lowering his head. "Then, I must take you back inside or the gossips will be saying that I brought you into the garden with ravishment on my mind."

"Did you?" she asked as his lips brushed lightly over her.

"Don't tempt me."

Fitch looked at her once more, still unable to define exactly what it was about her that drew him so. There were women who could produce love in a man, not just in bed, but beyond the bedroom, something deep and loyal and abiding. A primordial instinct rose within him at that moment, the elation from a woman willing to fight for what she believed was right, to care when others turned away, to risk when others would flee to safety. Hilary was all of these, and more, and soon she would belong to him.

It was a staggering thought for a man who had thought to marry only for convenience. He wasn't sure when the convenience of the arrangement had been replaced by the growing necessity to simply be with her, but it had.

The kiss that followed his thoughts was long and possessively passionate.

"Inside with you," he commanded, turning her toward the open terrace doors and the crowded ballroom.

Hilary went with a smile on her face. Fitch had brought her outside to rain disapproval; instead he'd laughed, kissed her, then held her affectionately in his arms. Another small victory, another dent in his armor.

Much later, she'd remember this night, and realize that the armor she had thought she dented was still very much intact.

Ten

It wasn't until the minister came to "as long as you both shall live," that Hilary realized the magnitude of what she was doing.

The ceremony was taking place in a brownstone church with a towering steeple, polished walnut pews, and soft light diffused by stained glass windows. The bride was wearing a gown of ivory brocade embroidered with threads of gold and silver. A veil of sheer lace covered her face. The groom's attire was that of an elegant English aristocrat, a gray tailored suit and silver waistcoat. A diamond stickpin gleamed in the folds of his white cravat.

Lizzie sat on the front pew, bookended by Annie on her left with Lady Felicity Forbes-Hammond and the Duke of Morland to her right. Like the bride, she wore white, a very pretty dress with a blue sash and wide bow. She was on her best behavior and smiling from ear to ear.

Hilary repeated her vows in the reverent silence of the chapel while the guests listened intently. But for all the richness of the words, there was nothing to keep them from becoming a mockery. Hilary heard her own voice and imagined Fitch coming to his senses at last, realizing how desperately he loved her, professing that love, and with those words truly making her his wife.

One part of her mind, the reasoning, sensible part, told her not to build her future on a dream. There were goals in every woman's life, most of them leading to the acquisition of a husband. A prudent woman married as much for security as she did for love. Hilary had thought herself different, but in reality, she wasn't entirely exempt. She wanted a home and family, but most of all, she wanted to win her husband's heart.

Then she was listening to Fitch, pledging his troth, vowing to cherish her above all others. But cherishing wasn't love; theirs was a business arrangement. During the weeks she had known the Earl of Ackerman, he had surprised her with his kindness and generosity, but there had been no words of deep affection, no whispered devotions. Now he was reaching for her hand, slipping a gold-and-diamond ring on her finger.

The minister had more words, a prayer for their marriage, and instructions for them to leave the church with the unity of God's blessing. It was over. She now belonged to the tall, dark-eyed man who possessively turned her to face him, then lifted her veil in preparation for their first kiss as husband and wife.

"My lady," he said solicitously.

Fitch held her by the shoulders and for a moment they stood in front of the altar, breaths merging, hearts pounding, eyes locked. Then he touched his mouth to hers. It was a very soft, very respectable kiss.

Someone in the audience murmured their approval and someone—Hilary was sure it was Lizzie—clapped their hands.

Her new husband led her from the church, piloting her down the carpeted aisle, through the archway, and outside to where a white and gold open carriage stood waiting.

It was a vivid day, the air sharp and clean, the sun falling pale on the pavement stones. In the tower, church bells pealed while rose petals were tossed by the guests who had gathered outside. There was to be a reception, hosted at the home of Lord and Lady Granby, followed by a wedding night in Eaton Square.

There was no way for Hilary to express what she felt as Fitch handed her into the carriage, then took his place beside her. She let out an audible sigh as the liveried driver gave a quick snap of his wrist, making the whip crack to start the horses. They moved away from the curb with shouts of well-wishers following them.

"We are married," she said, realizing that the statement sounded trite once it was spoken.

"Yes." Fitch took her hand, folding two larger, stronger ones around it. "I have a wife. A very exciting bride and hours before I can claim her."

Hilary tried not to blush, but failed. There would be no stopping tonight, no reason to deny the passion that sparked between them. What would happen between them had been sanctioned by church and law. Their desire had been legalized. A new path had been laid for her life. All she could do now was follow it.

"Blast this open carriage," Fitch said. "It's Felicity's doing, making sure I don't wrinkle your dress or muss your hair with impatient kisses."

Hilary laughed. "You sound like Lizzie. She was most upset when I told her that she couldn't stand at the altar with us. Be prepared. She's sure to ask if she can spend tonight in her new papa's house."

"I have denied her little, but tonight is for us." His gaze moved possessively over her. "Tonight we shall share the same bed. We shall share ourselves and hours of pleasure. I have prided myself on patience since your arrival in London, madame, but no longer. You are mine, and before the sun rises again you will know it well."

Share ourselves.

Oh, how Hilary wished it to be true, prayed that the ring she now wore was the key she'd been searching for these past weeks, the key to knowing the man she had married. But she knew Fitch was speaking of physical love, not the sharing of hopes and dreams and thoughts so private they must be whispered only in the quiet hours of the night.

He wanted nothing else of her, and yet she had risked her heart, surrendered her most personal principles to become his wife. The irony was as pitiful as it was comical, but Hilary had little time to dwell on the cause. The effect was still taking place—her wedding day was far from over. There were guests to greet and iced cake to be sliced and champagne to be poured.

"Please, Papa, I want to go with you and Hilary," Lizzie pleaded. "We're married now, aren't we?"

"Yes, pumpkin. We're married now. A real family, just as I promised we'd be."

Fitch and his daughter were in a small parlor on the second floor of Lord and Lady Granby's resi-

dence. The guests were lingering downstairs, waiting to give the bride and groom a proper send-off.

"If you're really my papa now, then why can't I
go with you?" Lizzie said, forming her mouth into
a perfect little pout. She was sitting on Fitch's lap,
and looking very set on getting her way.

"I will fetch you first thing in the morning," he
promised, "and we will all live together from that
point on. You and I and Hilary."

"And Annie, and Sylvester, and Hattie, and the
kittens? I do so miss my kittens."

"All of us." Fitch patted her hand. "I promise.
But now you must go with Annie. Weddings are
very much grown-up affairs with lots of pomp and
circumstance. I suspect I'll have to face yours one
day. I shan't like it, of course. Papas are a selfish
lot. We like to keep our little girls close."

Lizzie clasped her tiny hands around his neck,
then kissed his cheek. "I shan't leave you, Papa.
Not ever."

"Nor I you," he vowed. "Now, I shall have your
promise. Not one word to your aunt, or Annie, or
Mrs. Grunne that I gave you a sip of champagne. It
will earn me a fate worse than death."

"I promise, Papa."

"Good girl. Now, give me another hug, then off
with you. Annie is waiting."

Fitch smiled as she climbed down from his lap
and walked to the door. One last look from those
big brown eyes, a quick inquiry to see if he'd
changed his mind, then a bounce of curls and she
was gone.

Fitch finished off the champagne he'd brought
upstairs with him, remembering the way Lizzie had
wiggled up her nose after tasting it. She was an
adorable little girl, destined to be a pure hellion if

he didn't take her in hand before she realized just how deeply embedded she was in his heart.

"Your Grace," Fitch said, coming to his feet as the Duke of Morland stepped into the room.

"Just wanted to give you my personal congratulations. You have managed to acquire yourself a charming wife. And a daughter who strongly resembles your mother."

"Sir?" Fitch drew in his breath.

"I'm not sure what charade you hope to carry off, lad, but there's no fooling an old fool. Lizzie is *your* child, is she not?"

Fitch knew there was no point denying it. Morland had known his parents for more years than their son could count birthdays.

"Yes. She's my daughter."

"And the mother? Is she the lady you just took to wife?"

"No."

The duke settled himself into a chair. The guests could wait until he'd finished with the groom. "Your decision to do the right thing by the child is admirable, but I must admit confusion regarding the mother. Care to enlighten me?"

Fitch told him the truth, beginning with the night Hilary had called on him in Eaton Square. Morland listened, his expression revealing nothing of his thoughts until Fitch finished his recitation. Neither man was aware that Hilary was standing just beyond the door, having come upstairs to inform her new husband that it was time to accept the final well-wishes of their guests.

"I will do my best to be a good father to Lizzie and an acceptable husband to Hilary," Fitch said.

"Oh, I have no doubt that you will be both," the duke replied. "Never known anyone who could fault you when it comes to duty. The marriage doesn't disappoint me. On the contrary, I'm well satisfied with the bride you've chosen. But duty can grow cold if there's nothing else to hold a man and woman together."

"Hilary pleases me," Fitch said. "And there will be more children."

Hilary continued to listen. It was all well and good to hear that she *pleased* her husband, but the word rang dull against the excitement of what should be the most memorable day of a woman's life. The sight of the ring on her hand aroused her to the fact that there was no going back, no room for doubt. She had married a man who did not love her. Oh, he would be kind and solicitous, passionate and caring, while she loved in return.

What had begun as a promise to Beth had grown into a commitment of a lifetime, a web of passion and shared futures. With a silent sigh, Hilary admitted it was too late to dwell on the way of things. The ceremony was over, the future as unknown as the past Fitch kept so well hidden.

Not yielding in nature, she lifted her head. She had never meant to have a husband, never thought to be standing where she was standing today, in a satin gown adorned with lace and pearls. Having had one dream come true, she fortified her heart with the belief that another could come to pass.

"Your bride is waiting," Morland announced.

Hilary heard the soft tap of the duke's walking stick against the floor. She turned, hurrying to the top of the staircase, where she made a quick turn, gave the shimmering white of her skirts a hasty shake, and tried to appear as if she'd only just stepped into the hallway.

Fitch exited the parlor, behind the duke. He smiled when he saw her. Hilary smiled back.

When he held out his hand, she went to him, treading carefully lest she shatter the tenuous vision of the day, to take her place by his side. They would walk downstairs together, man and wife.

Later that evening, Hilary sat alone in a handsomely furnished bedroom. The mirror above the dressing table reflected the high oak headboard and blue-and-white coverlet of the large double bed. A snug little fireplace with an Italian marble mantelpiece was empty of flame. A basket of flowers had been set on the grate in lieu of firewood. The night was warm, the windows open to gather the breeze.

For a while the long turmoil of the day slipped away and she surrendered her thoughts to the upcoming night, to the spell of warmth and silence that invaded the room.

She was wearing a gown of carefully cut satin with a net yoke, the edges bound with white lace, and transparent except for strategically embroidered leaves and flowers. Pale pink chrysanthemums and white French knots created a shadow between her small breasts. The design erotically hinted of what it barely concealed.

Slipping a matching robe over her gown, she turned away from the mirror and studied the room instead. It was large and comfortable and connected to her husband's suite by a gilt-trimmed door. Even in a marriage of convenience she had an obligation to comply with his wishes—his desires. Not that she didn't share them. She did. Still, she realized with a sinking desperation how completely a married woman gave herself into the keeping of her husband. How much control Fitch would have over her from this day forth.

Tears burned in her eyes, and she brushed them away. It wouldn't do to have Fitch find her so. He was a good man, and she was certain he would prove himself a devoted husband and father.

More time ticked away and Hilary was overcome by a dreamy lethargy as she recalled the ceremony, the way Fitch had stared at her when she'd walked down the aisle. Never distant was the hope that this day, this night, would be the beginning of a new happiness for both of them.

Then the door was opened, and her husband stepped inside. He was wearing a robe, dark blue with black velvet lapels and sashed about the waist. His hair was brushed back from his face and darker than normal from a recent dampening. Silently, he appraised her, his gaze intense. Uncertain, afraid of outright rejection as he saw more closely what his proposal had gotten him, Hilary stood, hands at her side, and waited.

"Good evening, wife," he said, closing the door.

"My lord," Hilary replied, hating herself for feeling like a fish that had misplaced its pond. The embarrassment of how she'd come to be married to the earl swept over her, and she wished they could have chosen to wed for love of each other rather than a mutual love for Lizzie.

In the trembling light of the candles the maid had left burning to add a touch of romance to the room, Hilary's mind filled with a torrent of emotions, but she was unable to articulate a single word.

Fitch was having a similar problem. He knew Hilary needed to be reassured—any virgin would—but he was having trouble finding the right words.

He looked at her, at her slender form in a long, pearl-white gown and robe. She was softly beautiful in the flickering candlelight. And that hair! He'd never imagined there'd be so much of it, long and thick and flowing past her hips.

"You look lovely."

Hilary smiled, her heart beating more strongly now than it had during the wedding ceremony. She was thoughtful a moment, then said, "The maid left some champagne. Would you like a glass?"

"Perhaps later."

There was a softness in his voice. He wasn't going to rush her, or force her, but he wasn't going to leave, either.

"Shall we begin with a kiss?" he asked, stepping closer.

When he was standing close enough for Hilary to see the tiny lines that radiated from the corners of his dark eyes and the minute amount of gray at his temples, she gave a small nod, then smiled, realizing her nervousness was silly. This was Fitch. He had kissed her before, touched her more intimately than any other human being, and none of it had brought her shame or displeasure.

"Trust me," he said, and the kiss began.

It was a tiny kiss, a peck, that gradually developed into a more serious embrace. He contained his desire, managing it while he taught her the gentleness of passion, the degree of intimacy a man and woman could share when they were free to do as they pleased.

He removed the mother-of-pearl combs from her hair, and buried his fingers in its richness. "I've never seen more beautiful hair."

Hilary smiled again.

He would have picked her up then and carried

her to the bed, but it was too soon. Instead, he passed his hands over her silk-covered curves. Her slenderness pleased him. The way her back arched and her nipples hardened aroused him.

He gathered her into his arms, her softness molding against the muscles of his arms and stomach and legs, the warmth of her body melting into his. Her face lifted and he kissed her again, tasting the coolness of the night on her lips.

"I want you," he said.

"Yes," she replied. Her mind had finally stilled. There was nothing but the warmth of his body and the urgency of his touch, the meeting of their mouths and a world that could wait until morning.

It was all Fitch needed to hear. With a sly grin he slipped the robe off her shoulders and untied the bodice laces of her gown, but he didn't remove it. He stepped back and stripped off his robe, revealing a body that was even more powerful, more intimidating than Hilary had imagined.

Her eyes traveled over him. The rolling slope of his shoulders, the dark mat of hair on his chest, the leanness of his hips and stomach—all of him was very male and very desirable.

"Take off your gown," he told her.

Hilary did as he asked.

Fitch drew in his breath and held it. Naked, she was even more perfect: her waist tiny, her breasts firm. Her skin glowed pale in the candlelight, the only color that of her rose-colored nipples and the dark curls at the junction of her thighs.

"Come to me." He held out his hands.

Once again, Hilary did as he asked.

He drew her to him, every muscle in his body taut with wanting. He kissed her, letting his hands roam free. Her skin was scented with soap. She was delicately made; he cupped a hand over her hip and felt the marvelous play of muscle and bone as she pressed against him. The lust that had tormented him for days suddenly drained away, leaving him with a worshipping sense of awe at the female creation she represented.

They made their way to the bed.

He ran his hand over her smooth skin, down the white flesh of her belly, then down the outside of her thigh. He looked at her face and saw her eyes watching him. Bending over her, he sealed them with a kiss, then let his lips wander over her face, her throat, the slight swell of her flushed breasts. At the touch of his tongue the sensitive nipple stood erect in its dainty pink aureole. He pulled it into his mouth and began to suck—first one, then the other.

Slowly, his lips moved over her body, drinking in her scent, the softness of her luminous skin, down her belly to the cluster of curls.

He touched every inch of her, turning her at will, caressing her until she was moaning his name, begging him to finish what he'd begun. But he wasn't in any hurry. Dawn was hours away and he meant to make the night last.

Hilary's body felt like a liquid flame. Everywhere Fitch touched, she burned. She was poised on an invisible precipice, pulsing wildly as he loved her with his tongue and mouth and hands. She was helpless, unable to think, unable to do anything but feel the fire burning hotter and higher inside her.

She wanted instant relief—she wanted to burn forever.

Sensation after sensation streaked through her as he came to know her as thoroughly as any woman could be known by touch. He traced the inside of her thighs, his fingers moving slowly upward. He touched the hot, wet center of her and Hilary moaned out his name, shuddering beneath his hands.

"Yes, moan. Tell me what you like, how you like it," he whispered in a deep, rich voice. "Move against my hand, touch me, let me touch you."

He eased his hand between her legs again, stroking her up and down, then in small, tantalizing circles that stole her breath. The feeling was incredible—tiny flames that pierced her very soul.

Suddenly, Hilary wanted to spread the fire, to share it with her husband. Her hands began to explore his body in return, touching hard muscles and skin growing damp as he asserted control over his desire. When her hand moved low, brushing against the thick patch of hair surrounding his erection, Fitch tensed.

"I want to be inside you," he said. "Now. *Right now.*"

He pinned her beneath him, forcing her legs wide with his knee. Supporting himself on his arms, he rubbed against her, letting her feel the power of his need, the burning touch of his naked body against hers.

They kissed, long and deep, as he rocked against her. "Open yourself for me," he whispered. "Open and take me inside."

Slowly, Hilary pushed herself against him, spreading her legs to make room for his hips. She gasped as he began to push inside her, stretching her as he fitted their bodies together.

He pressed his lips to her forehead. "You feel so hot, so very, very hot and silky wet. I could stay inside you forever."

Hilary inhaled a breath, the first she could remember taking since Fitch had started kissing her. She tilted her hips to take more of him. Her husband gave it, easing into her until they couldn't get any closer, until his possession couldn't be any more complete.

He pulled out and pushed in again.

Hilary's eyes drifted shut.

She gloried in his possession, feeling infinitely precious, totally cherished. And strong. Strong in her own power as a woman, a passionate strength she'd refused to acknowledge for years. She and Fitch were more than lovers, they were partners, giving and taking, pleasing and being pleased in return. She felt limitless, as if anything was possible.

It didn't matter that their relationship could be measured in weeks and hours. Her previous life had been nothing, an emptiness that had existed only until he had filled it with his presence.

She heard him groan deep in his chest as he retreated again, then pushed back inside her, rekindling the fire.

It was all fever and flame after that.

His thrusts became less gentle, his desire more demanding as he forced her to surrender completely. Through parted lips, he breathed her name as he rode her hard and deep, until she thought she was going to die from the pleasure of it.

Her heart was going wild, her body even wilder as she arched up to meet his hips, to keep him inside her. It was burning and needing, only to burn and need even more. To want, and feel that wanting being satisfied, but knowing there was more. She gave herself to the mating dance, guided by instinct and love.

Fitch felt her climax begin, felt her inner muscles clench tightly around him, demanding that he give his essence in return for hers. It was beginning for him, too, the heavy weight in his loins, the intense, pulsating sweetness that had only one morality, one hot, blinding goal—to come inside her, to bring an end to the sweet agony.

"Please," she moaned, grinding her hips against him, letting go of all her inhibitions.

Guided by his movements, encouraged by his whispered words, she moved with him, enclosing him, taking him, giving of herself, one body, one goal.

Fitch changed his rhythm, forcing her to stay on the edge of ecstasy. He moved in and out of her in slow, powerful strokes that had her straining against him until passion and need blurred, until there was nothing but swirling flames of sensual fire and a pleasure so intense Hilary felt as if she was streaking across the heavens like a falling star.

Her nails dug into his back, clawing at his skin as she climaxed a second time. Fitch breathed out her name as he felt his own body slipping beyond his control. Then he was burning, too, dying in an explosive burst of heat that trapped his breath deep in his chest.

The pleasure was wave after wave of tingling sensation. When it finally ebbed, Fitch collapsed onto his side, wrapping his arm around Hilary's hips and bringing her with him, their bodies still joined.

She nestled in his arms and pressed a finger to the pulse beating at the base of his neck, then moved it up to his lips. She'd never imagined such a closeness. It was more than physical, more than emotional, it was simply the most perfect moment of her life.

Her husband smiled, looking very much like a man who had gotten exactly what he wanted.

"You're gloating," she said, taking the sting out of the words with a matching smile.

"How can I not, madame? I have gained a wife who accommodates me with the enthusiasm of a she-cat."

"A she-cat?" She pulled away, offended, but knowing he was right. She'd just participated in a feast of abandoned lovemaking that was more reminiscent of a street-girl than a lady of breeding. And she'd enjoyed every moment of it.

"A very nice she-cat," he murmured.

Hilary accepted his apology and the kisses that accompanied it. They lay together, content and silent.

Nothing about the circumstances of their marriage had changed, yet everything was different. They both sensed it, felt it, yet neither spoke of it.

"Sleep." He kissed her eyelids closed.

Hilary cuddled close, wanting to purr as waves of pleasure continued to flow through her body. She felt exalted, free to express a kind of love and giving she had never imagined in the silence of her spinster nights. She had secretly entertained what her aunt would have called *vain hopes*. But tonight hadn't been imagined. It had been another victory, a sweet victory, one she would always remember.

Eleven

Night was draining into the muted light of early dawn when Hilary came awake. A gossamer breeze ruffled the window curtains as the previous night's pleasure filled her mind like an unfinished dream.

A feeling of unfamiliarity brought a slow smile to her face. She was sleeping with her husband, his body warm beside her, his dark hair tousled from sleep. Coming fully awake, Hilary embraced the moment, catching it in her mind. Soon the day would take the moment from her; the servants would begin to stir, street vendors would take to their routes, singing hawking rhymes, birds would chatter as the morning sun warmed their nests, and the specialness of this second in time would become a memory.

But right now, right this very moment, she had the world all to herself. The sky was soft pink and blue-gray, and her hand itched with the feel of Fitch's chest hair as she laid her open palm ever so lightly over his heart. She realized that she had fallen in love with him almost immediately. From the first moment she'd seen him standing in the foyer of this very house, dressed in the finest of clothes, she'd decided that he was the most delectable man she'd ever laid eyes on.

Now, he belonged to her.

She studied him; the relaxed features of his face, the shadow of the beard that was beginning to show. Each time she saw him, he became more beautiful to her. With each kiss, her feelings became less surprising. Last night had been passion mixed with the fear that he might find her lacking. This morning she reveled in the knowledge that she'd pleased him, that their lovemaking had been a current so warm, so giving, it had taken them to a place known only to lovers.

Fitch chose that moment to move, turning over on his side. His hand found her hip, squeezing gently. When his eyes opened, they lay staring at each other.

"Good morning," she said, keeping her voice as soft as the light creeping over the windowsill.

"Good morning, wife."

His voice was sleepy and satisfied.

Suddenly it seemed very important to Hilary to make him smile, to fill the room with the sound of his laughter. Tossing the covers back, she began to tickle him.

Fitch came awake instantly. Grabbing her wrists, he held her at arm's length until he could untangle himself from the linens, then rolled her over onto her back. He straddled her hips, his muscular body fully aroused and in clear view of his wife's curious eyes.

"Madame, please tell me that you do not awaken each morning with such exuberance."

"Kiss me," Hilary demanded, freeing her thoughts

and responding to the liquid fire already warming her blood. "Kiss me so I know yesterday wasn't a dream."

" 'Twas no dream," he said. But instead of kissing her, he repaid her deed for deed, tickling her unmercifully.

They rolled around in the bed, all knees and elbows and giggling laughter. The coverlet slid to the floor, followed by one of four pillows, until Fitch once again gained the advantage and pinned her to the mattress with his body.

Hilary could see the glint in his eyes as he held her down and looked at her, at her breasts and belly, her hips and upper thighs, and the dark nest of curls between them.

"I've never met a woman who blushed so beautifully," Fitch said as he trailed one hand slowly down her body, exploring its surface like a mapmaker. Finding a tiny mole near her navel, he lowered his head and kissed it, then made his way up to her breasts to lick at first one nipple, then another.

Hilary began her own investigation, measuring him from rib to thigh. He sucked in his breath when her hand found the warm stones between his legs, shuddering when she examined them as thoroughly as he'd investigated her feminine secrets the previous night.

"My God," he groaned when she measured him, her fingertip trailing lightly over the end of his erection. He pushed himself into her hand, grimacing from the painful pleasure of her touch.

Wordless after that, Fitch moved, bringing them closer together, pressing against her, until they were touching hip to hip. She was warm and wet. He was hard and ready. Gently, in slow, small motions, he pushed inside her until ripples of pleasure began to shake his body.

"Yes," she whispered. "Oh, yes."

Their lovemaking was as delicate as the dawn— gentle thrusts and retreats, soft gasps of pleasure, whispered words, and clinging, caressing hands. Neither one was a person who found it easy to surrender, but surrender they did, giving themselves over to the pleasure and to each other.

Hilary's heart was stirred by Fitch's tenderness. She looked into his dark eyes, searching and finding her own pleasure mirrored there. She curled her legs around his waist, arching her body as he entered her again.

Fitch took her slowly and completely until the satisfaction peaked in a rolling wave of sensation that began as a pinpoint of light and ended like a blazing sun.

Afterwards, he retrieved the coverlet from the floor and joined her under it, pulling her snugly into his arms. "You, madame wife, are far more distracting than I had ever imagined."

"Shall I apologize?"

"No." Fitch grinned. "Go back to sleep, sweetheart. We've no one to attend to right now but ourselves."

They slept.

When Hilary awoke a second time, it was late morning, and she was alone.

After a leisurely bath, she donned a raspberry silk dress that showed Lady Waltham's influence in its classic lines. Then, descending the staircase, she made her way to the breakfast room with its silver chafing dishes aligned on a marble-topped, walnut sideboard. Slightly disappointed that her husband wasn't seated at the table with his morning paper, Hilary served herself and made fast work of her breakfast. She'd been too nervous to eat more than the smallest portions of the delicious food that had been served at the wedding reception, and she was hungrier than usual.

Raskett appeared to pour her second cup of tea. "His lordship has gone to retrieve his daughter," the butler said when asked.

"Then you know?" She was unable to hide her surprise that a servant readily knew what all but a select few did not.

"Aye, I know," Raskett said. "He told me that first night, after you came to call. But you needn't worry. I'll not be telling anyone else what's none of their business."

"How long have you worked for the earl?"

"I've been with him since he joined the regiment. Went to war with him, stepping off the boat in '54. The French got there before us. Had pickets four miles inland before we ever set foot on the beach. God-awful place, that peninsula. Cold and rainy and wracked with cholera."

Hilary sipped her tea, listening with interest. Butler or not, Raskett knew her husband far better than she did.

"Funny lot, those Frenchmen," Raskett went on. "Smart, too. They claimed the right to march on the right of the line, the sea protecting one flank while we protected the other."

"I've read accounts of the war. It must have been terrible."

"If they weren't, folks would be having 'em as regular as soirees."

"And the earl, my husband, fought with valor.

I'm told he was decorated by the queen upon his return."

"Fitch fought, all right. Never gave an inch of ground he didn't have to. And he never forgot his men," Raskett said with pride. "Course, things don't always go the way some fancy general plans for them to go. Balaclava was a prime example. Damn near got us all killed that day."

"Are you referring to the charge of the Light Brigade?"

"The Light wasn't the only division on the field that day," Raskett told her. When she motioned for him to take a seat, he hesitated, then sat down. Like most men, he couldn't resist a good war story. "There was the Second Division under Sir Evans, and the Duke of Cambridge gave orders to the First. We had the Fourth Division under Sir Cathcart and the cavalry under Lord Lucan, but it was the Ninety-third Highlanders that took the glory that day. Never thought I'd say it about a Scot, but I'll sing their praises now and forever more."

"My husband was there, amid the fighting?"

"No better lieutenant in all the Hussars," Raskett said proudly. "Made commander after that. But the amount of braid on his uniform never meant anything to him. Still don't. Braid don't make a soldier. God knows Balaclava proved that. The First Division had already crossed the river, but the Russians knew they were coming. They could see them from the top of the hill. That's where they were lined up, waiting to pluck us like feathers off a goose. But they couldn't see the Highlanders. Three battalions."

"Three battalions," Hilary replied, wondering just how many men that might be, but not wanting to interrupt Raskett long enough to ask.

"The Ninety-third Highlanders, the Cameron Highlanders, and the Black Watch. All decked out in kilts, red tunics, and black bearskin bonnets. They never stopped advancing. Just kept blasting away at the Russians. The smoke was so thick the spotters couldn't see that the rank was only two deep."

"And the queen's men were victorious."

"Aye, we were," Raskett said, though a bit sadly. "The road to Sevastopol lay between those hills. Once it was opened, we marched through to lay siege to the port."

What he didn't tell Hilary about the Battle of Balaclava was that it had taken two days for the wounded to be collected from the field and another day to bury the dead.

"You came to work for the earl after the war?" Hilary posed the question with only mild curiosity, though she was aching to question Raskett on every detail of Fitch's life.

"He wasn't an earl yet, but aye, I followed him home and took up a place at his side. Same as in battle, but things were a mite calmer once we got back to England."

Hilary didn't comment on her husband's unwillingness to discuss the war or his life since leaving the military. She'd promised herself to be patient. Now that they were married, day-to-day life was sure to remove the last of the barriers, and after the intimacy they had shared last night, she couldn't imagine them continuing as polite strangers.

"Tell me about Winslow," she prompted the butler.

"It's a fine estate, milady. Fine, indeed."

Before Raskett could elaborate on the Minstead family home, the door opened and Lizzie came boiling into the room, singing out Hilary's name.

"Papa came and got me, just like he promised!" She ran into Hilary's open arms. "Isn't this a pretty house? Papa said I'm going to have my very own room, and that Annie can sleep across the hall, and that we won't be here very long because the Season is going to be over soon, and we'll be going to Winslow, and I can see my kittens again. I hope Hattie hasn't gotten so prickly I can't hold her."

"Take a breath," Hilary said laughingly. "Lizzie, this is Mr. Raskett."

Lizzie bobbed into a hasty curtsy, unaware that servants weren't awarded such a greeting.

"She's a mite on the energetic side, isn't she, milord?" Raskett replied seriously. He then held out his hand, and with an offer to conduct Miss Lizzie on a thorough tour of the residence, won her undying admiration.

"She was up waiting for me, staring out the window," Fitch said as he came to stand by Hilary's chair. He leaned down and gave her a quick kiss. He smiled at the sound of Lizzie's voice, asking Raskett one question after another. "She hasn't stopped talking since we got in the carriage."

"She talks when she's excited," Hilary said. She poured her husband a cup of coffee, wondering how they would spend the day.

"She talks whenever she isn't sleeping." He settled himself into the chair at the head of the table before reaching for the coffee. "She wants me to tell Parliament to adjourn early. It seems my daughter thinks government a waste of time."

"It is. At least it is for the remainder of this day, my lord. Need I remind you that we are newly married and that this is our first full day as husband and wife."

"I need no reminder," Fitch said. He was smiling

and his expression gave Hilary hope. "What shall we do with ourselves? A leisurely walk in the park? It's a pretty day. Or would you prefer to have a tour of the house? It's not as large as Winslow, but I know one or two rooms where we might entertain ourselves."

Knowing just how her husband thought to entertain her brought a rush of heat to Hilary's body and a flush of color to her face. "I have been wondering how I would pass the time. Having never been a countess before, I'm unsure where to begin."

"You may begin with joining your husband in a discussion of the governess who will need to be employed for our daughter," Fitch told her. "This morning confirmed what I have suspected since your arrival in London. Annie is attentive, and has served well in the interim and excitement of our wedding plans, but Lizzie requires the education and discipline of a formal classroom."

"She's a bright child, not difficult to instruct once you have her attention. Her curiosity keeps the door open for all types of training. One has merely to keep the conversation going in the right direction, so to speak."

"I know you taught her in Nottingham. But that was before you became a countess. Our schedule here in the city will not permit the habit to be taken up again. I also think it best if you begin to take the position of a mother, rather than an aunt. A governess can supervise Lizzie in the classroom, while you see to her education in other ways."

"Lizzie isn't going to forget Beth," Hilary said, feeling a twinge of disloyalty to her former friend. She had, after all, married the man who had once been Beth Bradstreet's lover.

"I don't expect her to. However, I plan on filing

the adoption petition before we leave for Winslow. The court will take its time, of course, but in the end Lizzie will take the name of Minstead, just as you took it yesterday."

"Mrs. Minstead. I rather like the sound of it," Hilary said. "Pity, I shan't hear it spoken out loud. Lady Ackerman sounds so very proper and so very unlike me."

"You'll warm to the title, just as you've warmed to your husband."

Hilary left her seat and walked unabashed to where Fitch was sitting. Standing behind his chair, she wrapped her arms around his neck and whispered, "Have I warmed to you?"

"Not nearly as much as you will as soon as I can get you alone again," he promised with a cocky smile. "And not until I've had a proper breakfast. A husband has to keep up his strength, if he wants to keep his wife satisfied."

The next few days followed the same routine: nights spent in passionate splendor, days spent in witty conversation. It wasn't until one morning a full week after their wedding day that Hilary took up the formal duties of a wife. Fitch had announced at breakfast that his desk would soon collapse if he did not attend to business.

Hilary decided to do the same, needing to reply to the invitations that had arrived, requests to attend more social functions than she could list on one sheet of paper, and notes of congratulations from those who had not attended the ceremony but wished the earl and his countess endless happiness.

Endless happiness. It wasn't a practical thing,

Hilary supposed, but she liked the idea of it. And she *was* happy. Fitch was more than an attentive husband; he was a wonderful man who needed a family. It was that need, that wanting in him, that kept Hilary's hopes burning bright.

One day, perhaps sooner than she had first planned, she would be giving Fitch another child. He did not seem inclined to hinder the prospects by using any method of prevention. Hilary knew of a few, having read what would have been prohibited material to other women, but she couldn't bring herself to use them, especially when Fitch fell asleep with his hand spread wide over her stomach, as if to protect what he may have seeded during their lovemaking.

Tomorrow they would begin interviewing applicants for the position of governess. She would attend the appointments, Fitch insisted, knowing Lizzie's educational needs better than he.

"I value your opinion," he had said that very morning while they'd been sitting in bed, naked under the covers, their hands wrapped around cups of hot chocolate. "I want no one too stern, but anyone with less constitution than a field-seasoned general will be turned into mush by Lizzie's first smile. Raskett has, and I'd have wagered nothing short of a bonfire could melt his crusty exterior. He's clay in those little hands of hers."

Thinking of the butler, Hilary smiled as she sat down at the art nouveau desk in the morning room. She was sure the white-lacquered oak furnishings that now dominated the room had been added after the earl's proposal in an effort to make the house less of a bachelor's residence. Drawing out a sheet of fine parchment paper, she set about making a list of questions to put to the applicants who would begin to arrive promptly at ten tomorrow morning.

She was midway of the list when she heard the bell over the front entry door jingle, announcing a visitor. Displaying his normal proficiency, Raskett had the door open and the caller greeted before a second ring was necessary.

"I will see if his lordship can receive you, sir. Please wait here."

Hilary rose and walked to the door, looking into the foyer. A man, dressed in a black suit and looking very much like either a vicar or an undertaker, stood in the center of the tiled reception area. His face was pale, as if it had lacked the touch of sunlight for as many years as it had taken to accumulate the wrinkles that weighed down his cheeks and forehead. Whoever he was, he presented a forbidding presence on what was otherwise a bright and cheerful day. It was more than his attire and the gaunt expression on his face. It was as though he were accustomed to being the bearer of bad news.

Hilary left the morning room. She wasn't entirely sure how a countess went about introducing herself, having never had the opportunity as yet, but she went nevertheless.

"Good morning, sir," she said, smiling. "I am Lady Ackerman."

"Milady." He nodded, but said nothing more. His hands, blue-veined and slightly crooked about the knuckles, giving one the impression that they pained him terribly when the weather was cold, remained folded in front of him.

"Have you business with the earl?" Hilary supposed he could be a merchant, or more likely a clerk of long service entrusted with the monthly delivery of vouchers for payment.

"Yes."

The one-word answer was all she was to receive. Raskett showed himself again, having handed over the man's card to her husband. "His lordship will receive you in the library. This way, if you please, sir."

The man followed, hesitating only long enough to give Hilary a slight nod. She watched as he was shown into the library. Raskett exited a moment later, pulling the double doors closed.

"Who is that strange little man?" she asked.

"A Mr. William Hart," Raskett answered her. "His card carried no mention of his occupation."

"And his business?" she inquired, thinking he must have given some reason for his appearance in order to have gained her husband's audience.

"Of that, I am uncertain, milady. He asked me to deliver a note to his lordship along with his card. Upon reading the message, the earl requested that I show Mr. Hart into the library."

"Thank you, Raskett. Please continue with your duties. I meant no interruption. At times, I'm as curious as Lizzie."

The butler retired to another part of the house, leaving Hilary to feel as if a dark cloud had suddenly taken position over the Eaton Square residence. Unfortunately, her premonition proved to be right.

Twelve

When William Hart stepped into the library, Fitch assumed the man's business was that of soliciting funds for charity. Granted, such requests were normally made at parties where the host or hostess was sponsoring a needy cause, but some of London's less fortunate institutions had to depend on a more direct means to keep their doors open.

"Lord Ackerman?" the stern-looking man inquired tentatively. "The same Lord Ackerman who served with distinction during the Crimean War?"

"Yes." Fitch came to his feet, assuming a benign expression and indicating that Mr. Hart should take a chair. "Your note was a bit vague. You are employed by Debrow's Hospital. Sorry, but I can't say I've ever heard of the place."

"It's a small, private hospital in the St. Luke's District, my lord." He sat, his back straight, his eyes unreadable.

"How may I help you?" Fitch inquired, resuming his own seat. He was prepared to give the hospital, private or public, a donation once the man had had a chance to recite the speech he used in soliciting such funds. It would be rude to prevent him from performing his job, though Fitch thought Debrow's might be better served if they employed someone less sinister in appearance.

Relieving his host of any further preliminaries, Mr. Hart came directly to the point. "I am here at the request of James Hutton. Mr. Hutton served under you during his tour of duty in the Balkans. You knew him as Ensign Hutton, though he gained promotion later, by buying the commission of a retiring lieutenant, one Victor Atkinson, the fourth son of a viscount."

"The buying and selling of military commissions doesn't normally warrant a morning call, Mr. Hart."

Fitch controlled his voice, but not without some difficulty. The last thing he wanted was to have his honeymoon overshadowed by memories of a war he wished he could forget.

"My call has nothing to do with buying or selling, my lord, but with the delivery of news and a small parcel entrusted into my keeping by Mr. Hutton."

The parcel was withdrawn from a black jacket pocket and placed on the corner of Fitch's inlaid mahogany desk. He reached for it, untying the string that kept a sheet of inexpensive brown paper in place.

It was a journal, bookmarked by a gold military braid.

Fitch didn't open the book. Instead, he looked across the desk. "Mr. Hutton asked you to give this to me?"

"Yes, my lord. I was also asked to extend an invitation."

"An invitation?"

"To Mr. Hutton's funeral."

Fitch placed the journal on the green felt blotter that covered the center of his desk. "I will send my condolences to the family. James was from Cornwall, was he not?"

"Yes. You recall serving with him, then?"

"I remember."

"Mr. Hutton will be buried on Wednesday. At Pitfield Road Cemetery."

"Not in Cornwall?"

"No, my lord. He requested that his family not be notified of his death until after the funeral. I will post the letter tomorrow afternoon."

Fitch didn't care for the direction the conversation was taking, or for the conclusion he was drawing. "How did James die?"

"Mr. Hutton shot himself."

Fitch removed his hand from the journal. He recognized it, just as he'd recognized James Hutton's name the moment it had passed William Hart's lips. James had carried the small leather-bound diary in the Crimea. He'd fancied himself a journalist at heart and had taken some heavy teasing for his penmanship from his fellow soldiers, none of whom had had his flair for words.

"What time?" Fitch asked as Mr. Hart came to his feet. He disliked the idea of attending a funeral so soon after his wedding, but the memory of a fallen comrade required otherwise.

"Eight in the morning. The caretaker prefers such services be completed as early as possible."

"I will be there."

Mr. Hart turned, preparing to leave, but Fitch stopped him with a question. "Debrow's Hospital is a sanitarium, is it not?"

"Yes, my lord. Very small and very private. Mr. Hutton resided with us for several years."

"How in the hell did he get his hands on a bloody gun? Don't you people watch over those placed in your care?"

Understanding Fitch's anger, Mr. Hart replied without offense. "There are no locks on the door at Debrow's. Those who come to us, come willingly, and are free to leave whenever they choose. Mr. Hutton left the grounds last week."

"Is that when he gave you the journal?"

"Yes. He asked me to bring it to you when the time came. I regret that it was so soon. He was a fine young man with a keen mind."

"Yes. Yes, he was," Fitch replied sadly. He had seen so much death, so much injustice. So much that he'd once thought his capacity for feeling anything exhausted. "Thank you," he said, unsure if it was the right way to end the conversation, but unable to think of anything else at the moment. "I shall keep the journal. I know how much it meant to James."

"Good day, my lord." With a slight inflection of his head, Mr. Hart took his leave, exiting the house without the aid of a servant to open or close the door.

Fitch stared at the journal with a complexity of feelings, all bittersweet and painful. James Hutton was dead, and by his own hand. Walking to the cabinet, he poured himself a drink. The whiskey caused his stomach to tighten and his mouth to clench into a hard line. He swallowed hard, sending the last of the numbing spirits into his system, wanting the anesthetizing effect the drink would bring.

He turned toward the window, toward the light of a late sunlit morning and the rejuvenation of a new day, but the darkness of war had entered the room in the guise of a man delivering a package, and it wasn't to be ignored.

Returning to the desk, Fitch opened the book. The inside cover bore the name and birth date of its owner. James Hutton had died at the age of thirty. The first entries were what Fitch expected them to be, the ramblings of a young man excited by the prospect of battle. He flipped through them, all too aware of what James had written. As a soldier, he'd shared those same feelings of jubilation, followed by despair.

A third of the way through the book several pages had been left blank, as if to signify the beginning of a new chapter in Hutton's life. The first entry after the war was dated the eleventh day of October, 1860.

The nightmares will not cease. They accompany me to bed each night, the most vigilant of companions, as dutiful as any wife resting her head on the pillow next to mine. But I find no tender release in their arms. Fear brings me awake.

Fitch closed the journal.
No.
The word echoed inside his head. *No.* I will not allow this day to be ruined by memories of war. But even as he opened the drawer of his desk and placed the journal inside, Fitch feared what he knew James Hutton had feared—that the war was still claiming casualties.

Leaving the library, Fitch went in search of his wife and daughter. Hilary was found first, in the morning room at a small desk, her head lowered in concentration.

He stood in the doorway for a long while, looking at her, absorbing all that she represented. As a woman, she surprised him. As a wife, she pleased him. And as a lover, she delighted him. Her response to him was as candid, as thoroughly honest, as her outspoken nature. She offered herself without question or hesitation, always open to the possibility of pleasure. Their recent nights of lovemaking had eliminated the last of her inhibitions. Whatever Fitch asked, she gave.

She looked up and their eyes met, sharing the moment.

"Good morning, my lord," she said, leaving the desk and walking toward him, her slender body gracefully draped in raspberry silk, her brown eyes aglow with life.

"Good morning, wife."

He smiled, opening his arms, and she came to him. The kiss they shared was long and leisurely.

"I saw Mr. Hart," Hilary said. "What a strange little man."

"Yes."

She looked up. "May I inquire into his reason for calling?"

"The death of an old friend."

"I'm sorry."

A silence ensued. Fitch knew she wanted details. Hilary knew he was struggling to tell her as little as possible.

"His name was James Hutton. He served with me, as George Aimes did, in the Crimean."

"You were his commanding officer?"

"Yes."

Despite Hilary's good intentions, she could not help but wish that Fitch would volunteer some sort of information about James Hutton. Had he been a close friend? A good soldier?

The fact that there was a wall between them, invisible but still very much intact, didn't lessen her need to wrap her arms around her husband and hold him close. She did so, resting her cheek against his chest, so she could listen to the beating of his heart.

"The funeral is Wednesday morning," he told her.

"I will attend it with you."

"Funerals are dark and dreary affairs, and this is our honeymoon," he said. "A rather unconventional honeymoon, since I've yet to take you beyond the garden, but it is our wedding week at best and I'll not have your spirits dampened by attending a funeral service."

Hilary wanted to argue. Wanted to insist that as his wife it was her place, her right, to be by his side. But she didn't. Like Fitch, she didn't want to lose the spirit of their time together. Next week he would return to his parliamentary duties and they would be seen in the evenings, a married couple attending balls and dinner and the theater.

"Very well," she relented.

"Where is Lizzie?" Fitch asked, needing his daughter's smile more than usual.

"Annie took her for an outing in the park."

"Then come upstairs with me," he said, removing his arms from around her and taking hold of her hand. "I can't think of a better way to pass the time until luncheon."

Hilary laughed. "Are all husbands so demanding?"

"This husband is," he replied, leading her from the room and up the stairs. They passed Raskett on the stairs, and even though the butler could discern with one glance what they were about, he was discreet enough to act as if nothing was amiss.

Once inside Fitch's bedchamber, a masculine

room done in tones of chocolate brown and ivory, Hilary found herself quickly being divested of her clothing. She stood in the middle of the room, naked, smiling the kind of smile that made Fitch wonder what was going on inside that intelligent head of hers.

"What are you thinking?" he asked as he sat down to take off his boots.

"What will happen with us?" Hilary knew her voice betrayed her feelings, but there was nothing she could do about it. She loved this man.

"What do you want to happen?" His hands went to the buttons on his trousers.

"This," Hilary whispered, raising on her tiptoes and offering herself to him.

The kiss they shared was an explosion of feelings: desire, need, and an urgency that neither one of them could explain.

Nothing mattered but being able to touch each other, to confirm the things that had yet to be spoken between them.

In the soft sunlight of the late morning, Fitch gazed at Hilary lying naked on the coverlet, quivering for him, open for him, her arms lifted to embrace him. He placed his hands on her ankles and ran them up the length of her slender legs, between her open thighs, gently, slowly, so she knew exactly what he was going to do, so she could anticipate their joining as much as he was. Then he let his hands roam some more, over the soft flesh of her stomach and rib cage. She moaned when he finally pressed his hands over her breasts.

He knelt between her legs, his mouth roaming over her body as hungrily as his hands. Wrapped in sensual fire, Hilary twisted and moaned, sending out the sensual message of a woman who wanted to be joined with a man in the most intimate way possible.

Fitch put his cheek against her breast and breathed in the scent of soap and woman. He licked her nipples until they stood erect, like tiny, wet jewels. He gathered her close, his face buried in the curve of her shoulder, his hands still moving, arousing her to the next level, promising her more pleasure with each stroke of his fingertips.

He brought her closer to the edge, slowly unraveling her, then pulling her taut again as his fingers entered her, stretching her, feeling the heat and softness that waited inside. Waited just for him. He rubbed her some more, until she couldn't contain the pleasure, until she convulsed and trembled like a fragile flower caressed by a gentle wind.

It was sweet. So sweet. God, he loved pleasing her, knowing he could please her even more. "I want to be inside you," he said. "But it will be over too soon if I do, so I'm going to make myself wait."

"No," Hilary moaned, clawing at his damp shoulders. "I can't wait. I'm burning alive."

"Not yet," he laughed. "I want to enjoy you like this, naked and lying open for me, waiting for me to take you, wanting me so much you're trembling with the need."

"You're killing me," she said, trying to laugh but too aroused to do more than make a sound that was part pain, part pleasure.

"No, madame, I'm pleasing you. And the pleasure has only just begun."

Hilary relented and let the sensual rhythm take hold of her again. Her heart was wild, her body throbbing with sensation, her breasts aching for Fitch's mouth, her heart wanting all of him. Her hands reached out to hold him, to touch the hard, velvet length of him pressed against her thigh. He moaned as she measured his strength, touching the place he was the most vulnerable and loving the heat that filled her hands. He trembled, and she knew that he wouldn't stay separate from her much longer. She could feel the intemperate hunger in his body and in her own, that irresistible need to join, to become one with each other.

"Now, you're killing me," he whispered hoarsely. "Open for me. Let me inside you. Keep me inside you."

Slowly Fitch pushed himself into her body, inch by inch, until he was buried snugly within her tight channel, until he could feel the velvety clasp of her inner muscles around him.

He sighed as his hips rested completely against hers, content for a moment, satisfied to be where he belonged. "I don't want to move," he said as her hands began to stroke up and down his back. "You feel too good."

"Move," Hilary whispered. "Please."

He did, pulling slowly out of her, then returning with a deep stroke that stole her breath. "Like that?"

"Oh, yes. Just like that."

Fitch pulled all the way out and pushed himself all the way in again, then listened as his wife let out a sigh of pleasure that rose into the air like the song of a bird, sweet and soft. He continued to make love to her in long, slow strokes that fed the fire, building the need until they were both gritting their teeth, their bodies gleaming with sweat, their eyes locked on each other.

Slow and steady, excessively and absolutely, deeper and deeper still, until the fire was raging out of control, until she was arching her hips to take more of him.

"Harder, faster," she breathed. "I'm dying."

Fitch stilled for a moment, holding himself inside her, feeling the magic, wanting it to last forever. He flexed his hips and drove into her again, letting the wildness take him, pushing in and out so hard and fast that Hilary thought she was going to faint.

And still the fire raged. Primal, awesome, touching her senses and her heart, her very soul. The tiny tingling inside her grew and grew as ripples of heat and excitement played havoc with her nerve endings.

As the moment arrived, she looked deep into Fitch's eyes. Mysterious eyes—bright and focused on her, on conquering her, and on pleasing her.

Fitch cupped her bottom, lifting her as he pushed down and into her, forcing her to feel every inch of him, every sensation, every ounce of pleasure he could create. He kissed her until the flame turned to vapor, until the fire burned hotter than any sun, until she was mindless and boneless and thoughtless.

It was always like this when they made love, but somehow today was different. When he wasn't with her, there was an emptiness to him, an illogical void that making love to her filled to overflowing.

"Stay inside me," she said, when he would have moved away to spare her his weight. "I like holding you."

He smiled, then nudged at her neck, his tongue flicking out to taste the saltiness of her skin. "I like holding you. Underneath, on top of me, any way I can get you. I like making love to you in the sunlight so I can see you, see your eyes go soft and feel your body catch fire."

"I'm surprised I haven't melted away."

Fitch eased away just enough to take a nipple into his mouth. He sucked in a leisurely way, liking the taste of her, the sound of contentment in her voice when she asked him not to stop. He never tired of her, never ceased to be aroused by the sight and scent and sound of her

He was happy. Perfectly content to stay where he was and to let time go racing by as fast or as slow as it liked.

Finally, he moved because he knew his weight was too much for her. She moved with him, her arm coming across his chest, her leg overlapping his loins. He could feel the silky heat of her inner thighs and the damp evidence of their recent coupling. A smile curved his mouth as he remembered what it had felt like to come inside her, to give up a part of himself.

It was all he dared to give.

He had long thought that a man was what he believed himself to be, not the identities given to him by others, titles and rankings that meant little in the final hours, but a combination of thoughts and dreams and actions, a creature molded by his own experiences, accountable to himself as much as to God. And yet, who was he? It was as if some part of him had been stripped away during the war and he'd come home incomplete.

Hilary felt a small part of Fitch withdraw from her—not his body, but his mind. He was thinking of something else. Being selfish, wanting him totally to herself for as long as she could have him, she began drawing small circles on his chest, random spirals with a touch as delicate as a butterfly's wing. His nipples stiffened and she smiled. Leaning over, she replaced her fingertips with her tongue.

Fitch shuddered and forgot the worries that had

resurfaced so quickly. Hilary's tongue continued to lick at his chest, painting visions of delight on his bare flesh. He groaned as she moved lower, setting fire to him with her mouth, her hands stroking his thighs, arousing him again.

Wherever he ached, she kissed him. Wherever he wanted the feel of her hands, she touched him. Wordlessly, she brought him to a fresh peak of desire, his body belying the fact that he'd had her only minutes before.

He tugged gently to lift her and she flowed upward in one easy motion of such fluid grace his heart constricted with the pleasure of seeing it. His eyes devoured her as if he'd never seen a woman unclothed before, never touched naked female flesh, never felt the pleasure that could burn a man all the way to his soul.

Her shoulders sloped into slender arms that held more strength than he'd first suspected. Her breasts were small and firm, the nipples dark against her fair skin. But there was a weight to them, a womanly ripeness that he loved to touch and taste. He looked at the curve of her hips, at the tempting nest of curls between her legs, at the softness of her belly. Her skin smelled of soap and him.

She moved then, her hand guiding his erection to the softness between her thighs. A soft trembling started inside him, and Fitch knew a moment's fear; if he ever lost this woman, lost the beauty of her smile and the warmth of her body, his life would never be the same. The acute awareness that she had become more to him than he'd ever imagined she could become pulled at his heart.

Unaware of his thoughts, Hilary loved and conquered the way only a woman could love and conquer, until beads of sweat gathered between her

breasts and rolled down her stomach to the tight
junction formed by their joined bodies. The sensations built and gathered; a sweetness, an intense
concentration of pleasure so close to pain it was almost unbearable, a maelstrom of feelings and desires and needs that spiraled downward and inward
until all control was gone.

Finally, they lay on their backs, eyes closed, their
breathing a perfectly merged duet of sounds. Their
lovemaking had drained them both. They lay
silent, hearing the sounds of the encroaching day,
feeling the cooling texture of the wind as it flowed
through the window and touched their bare skin.

Fitch rolled to his side and studied Hilary's features. There was nothing in them that disappointed
him, not one plane or curve he would change.

Suddenly, and without warning, a single thought
buried itself in his mind and heart: he loved this
woman.

She brought joy to his life, unleashing a tide of
feelings that he'd managed to keep dammed for
years because acknowledging them meant he wasn't
in control. His ring glittered upon her hand, and
it seemed to Fitch that the shimmering gold was
burning through him, to the part that had slept
while other men lived and loved and built futures
for themselves.

Hilary's touch loosened the sorrow of the years
he had spent alone; he could feel the bands of iron
that had once encased his heart falling away, fet-
ters of loneliness cracking like ice at winter's end.

The pleasure was too strong for mere words, but
there was more than brightness to the feelings.
Love came with a responsibility Fitch didn't bear
lightly.

Love required all of a man. It demanded that he

reveal his very soul to another person, that he open his most private thoughts, that he expose himself in every sense of the word.

It meant no secrets. Nothing hidden or disguised.

It meant unlimited sharing. Unlimited giving.

Fitch turned his gaze toward the ceiling, thinking about all that had happened in his life. The victories and the defeats, the treasured moments of joy and the desolate hours of despair. Love was said to triumph over all, and yet if he closed his eyes, he knew the memories of the war would be waiting for him, always vigilant, just as James Hutton had described them.

How could he give Hilary his heart, all that he was, when so much of him was tainted by death and destruction?

Thirteen

The funeral of James Hutton was attended by no one but the Earl of Ackerman, two grave diggers, waiting to fill in the hole once the casket had been lowered and a few decent words spoken by the fourth man attending the service, a minister who leased himself out to local undertakers. He was a thin man, above medium height, dressed in a long, loose-fitting frock coat that flapped about his legs when he walked. Graying black hair straggled down to his collar. His mouth was narrow-lipped and turned down at the corners in a perpetual frown that came from too many years of performing services like the one today.

A funeral wagon sat just beyond the wrought-iron gate of Pitfield Road Cemetery, the black plume set into the horse's bridle limp from age. There were no crests on the door; the carriage had been hired. The portion of the cemetery where the grave had been dug was unhallowed ground, reserved for those considered unworthy of heaven.

Fitch stood at the graveside, his head bowed in

respect, a band of black crepe wrapped around his upper arm. Everything was done in muffled tones; the lowering of the casket by the two burly diggers, godly words of guidance presented by the minister, the crush of earth against the lid of the casket as Fitch tossed a handful of damp, dark soil onto the top of the wooden coffin in a display of final farewell—ashes to ashes, dust to dust.

It was a fitting day for a funeral. The thickening clouds that had covered the sun since dawn had increased in size and strength until their charcoal bellies looked ready to burst. The wind was reverently mournful, moving through the trees, carrying the scent of the upcoming storm.

The pale daylight showed dozens of stone markers, each identifying the resting place of some lost soul. For only lost souls made their way to Pitfield Road. It was a lonely cemetery, set in the northeastern rim of London, its fence rusted with age, the hinges on its solitary gate creaking each time it was opened or closed. It wasn't a pauper's burial ground, but one set aside for those who could afford only the barest of luxuries in both life and death.

It was this small plot of earth that James Hutton had chosen as his final resting place. But would he rest? Had the taking of his own life brought him the peace he had craved, or had it simply opened the doors to a new purgatory? Who could say from this side of the grave? What man could honestly judge another, know the inner workings of his heart and mind during the last moments of his life? Certainly not Fitch.

The minister finished his prayer, a final amen murmured under his breath, the Bible in his hands closed with solemn respect as the wind picked up, rattling the leaves overhead in what seemed a fitting eulogy.

"May he rest in peace," Fitch added, his voice resigned. He stepped back from the grave, turned, and walked away. He had come as James had requested. There was nothing more he could do.

It was raining by the time he reached the inner city, a slow, dreary drizzle that promised to turn into a full-fledged downpour before he reached home. Mindless of the traffic around him, hansom cabs and carriages, vendor carts and delivery wagons, Fitch guided the curricle along Fleet Street, past Waterloo Bridge, then south toward the towers of Westminster and Buckingham Palace. Pitfield Road was a long way from Eaton Square and he used the time to think. Not of James, but of himself, of the changes that had come upon his life since learning that he had a daughter.

James had never taken a wife, never fathered a child.

What a waste, Fitch thought, as he neared his London home and his waiting family. Thoughts of his old friend shifted from memory into a cold, bitter feeling that curled deep in the pit of his stomach.

A surge of pity for the lonely man he'd just seen buried rolled over him, leaving Fitch weak and angry, wanting to help and knowing it was too late. It also left him acutely aware of his own vulnerability.

How many men had he seen killed in the war—hundreds in a single day. So many that he'd stopped counting, stopped feeling. Numbness had been as much of a weapon as his pistol or saber. He had survived because he'd forced himself to stop counting the number of men he himself had killed to stay alive.

Hilary was waiting downstairs.

"You're soaked to the bone," she said, frowning at the rain that dripped off his clothing and onto the foyer's pristine tile. "Upstairs and into some dry clothes, my lord. I'll have a tray sent up. Something hot to ward off the chill."

"A brandy will do," Fitch said, walking past her and into the library—the one room he should have avoided at all cost, but didn't. Perhaps it was because the day and its gloomy circumstances brought out the need for penance. Whatever the cause, he poured himself a drink before turning to look at his wife.

The feelings inside him were a contradiction. Sadness and grief for James Hutton. Contentment and joy for himself. A battling set of emotions that allowed neither to be victorious.

A game of chance, that's what it was. If Hilary hadn't come into his life, he would have married someone else in the future, married and been content because that was what life demanded of a man in his position. And the war. That had been a game, too—more deadly, but just as risky as everyday life with fate's unforeseeable hand in the scheme of things.

Hilary watched as her husband tilted the brandy glass to his mouth. She felt the same curious sense of loss that she'd felt that morning when he'd come downstairs wearing a black arm band.

She'd been restless since his departure, and she'd half toyed with the idea of following him. Instead she'd sat in the parlor, reading a novel and wishing he'd allowed her to take her rightful place at his side.

Fitch splashed more brandy into his glass, then turned to face the window, to stare out as though he were searching for something beyond the opaque rain. A flat, absorbed silence filled the room. Rain beat against the glass, trickling down like tears.

Hilary stood silently for a moment, unsure how to offer the comfort she wanted to give, sensing that more than the death of a single friend burdened her husband's heart.

She understood grief, had felt it in a child's heart when her parents had died in a fire, and as an adult, standing by Beth's grave, then again only a few months later when Edwina had died. But in spite of her experience with what she thought Fitch was feeling, Hilary was still at a loss for words. People had to deal with death in much the same way they dealt with life—each in their own way.

"Have you unfinished work?" she asked, offering them both a way out of the awkward silence. "If so, I shall leave you to it. I'll have Raskett bring in a luncheon tray."

"Thank you." His back was still to her, the glass in his hand nearing his mouth a second time.

It wasn't until she turned to leave the room that Fitch realized he'd been rude. He set aside his drink and walked to where she was standing, her hand poised to reach for the doorknob. He kissed her gently. "My apologies, madame. Funerals breed feelings that are best dealt with alone. A few hours with my ledgers, if you please, and I shall escort you to the theater a different man."

"I understand," she said, wanting him to know

that she did, at least as much as he'd allow. "I felt so empty after Edwina died. And Beth—she was so young."

He looked at her then, his gaze bleak. "So was James."

Hilary looked deep into his eyes and realized that the chasm between them was much wider than she'd originally thought. At that moment she almost abandoned the hope she was holding so dearly in her heart, thinking it impossible. Yet in another corner of her heart, she knew that if she gave up on this man, he would one day give up on himself. Where the thought originated, she couldn't say, but she believed it to be true.

As the days progressed, Hilary did indeed find herself married to a different man. Fitch spent more and more time in his library, cloistered away from her. Lizzie became their common focus, the thing that gave their relationship normality.

They seemed caught in an exasperating game of light and shadow that left her starved for the kind of intimacy she knew could exist between them if only he would *talk* to her.

Whenever she reached the point of bursting into frustrated tears or felt the urge to rant and rave, Fitch would suddenly ask her to take a walk with him or stroll into the parlor with a smile on his face, turning her disappointment back into hope.

When they attended parties, he was attentive and polite. Hilary knew other women eyed her secretly and enviously, and with good cause—she was married to the man so many of them had coveted. Society now saw her as a woman who had accom-

plished her principal role in life: she'd married a
handsome, titled man of impeccable breeding. What
more could she possibly want?

Despite her misgivings, Hilary made sure she
glowed with cheerfulness whenever she and Fitch
were seen in public. To the unsuspecting eye, they
were a happily married couple.

Tonight was one of those nights. As she dressed,
Hilary disliked the idea of another evening of
feigned contentment, but she had little choice.
The invitation to Lady Winchilsea's ball had been
accepted weeks ago.

They arrived amid a crowd of polished carriages.
Taking her husband's hand, she was led into yet
another grand London house, into a blaze of lights
and glittering jewels. The sound of music and laughter and endless chatter filled the ballroom.

Hilary looked around at the sea of lace and silk.
The party was being held in honor of a very pretty
young girl of eighteen who was having her first
Season. Hilary had been introduced to Prudence
the previous week, at a tea held by Lady Forbes-
Hammond. She had found the young lady to be
shy but charming, soft-spoken but sincere.

In spite of the small amount of time they had
spent together, Hilary retained the impression that
there was more to Prudence Tamhill than met the
eye. There was a courage in her gaze that belied
the vulnerability one usually associated with someone so young.

She was of average height, slender, and quite
the most beautiful young lady London had seen in
years. Her hair was a rich brown. Eyes as black as
jet gleamed under finely arched brow. Demurely
dressed in a fashionable gown of white and the

palest of pinks, Prudence stood next to her hostess as more and more guests arrived.

Hilary noticed Rathbone eyeing her from a distance. The viscount seemed more amused than interested, and she hoped he wasn't sizing Prudence up for a night of scandalous fun.

"What has you brooding?" Fitch asked.

"Your friend," Hilary told him, directing her gaze across the room to where the viscount was standing slightly apart from the other guests. "He's eyeing poor Prudence as if she were a lamb to be led to the slaughter."

"Don't worry yourself, madame. Prudence Tamhill is the last lady Rathbone would seduce."

"Why?"

The orchestra began to play a waltz. Fitch offered his arm to lead her to the floor. Once they were dancing, she repeated her question, curious as to why Rathbone would detour himself from the prettiest female in the room when he was known to be a womanizer.

"The *why* is simple," Fitch replied. "Prudence Tamhill is the ward of the Duke of Worley, who is a very close, very personal friend of the Duke of Morland."

"I fail to see what you and your friends find so foreboding about Morland," she said, swirling gracefully in his arms as they negotiated a complicated corner of the room. "He is the most perfect of gentlemen."

"That he is," Fitch conceded with a smile. "Then again, you've never been forced to endure his gentlemanly meddling."

The music came to an end a few moments before the Earl of Granby arrived. He was minus his wife this evening, something Hilary noted immediately. When she inquired as to Catherine's health, the earl smiled.

"My lady is pleasingly plump and not at all happy to be left at home," he replied. "However, may I take the pleasure of introducing my father-in-law, Sir Warren Hardwick. I've solicited his help in getting Catherine to the country before the end of the Season. She refuses to listen to me."

"Not sure she'll listen to *me*," Sir Hardwick said, stepping forward. "She was born on the stubborn side of the blanket. Takes after her mother, of course."

Hardwick was a tall man with broad shoulders and a strongly sculptured face. A thin scar ran the length of his right jaw. "Lady Ackerman," he said, bowing over her hand. "I know your husband. Served in the Eighth Hussars myself."

"Hardwick," Fitch said in acknowledgement. "It's been some time."

"Yes, it has, my lord." His eyes scanned the room. "Nothing like Balaclava, is it?"

"Hardly," her husband replied, his voice devoid of emotion.

Hilary sensed he hoped to avoid any direct discussion of the war. Still, he seemed pleased to see Hardwick again.

They spoke of other things, of racing and politics and the upcoming summer and the possibilities of a good grouse season once the weather cooled again. Hilary listened, hoping to gain some insight into the time when Sir Hardwick had known her husband as Lieutenant Minstead, but the conversation didn't return to the war. Still, she caught one or two glances, a silent acknowledgement that her husband and Sir Hardwick shared a knowledge no one else in the room could fully comprehend.

By evening's end, she was so tired of smiling and looking happy, she retired to her room—totally miserable.

Thunder brought Hilary awake. The hour was late and there was no warm, comforting body beside her in the double bed. Nor had there been for the last six nights.

Knowing where she'd likely find her husband, she went downstairs. As expected, light shone from beneath the closed library door. Taking a deep breath and assuring herself that as adults she and Fitch could discuss things in a rational, reasonable fashion, she opened the door and stepped inside.

Her husband looked up from where he was sitting in a wing-backed chair. The glow of the gas lamp cast his features in shadowed hues that revealed his mood. For a moment Hilary regretted coming downstairs.

It was clear that he'd been drinking. A crystal decanter minus its corked top sat on the table at his side. A glass was resting within reach, empty for the moment. He had been reading something. The small book was closed now, but still in his hand.

"Madame?" he inquired dryly.

His lack of cordiality in not standing when she entered the room wasn't unexpected. He looked more than put out by her interruption, as if she had no right to venture beyond the bedroom once the sun had set.

"The storm woke me," she said, adding an air of

reserve to her greeting. Her husband wasn't the only one in a foul mood. Truth be told, she'd had quite enough of his evasive behavior. A roaring argument might be just the thing to clear the air.

Ignoring his dismissing tone, she made her way to a neighboring chair and settled into it like a lazy cat, curling her legs under her. "What are you reading?"

"Nothing." The book was set aside so he could refill his glass. "If you're looking for a similar pastime, there are a few novels that might appeal to you. Feel free to make a selection."

"I'd rather talk."

"I'm not in the mood for conversation." The edge in his voice was soft but discernible.

"You have been by yourself too much of late," she replied, refusing defeat. "Admittedly I am a woman and thereby unable to grasp the solace a man takes in his library, but hour upon hour, day after day, my lord? Something is plaguing you and I wish to know what it is. I am your wife. We should be able to talk without reservation. If all you require is a listener—"

"I am not in the mood to talk, madame—thus a listener is unnecessary."

Hilary didn't move a muscle.

Wisdom told her to leave the stubborn man to battle his own problems, but her heart felt too strongly to be denied. She was still confused by her reaction to Fitch, by the wanton cravings he aroused within her, and by the need to be important to him. Then again, if a man stirred a woman so deeply she no longer knew herself, perhaps it was a thing to be pitied. God knew, she had lost herself the day she had married. The bluestocking spinster of Nottingham no longer existed.

Now she was a wife, and as such, she refused to be ignored or relegated to the bedroom. So she simply sat in the chair, gazing about the library as if she had nothing better to do in the middle of the night.

Fitch felt his temper rising, fueled by too much drink and the sinking feeling that he no longer controlled his own life.

Hutton's journal had been whispering to him since the day he had locked it in the drawer, calling out in the voice of a silenced comrade to be read. Seeing Hardwick tonight had strengthened the idea that by reading what James had written, he might in some way be able to put the memories behind him.

But the more he'd read, the more vivid his recollections had become. The horror and loss were as clear in his mind as they had been that day at Balaclava. So many men. One moment they had been alive, fighting side by side, the next they lay dead or dying, their blood painting the mud a deep crimson red.

If only Hilary hadn't come downstairs. If only he'd been left to his brandy and his brooding. But she was here, and he was too drunk to care that she meant well.

He moved from the chair, staggering for a brief moment before righting his balance. His face was flushed with drink, but his eyes seemed empty as they gazed down at Hilary.

"Perhaps we can find a way to pass the time together."

He came to her then, lowering himself on one knee beside her chair. But instead of kissing her, he reached out and untied the laces of her robe, pushing them aside and exposing the sheer gown beneath it. As always the closeness of his body quickened her blood. His hands were warm, almost hot, as they caressed her, cupping the weight of her in his open palms.

Fitch could see the resistance in her eyes at the same time he could see her arousal. She thought to dissuade him, to insist that he bare his soul before he bared his loins. But he couldn't. There was no making anyone understand, not unless they'd been there. He blinked the images away. He didn't want to remember.

He focused his gaze on his wife, on the hardening peaks of her breasts, and felt the blood rush to his groin.

"Shall it be seduction tonight, madame? Do you require slow, passionate kisses and whispered words? Or are you as ready as I? Your nipples tell me you are. They're standing like tiny crowns atop your breasts. Bare them for me."

Hilary tried to close her robe, but his hands were in the way. He fondled her boldly, his smile sardonic.

"Please," she said, hoping to bring some sense to things.

"Please what, my dear? Please take you here and now, on the library rug, or would you prefer the chair? A good, comfortable chair can make for a very satisfying night."

Hilary pushed his hands away. He was drunk, but that didn't justify his actions. "Enough. I won't be treated in this manner."

Fitch stood up, hands clenched at his sides. "And what manner is that, wife? You come into this room in the middle of the night, dressed in silk—what response did you expect from me save the one you have received?"

"Please don't do this."

"Do what?" he asked sarcastically. "Dismiss you? Tell you that if you have no desire to be a wife tonight, then I have no need of you?"

For a moment there was nothing but silence and the cold darkness that had come with the storm. The disappointment Hilary felt was too sharp, too painful, to be put into words. It cut into her very soul. But like her husband, her pride ran deep.

She pushed herself out of the chair. Holding her robe closed, she returned his gaze. "Very well, my lord. I will go upstairs, and come morning, I shall descend those same stairs a wife of convenience. I shall keep your house in an orderly manner and attend whatever obligatory balls and afternoon teas are required of me. I will not, however, go about the house whispering as if there were straw in the street, nor bend myself so completely to your will that I become a marionette."

"Are you refusing me the comforts of your bed, madame?"

"If you think to be as perfunctory there as you have been here tonight, then yes, my lord."

With a fatalistic shrug, Fitch lifted the brandy glass to his mouth. In that same terrible moment Hilary saw their future crumbling like a wall that lacked mortar to hold the stones together.

Fourteen

Winslow Hall was near an arched stone bridge that crossed a bubbling creek. Thick trees and clinging summer vines hid the manor house from view. It was nearing evening and a mellow sun hung over the trees and the tea-colored stream that had been churned up by a recent rain. The water from a dozen tiny rock falls burbled and swirled, rolling up and against itself before spinning off in foamy circles and lacy, wet spirals.

It had been almost a full day since Hilary and her husband had left the Two Goats Inn, a coaching house where they and a troupe of servants had spent the night. Parliament was officially adjourned, the Season over. It was time for lords to take to their country estates, time for lawn parties and croquet matches, time for her and Fitch to stop pretending to be married.

The thought was a sober one, unfitting the circumstances if one looked across the coach to where her husband sat with Lizzie upon his lap. Fastidiously

dainty in a pink dress, she sat contently on her father's knee, knowing there was no need to de-
mand acknowledgement of her presence, knowing
she was loved.

Fitch was busy describing all the things they would
be doing now that summer had come—morning
rides and treasure hunts in the woods, picnics and
fishing in the nearby stream. It all sounded so perfectly, wonderfully normal, and Hilary prayed with
all her heart that the green meadows and misty
vales of Buckinghamshire would cure her ailing
marriage.

Not that Fitch had continued the rudeness he'd
displayed the night she'd intruded on him. Quite
the contrary. He'd come to the breakfast table the
following morning acting as if the incident had
never taken place. But it had, and there was no undoing it. It stood between them like a shadow, and
until it was gone there could be no real trust between them.

As a result, they spoke in pleasant tones at dinner, smiled when in public, and slept behind separate doors at night. For all intents and purposes,
their union had become a marriage of convenience,
except for the fact that there'd be no heir unless
things changed. Hilary wasn't pregnant, nor was she
likely to get that way unless one of them sought a
compromise.

She supposed in the end that it would be her.
Men were such stubborn creatures, and she did so
love this one. But she wasn't ready to give in yet.
There was still Winslow Hall and the hope that a
change of scenery could bring about a change of
attitude.

"Oh, look, Papa!" Lizzie said, pointing to a pond

with rippling water where a pair of white swans glided effortlessly, their wings tucked neatly at their sides. "Do they have names?"

"None that I know of, pumpkin."

As always, Lizzie was the delight of his heart and it showed. Hilary ached with jealousy. If only she could put a similar smile on her husband's face. He was such a complex man, restless and passionate, disturbing in ways that both pleased and puzzled her.

The coach rolled under a line of heavily leaved trees and along the gravel drive that led to the impressive house. Then suddenly the trees gave way, and Hilary saw her husband's family home.

Winslow Hall rose from a tablelike span of land, idyllic in a setting of scythed grass and manicured hedges. The house was in the Old Tudor style, resembling a fortress with hexagonal bays and turrets, high chimneys, tall leaded windows, and decorative roof balustrades. The entry steps were long and wide, quarried from local stone and bordered by large Grecian urns that dripped greenery onto the gray-white stone.

Raskett, who had arrived the previous day to see that all was in order for the Hall's new mistress, greeted them with a smile. "Welcome to Winslow Hall, milady."

Fitch had already handed her down from the carriage and was now listening to Lizzie rattle on about how large the house was and how she'd surely get lost.

"Come along," Fitch said, offering Hilary his arm and taking Lizzie by the hand. "I'll introduce you to the staff."

The staff turned out to be seventy-plus servants, beginning with the housekeeper. Mrs. Ellerbeck was a stout woman, a bit hard-faced but not unattractively stern. Her dress was of dark gray cloth, its skirt brushing the spotless floor, its front protected by a starched white apron. A jingling ring of keys hung from her belt.

The introductions took place in the main circular foyer that was two stories high. Hilary knew she wasn't expected to remember each and every name, nor the specific ranking of maids from parlor to between-stairs. Still, it was a bit intimidating to realize that she had a small army at her disposal.

Lizzie was, of course, the center of attention. Mrs. Ellerbeck needed only one look at the child to know that she was more than Hilary's ward. Fitch accepted the housekeeper's quizzical expression with an equally quizzical smile.

"My ladies have traveled far, Mrs. Ellerbeck. Would you be so kind as to show them above stairs?"

"Of course, milord. It's a pleasure to have a little one about the place again. I hope there will be more soon."

"I'm sure there will be," Fitch replied. He stepped aside, freeing Hilary to follow the housekeeper. "Supper at the normal time, then?"

"Yes, milord, and your favorite if the smells from the kitchen are any clue."

Hilary smiled, wondering what would be said once she and the earl had disappeared upstairs, or if Mrs. Ellerbeck would forbid any such chatter among the servants. Her appearance gave the impression that she ruled with a firm hand, but servants, being incurably nosey, would have their say nevertheless.

The furniture she was able to see from glancing through the open doors they passed was old and sturdy. Chair covers were made out of tapestry in bold and dim colors alike. The legs of the second-floor parlor settee were curved and carved into lion's feet and glossier than any pew she'd ever seen in church. There was a spinet piano in the music room, and cabinets with belly-fronted glass doors, filled to capacity with bric-a-brac and mementoes of the family who had lived in the same house for generations.

Hilary's intuition told her that the suite of rooms she was shown into had once belonged to Fitch's mother. Like the other rooms, there was nothing mediocre to be seen. The carpet was fir green, the windows draped in soft ivory velvet. Two dainty Queen Anne chairs, upholstered in a green-and-cream matching print, sat on either side of a pedestal table. The woodwork and mantelpiece were painted white, the chandelier brass and crystal. A wicker chaise thick with multicolored cushions added a restful ambiance to the sitting room.

The bedroom itself was peacefully beautiful. The color scheme had been reversed, the carpet a soft, rich ivory with dark green designs that swirled out from its center. Green velvet draperies were tied back from the tall, lead-paned windows, offering a view of the gardens to the east of the house.

"A balcony," Lizzie exclaimed, scampering outside through the open door. She raised her hands as if to touch the sun, then twirled around and around.

"Your room has one, too," Mrs. Ellerbeck told her. "And a carousel painted on the wall. Do you like horses?"

"Oh, yes," Lizzie told her. "And dogs and kittens and hedgehogs. I have a hedgehog. Papa found it and we named it Hattie."

Mrs. Ellerbeck smiled, beaming as if she'd inherited a grandchild to spoil. "Well now, I've seen some new kittens down at the stables. Came with orders, they did."

"Orders?" Lizzie pranced inside, forgetting about the wonders of the balcony.

"Aye, direct orders from his lordship to old Gilleon."

"Who's Gilleon?"

"He's the stablemaster. A fearsome old man, or so he likes folks to think, but you'll not find a softer heart when it comes to animals. He's taken good care of your pets."

"I want to see them," Lizzie said, turning pleading brown eyes on her aunt. "Please, Aunt Hilary, please."

"Later, once you've changed into clothes that a stable won't ruin. And after you'd had something to eat."

Lizzie's pout brought another smile to Mrs. Ellerbeck's face. "Oh, she's a charmer, she is."

"I'm afraid so."

"Nothing wrong with that," the housekeeper remarked. "We've been too long without children in this house. I was the first to say amen when Raskett sent the news of his lordship's marriage. Amen, and about bloody time, if you excuse me for saying so. You're not to have a worry here, milady. We'll take good care you."

Believing the housekeeper meant what she said, Hilary watched as she took Lizzie by the hand and led her away to discover her own room. A short time later, Annie appeared, ready to begin unpacking the trunks the footmen were carrying up the back stairs.

"Oh, it's a lovely old house, and so grand," Annie said once they alone. "I'll learn to be a proper lady's maid here, I will."

"You've always been proper enough for me," Hilary said. "Did anyone mention how long until supper is served?"

"Not until eight. I asked on the way up."

"Then I think I'll take a stroll about the place. I don't want to get in your way while you unpack."

That said, Hilary crossed the room to the chest of drawers where she removed her hat and gloves before setting out to familiarize herself with her new home.

The second floor of the house was intersected by two halls of equal width. One corridor began at the front and ended just beyond the wide staircase that climbed in leisurely fashion from the circular foyer. The second hallway accessed the bedrooms, the music room, and two secondary parlors.

The music room, which could be entered from opposite sides, had been left with both sets of doors open. The effect lent an air of spaciousness and elegance. It contained a marble fireplace, whose mantel was adorned by a clock of rose Pompadour porcelain. Tall, arched windows on either side of the piano were hung in tamboured lace curtains and blue brocade draperies. The material was repeated in the upholstery of two plumb and deeply tufted armchairs, a long sofa that sat in the center of the room, and the loveseat in the corner. The opposing corner was filled by a massive Chippendale cabinet with a bowed front, filled with Dresden figurines.

Hilary walked around the room, thinking how beautifully the sound of the piano would carry through the house when both sets of doors were open. She hadn't played since the night of Lord Waltham's dinner party. Thinking of future nights with her husband relaxing where she played brought a smile to her face.

She would play for him tonight, she decided, before leaving the room and continuing her exploration.

From a corner of the second-floor hallway, Hilary saw what looked like a conservatory. Deciding it was as good a place as any to spend a few minutes alone, she made her way downstairs.

In actuality the room was part conservatory, part parlor. Decorated in a Gothic design with fanciful gargoyles gazing down from stone columns, the room was alive with plants and herbs that added a wonderful, invigorating scent to the air. The furniture was wicker, like the chaise upstairs, ornate but sturdy with brightly colored cushions and skirted tables. The windows, polished as bright as a mirror, allowed the garden beyond to seep into the room, making them seem almost one.

"My mother loved this room."

Hilary turned to find her husband standing in an opposing doorway. "It's lovely."

"So was she," he said with a smile. "Father used to tease her, saying she had to be hiding Spanish blood in her veins. She loved the sunshine. In some ways, she suited this room as much as it suited her."

"What was her name?" It was the first time he'd mentioned either one of his parents directly, and it warmed Hilary's heart, making the hope flame anew.

"Lavinia."

"And your father?"

"Radcliffe William Fitzgerald Minstead." Her husband laughed. "The name suited him. He was a tough old bird."

She watched as he moved into the room, stopping to touch an embroidered cushion lying in a high-backed rocker. Dare she hope that Winslow Hall was already working its magic, that Fitch was beginning to feel a sense of peace now that he was home?

"Tell me, what do you think of Mrs. Ellerbeck?"

"She's charming."

"Only another woman would say that. She's almost as strict as my father was, but in a different way." A melancholy smile came to his face, then a low laugh. "She gave me my first thrashing. Said it was either a wooden bread board or a trip to my father's study."

"So you took the bread board?"

"Thought I was getting the better end of the deal, so to speak. I wasn't so sure afterwards. She blistered me good."

Hilary tried not to laugh. "What did you do?"

"I poured honey into the laundry tub."

"I'm surprised she didn't hang you from the wash line." The very idea of her serious-minded husband being a mischievous little boy lightened her heart.

"You don't hang six-year-old boys from the wash line—you intimidate them for the rest of their lives."

"Was your brother the paragon, then?"

"Christian? Not bloody likely. He was worse than one, more of a charmer. And he didn't hesitate to use that charm. But neither one of us could fool Ellerbeck. She knew exactly where to find us when trouble was about."

A wren came to roost just outside the window,

turning its brown head from side to side before pecking at the glass.

"I owe you an apology, wife."

It was the first they had spoken of the night they'd argued. Hilary feared the sunshine streaming into the room would be overcast by a cloud, but a moment passed and still the sun shone.

"Show me more of the house," she said, holding out her hand. "I've already seen the music room. It's beautiful. I can't wait to try the piano."

"You must play tonight. I insist." He closed the distance between them and took her hand. After raising it to his mouth for a kiss, he smiled. "There is a room of particular interest that I would like to show you tonight. The master bedroom."

"You, sir, are a rogue."

"Nay, a husband who has missed his wife."

"As I am a wife who has missed her husband."

He led her out of the conservatory and down a long hall, then up a flight of stairs and down another hall.

"Where are we going?" Hilary asked, tugging at his hand so he might slow down. "I would see my new home."

"Tomorrow, I shall give you a tour. Room by room."

"Where do you think to take me now?"

"Someplace where we won't be bothered by servants or little girls with bouncing curls."

The room was in the west wing of the house, small and neatly furnished as a sitting room for guests. There was a center table, mahogany, with a pedestal base and claw feet, draped in fine linen. The bentwood chairs were delicately made and upholstered in red damask.

Once the door was closed, nary a sound could be heard. Fitch leaned against the closed door, his smile pure devilry.

Hilary found herself smiling in return. "It is plain to see that you have seduction on your mind."

"Not seduction. I will have you to come to me willingly this time."

There was an unguarded gleam in his eye and a softening of his features that made Hilary's heart begin to flutter and her body grow warm. She glanced around the room. There were chairs, none of which looked *that* comfortable, and a settee that was too short to make good use of. The carpet was plush, but she disliked the idea of being on the floor.

Fortunately, her husband was a resourceful man.

He led her to the windowseat. "This will do nicely, I think. You can ride me."

A flush of color crept into Hilary's face. Her eyes were downcast, her lashes shadowing elegantly modeled cheekbones. She looked shy and unapproachable. "I should not give in to your charms too readily, my lord. I do not want you to think me so easily dissuaded."

"Then I shall have to use all my gentlemanly skills to convince you otherwise."

He advanced, very much like a panther stalking a wary prey. A strange tension began to take hold of Hilary's senses, making her breath come in short gasps.

She was surprised when, like a panther, he pounced unexpectedly, wrapping his arms around her and lifting her off the floor. She could feel his body, firm and lean, and the hardness that said he wanted her—now.

If she had any doubt as to his intentions, it vanished the moment he kissed her. It was a ravenous kiss, deep and possessive.

When the kiss was over, he looked down at her, into the depths of her brown eyes, eyes that told him she, too, had missed sharing the same bed.

Silence reigned for a moment, followed by the huskily spoken words, "I want you."

"I'm yours to have," Hilary whispered as the tension took hold again. But this time it was more anticipation than worry, more need than hesitation.

Suddenly they were upon the windowseat, his hands around her waist, guiding her to sit atop his thighs, straddling his legs in a most unladylike fashion. She spread her hands wide over his chest, then raised her face for a devastating kiss that left her weak in the knees. His hands moved from her shoulders to her knees, then began inching up her dress. The feel of gauzy silk creeping slowly, sensually up her legs, was an erotic sensation. She moaned softly when his fingertips found their way under the dress and brushed lightly over the thin layer of cloth she was wearing underneath it.

Fitch smiled a triumphant smile as he found the slip in her pantaloons. He combed his fingers through her private curls, then probed deeper. He teased her with his fingers until she was aching and swollen, arching her back and vowing if he didn't hurry she'd die from the wanting.

"I'm going to have you now," he whispered.

He opened his own clothing, then lifted her. Hilary wrapped her legs around his waist. He entered her in a long, smooth stroke that joined their bodies so intimately tears came to her eyes.

"I like it hard and deep," he whispered. "Do you want it that way?"

"Yes."

She made the monosyllable reply very expressive. It would be hypocrisy to pretend that she wasn't as hungry as he was, that she didn't want him with the same desperate need.

After that, Hilary couldn't speak; all she could do was moan as he pushed up inside her. Wanting him, needing to show her love, she matched his pace, move for move, kiss for kiss. His fingers dug into the soft skin of her bottom. She'd find bruises there in the morning, but she didn't care. All she wanted was the pleasure he was promising.

True to his word, her husband moved hard and deep, going deeper into her womb with each thrust until all she could do was surrender to the delicious sensations.

Fitch whispered her name just before his own surrender. He burst inside her, his body exploding with the convulsions he'd been able to control until Hilary had found her own release. He pushed deep one last time, dying a little as the sated feeling of being drained and renewed swept through him.

"You belong to me," he said, holding her close as she came back to herself. "I've wanted you for days, but I decided to wait until we were here. Until we were home. Sorry, I was too impatient to wait until I could make love to you properly in the master bedroom."

"Don't be sorry." She leaned against him, breathless but satisfied. "I've never been ravished before—it was nice."

Fitch laughed, then kissed her. "What else do you like?"

"Tea and an hour to rest before dinner," she mumbled, suddenly exhausted.

Things still had a long way to go before being

right between them, but Hilary couldn't discount the significance of today's events. Fitch had spoken of his family for the first time, and he'd waited until they'd reached Winslow Hall so he could make love to her in their true home, in the house where their children would be born. It was enough to renew the hope in her heart.

Fifteen

Life in the country soon became divided into two parts—the time Hilary spent with her husband and the time she spent without him. For the most part, her time with him was the early hours of the morning and the late hours of the evening.

Hilary couldn't decide which portion of the day she liked best. The time between waking up beside Fitch in the huge master bedroom and breakfast on the terrace outside the conservatory was spent in numerous ways. Some mornings they languished in bed, making love; others, they dressed and went for a morning ride. Wanting to please him, she was a good pupil and was soon sitting a lovely chestnut mare with confident grace.

In accordance with their mutual change of scenery and attitude, time ceased to tick away minute by minute, and instead was counted by the halcyon days of summer and warm, passionate nights.

Winslow Hall was a house of sixty-plus rooms situated in the center of an estate of over fourteen hundred acres. There was always something to see, but her morning rides with Fitch provided a special solicitude, as if the pattern of intimacy they had shared that first day in the conservatory might develop through repetition into something much more satisfying.

Some mornings Fitch had the look of a man with a secret he was patiently waiting to reveal; at other times he appeared to be just what he was—a well-bred gentleman who loved his home and the land that had given his family stability for six generations.

He spoke to her of his family, but only in terms of his childhood, a life spent growing up in the peaceful realm of a country estate. Nothing had been said of his time spent in the military or of the years since Christian's death. The dozens of questions that were waiting to be asked, still waited, controlled by Hilary's determination not to stir the waters so deeply that the fragile truce between herself and Fitch dissolved.

They took an easterly route after leaving the stables one morning, riding down the slopes of grass-covered hills to a sparkling stream. They sat motionless, atop their horses, gazing at the terraced fields that traced the contours of the green hills.

"The land is what truly holds a family together," Fitch said. "My father used to bring me here when I was a boy. He'd talk about crops and livestock as if they were the only thing on earth that mattered. It wasn't until I was older, much older, that I realized why he was so intent on transferring his knowledge to me. He wanted me to realize that our family was more than an aristocratic title—it was our estates, our land."

"You never begrudged your brother the title?"

Hilary asked, having sensed the loss he felt whenever Christian's name was mentioned.

"No. In most ways, being the second son was a
blessing. While I had to measure up to a certain
standard, it was not the one expected of Christian."

He shifted in the saddle, turning to look back
the way they had come, through a grove of apple
trees that was showing signs of fruit. For a moment, Hilary sensed that he was trying to look back
over his life, at the chain of events that had brought
him to the earldom. When he turned to her a moment later, the brooding expression had left his
face.

"Is Lizzie still complaining that Mrs. Crombie is
too strict?"

"Yes. She told me this morning that three hours
a day is far too many to be cooped up in a classroom."

Before leaving London, they had interviewed
half a dozen women for the post of governess. Mrs.
Crombie had been the last. She was a widow, forced
by financial circumstances to seek employment.
They had debated upon the choice, Fitch wanting
a more credentialed governess while Hilary had
leaned toward one with common sense and a good
grasp of the basics of education. The amiable argument had ended with Fitch relinquishing the
decision into his wife's capable hands. Thus Mrs.
Crombie had arrived last week and was now well
established in the classroom across the hall from
the nursery.

"She isn't so old as to be inflexible in her attitudes, nor too young to be taken in by your daughter's indisputable charm. The lessons I have
monitored have been well presented and Lizzie's
French is progressing nicely," Hilary remarked.

"My beguiling little girl has certainly won Gilleon over," Fitch said humorously. "He turns to mush the moment she shows herself around the stables."

"All the servants do. The older ones know she's your child, though they're too well trained and too respectful of you to say it aloud." She looked at Fitch to gauge his reaction. "The portrait of your mother is witness to the fact. The resemblance is unmistakable."

"I know, and I'm sure Mrs. Ellerbeck and the rest have speculated. Does it bother you?"

"No. Beth was my dearest friend. And I love Lizzie. The fact that she is your daughter is the very reason we married. To wish otherwise does not please me."

He nudged his horse closer. His lawn shirt was open at the throat, revealing the upper portion of his chest and a mat of thick, dark hair. He exuded power and a strong vitality that never failed to stir Hilary's blood.

With each passing day, she puzzled more and more over his character. He was a violently passionate man—she had only to think of his love-making to know that; yet at times he seemed more like a hermit, shutting himself away from the world, living within his own private thoughts.

"Having no illusions about finding the perfect husband every little girl dreams about, I cannot be displeased with the one I have now, my lord. A glance in the mirror each morning reminds me that I am still plain. My nose is a trifle too long, my jaw too firm, my eyes too direct. While I acknowledge that Lady Waltham's advice on fashion has helped immensely, there is no denying that if you and Beth had not been lovers, I would not now be Lady Ackerman."

"I am glad to hear that our marriage pleases you," Fitch said. "Though I don't like the reasons you list. Yes, Lizzie is the reason I proposed marriage, but there were others."

"Such as?"

"Has not our time together as husband and wife shown you the answer to that question, madame? We are well suited, as I knew we would be."

Fitch knew this was the time to tell his wife that he had grown to love her, that his feelings ran so deep they frightened him in ways he couldn't adequately express. But he held his tongue. He had come a long way toward recovering his former self since they had arrived at Winslow, but James Hutton's death still haunted him. The more he read the bequeathed journal, the more he realized that he was a victim of the same thoughts, the same nightmares. During the daylight hours he could struggle and win, but at night, lying in bed with Hilary at his side, he was still reluctant to let sleep claim him for fear that he'd be unable to dissociate himself come dawn.

"Are we, my lord?" Hilary asked, unaware of his private thoughts because he masked them so well.

"Have I done something to make you think otherwise?" He dismounted and reached for her.

Hilary came away from the sidesaddle and into his arms. They left the horses to graze while they walked toward the stream, hand in hand. Along the way, they chatted of the summer's successes and failures, of the new irrigation system and Lizzie's dislike of the French language, but Fitch wasn't deceived by his wife's amiability. She was not being her usual outspoken self, which meant there was something on her mind.

"Have I a scolding due?" he asked, once they stopped near the edge of the stream.

"No. Have you done something to warrant one?"

"I'm not sure," he said, relaxing his shoulder against a large tree with limbs that twisted and turned their way toward the sun. "My wife tells me she is pleased to be my wife. I tell her that I am just as pleased to be her husband, but I sense something more is to be said. What is it?"

Knowing the importance of her answer, Hilary took her time in composing the reply. "I love Winslow Hall," she said. "Since walking through its door I feel as if I were predestined to live here."

"Perhaps you were." He pulled her close, shifting her so her back was to his chest, his arms wrapped possessively around her waist so his hands could rest over her lower stomach. "I gave up trying to outguess fate long ago."

"I never expected my life to take a turn to match yours," she said, snuggling close because every moment she spent in his arms was precious. "What do you suppose you'd be doing today if you hadn't become the earl? If Christian hadn't died?"

It was the wrong question. Hilary didn't have to see Fitch's face to know that he had resumed his brooding expression. He didn't slacken his hold on her, but she could feel the tension in his body.

"Christian is dead and I am the earl. Romantic notions and questions won't change either one." He knew where the conversation was going, knew it would only lead to an argument if he didn't turn her attention to other things. "Have you sent out the invitations to my dreaded birthday ball?"

Hilary allowed the change of subject. She had stood at her parents' grave, and the graves of her

aunt and Beth Bradstreet. She knew that time healed
most wounds, but there was always a twinge of
memory in the scars. She'd be patient a while
longer.

"Yes. Lots of invitations. The house will be filled
for an entire week."

It was to be her debut as a hostess. The ball
would take place in three weeks, in honor of her
husband's thirty-third birthday. The guest list was
mostly close friends, plus members from the local
gentry who would expect to be included in such
an affair. Hilary had yet to meet most of them.
Since arriving at Winslow, she and Fitch had kept
to themselves, savoring the time like the honeymoon they hadn't taken after their London wedding.

"I should deduct a sizeable sum from Mrs. Ellerbeck's wages for telling you the date," Fitch said
good-naturedly. "A man's birthday should be a
time of reflection, not celebration."

"A wife shouldn't have to be told her husband's
birth date by the housekeeper."

"So I'm to be scolded after all."

"Yes. I suppose you are. We've been married for
months and you're still a mystery to me."

So much for leading the conversation elsewhere,
he thought. "What do you want to know?"

"Everything." She turned in his arms so she
could look at him. "Every thought, every dream."

"At the moment, my thoughts are lustful." He
lowered his head and kissed her. "As for my dreams,
I would like to see Winslow's nursery as filled with
children as its guest wings are soon to be filled
with visitors."

Hilary hesitated. She could be pregnant, but it

was too soon to tell. Another week, maybe two. She would not raise his hopes only to shatter them.

"There should be more to a marriage than children," she said, looking down at where she was resting against him, hip to hip, belly to belly.

"Granted. But it is a primary obligation when a man holds a title."

"Will you name our firstborn after your father or your brother?"

Fitch looked past her to where the field lay ripe with crops. The land represented the best part of his life, the time spent growing from boy into man. After the war, he had returned to England, yearning to recapture those years, but there was no going back, no undoing the past. There was only the present and the future—if he could hold on to them.

"Give me a son, madame, and I will give him his own name."

The nearness of him added to the sincerity of his words and Hilary saw fleeting images in her mind: the night she had gone to his home in Eaton Square; the smile on his face when he'd seen Lizzie for the first time; their wedding day; the night he'd dismissed her from his library; this morning when he'd made love to her so gently it had brought tears to her eyes. Each time she thought she had a clear picture of him, he revealed another facet of himself. It was like being married to a dozen different men, yet she loved each one.

"We should be getting back," she told him, suddenly frightened by all that she felt without knowing how he felt in return. "Lizzie will be done with her lessons soon, and you promised her a ride in the pony cart."

"So I did." He led her to where the horses were

waiting. "Tonight, then. We shall endeavor to make a child."

Hilary took the reins from the mare's neck and, stepping into Fitch's cupped hands, mounted the docile horse. Settling herself in the sidesaddle, she adjusted the long skirts of her stylish blue riding habit over the tops of her boots.

"Tonight," she said, meeting his gaze. "Until then, you must resume the role of country squire and I that of a nervous wife planning her first ball."

"It will be a success," Fitch assured as her as he gained his own saddle. "If I've learned anything about you, it's that you'll settle for nothing else."

Just as I'll settle for nothing less than your heart, Hilary vowed, as they made their way back to the stables.

It was impossible to gauge the time when Hilary awoke in the middle of the night to find herself alone. The room was completely dark. A storm had arrived sometime while she slept, and outside a brash wind was hurling raindrops at the windows. The turbulent air prowled around the house, whistling across the chimneys and sending a mournful sound down the brick stacks to escape in a ghostly whisper through the fireplaces.

Hilary lay in the bed, shivering as a sudden torrential burst of rain pounded against the stone walls as if trying to rip the house apart.

Something had awakened her, but there was no thunder, only the rain and the guttural sound of the wind as it carried the storm across the meadows and woods that separated Winslow Hall from its namesake village a few miles to the south.

Wondering if the storm has awakened Fitch as

well, Hilary sat up and called his name. There was no answer.

He'd been with her earlier, had fallen asleep on the pillow next to hers after making love to her so thoroughly she'd faded into slumber, exhausted.

She left the bed and found her robe. Tying the sash loosely about her waist, she made her way to the door of the master bedroom. Her adjoining room hadn't been slept in since their arrival at Winslow. She bathed in her own suite, dressed there, and occasionally used the sitting room when she needed to write a letter, but she slept with her husband.

Making her way through the vacant corridor and down the stairs, past the flickering gaslights that Raskett had seen turned low as part of his closing duties for the evening, Hilary met only the sounds of the storm and the eerie silence of a house whose occupants had long since retired.

She stopped to look into the conservatory. Beyond its huge glass windows, the night was still dark, though she thought she could see a slight color on the horizon, as if the sun was battling to make itself known. A few moments later, the tallcase clock in the foyer softly chimed the hour, confirming her suspicions. It was nearly dawn.

Thinking she would find her husband in the library, she made her way there. The door was slightly ajar. She took a deep breath, remembering the last time she'd confronted him in a similar fashion.

The room was dimly lit by a fire that was near to going out. Hilary glanced from the fading embers to the long horsehair sofa that faced the hearth. Fitch lay sleeping there, his robe open almost to the waist, his feet bare. A decanter rested on the table beside the sofa, uncorked and nearly empty,

but it was the book clutched in his hand and resting against his chest that captured Hilary's attention.

It was the same small journal that she'd seen that
night in London, the night he'd dismissed her so
rudely.

Stepping closer, her footfalls silent on the plush
carpet, she looked for some identifying mark that
would tell her what her husband had been reading. There was none. The book was a plain, leather-
bound journal, the sort that could be purchased
anywhere and put to countless uses.

She looked at her husband fully for the first
time, trying to judge if the book had driven him to
drink or if something less tangible was the reason
he'd deserted their bed. Even in sleep she could
see something of the worry in his features, and
knew it was real, though of course he would not
admit to it were she to awaken him. His damnable
pride refused to allow his defenses to be lowered
even for a moment.

Once again, her eyes sought the room. It was
large and heavily furnished with a massive desk behind which sat a thronelike chair of stained chestnut with a high baluster stile back and scrolled arms.
The drapes were closed, their deep burgundy appearing almost black in the shadows. There were
the expected accessories: a globe stand and a smaller
davenport desk fashioned in a severe military style
with brassbound corners and a hinged lid that allowed it to be raised and used as a writing easel.

She supposed Fitch felt at ease in this room, as
had his father and grandfather before him. There
were portraits on the walls, separately framed but
each depicting a man of strong character and un-

yielding ways. A smaller portrait, to the left of the desk, revealed what Christian Minstead had looked like just after assuming his father's title. Like most Minsteads, he had possessed dark eyes, but his hair had been light—blond, thick, and wavy. He had been a young man, barely thirty when he'd died, and quite handsome.

Hilary scanned the walls for a portrait of Fitch in full regimentals, the sort any proud father would display in a room as personal as his private library. But there was no likeness of the second Minstead son, scarlet tunic ablaze above the white pipe clay of his skintight breeches, gleaming sword held shoulder-high as he posed for the artist. Intuition told her one existed somewhere in the Hall, but she'd yet to see it.

Having surveyed her surroundings, Hilary took a moment to analyze the situation. Should she awaken her husband, and if she did, would he receive her favorably?

Before she could reach a decision, the library door was opened, this time by Raskett. The butler looked his usual impeccable self, so much so that Hilary suspected he slept upright in a vat of starch.

He showed no surprise at seeing her dressed in a robe with her hair undone or at the view of his employer, sleeping off the effects of a decanter of whiskey.

Retracing her steps to where the butler stood with a tray of steaming coffee and dry toast, she smiled. "I was just about to wake him."

"I would suggest just the opposite, milady," Raskett replied in whispered tones. "His lordship would not take kindly to having you find him so out of character."

"Is Cook in the kitchen?" she asked.

"Mrs. Travers adheres to the firm schedule of not showing herself until precisely six A.M."

"Good. I shall like a word with you," Hilary said. "Leave the tray."

If Raskett thought the request unusual, he said nothing to contradict her. Instead he nodded, set the tray on the same table as the whiskey decanter, then turned to follow her out of the room, leaving the door precisely as Hilary had found it, slightly ajar.

The kitchen offered more light than the rest of the house, attesting to Raskett's previous visit and the preparation of coffee. Hilary tucked her robe closely about her, then sat down, taking one of the six straight-backed chairs at the rectangular table.

Even though the oven was cold, the room had all the familiar smells of a kitchen. The gas lanterns, hung high to be out of the way, cast a friendly glow on the well-scrubbed tables and an equally spotless red tile floor.

"You've done this before," Hilary said. "Gotten up before dawn to make sure my husband has coffee to clear his head."

"I am his man, milady. His valet may shave him and lay out his clothes, but I have always seen to his other needs."

"He trusts you."

"I would hope so. Would you care for a cup of coffee? I had planned to return and have one for myself."

"Yes, thank you."

Once the coffee was poured, Raskett placed a sugar caddy and a small pitcher of cream on the table. Hilary used only the cream. She stirred it into the dark, hot coffee, knowing full well there would be hell to pay if Fitch discovered her and Raskett in the kitchen. But what choice did she have? If her husband refused to talk to her, then she had few options left.

"You served with my husband during the war? In the Crimean?"

"I was his man there as well, milady."

"He rarely speaks of it." The truth was he never spoke of it, but Hilary knew Raskett grasped her true meaning. If anyone in the household understood her husband, it was this man.

"Talk of war isn't meant for a lady's ears."

"Yes, well, I hate to disappoint you, but I'm not that much of a lady. Not in the sense to which you refer. I'm his lordship's wife first and foremost and I'm concerned by his behavior."

"And what behavior would that be, milady?"

"You know very well to what behavior I refer— that of my husband drinking himself into oblivion on nights such as this. Is it memories of the war that cost him peace of mind or something else? The death of his brother? The title he inherited when he thought to continue life as he had started it, as a second son?"

"If you want to know what plagues me, you can bloody well ask me." Fitch stood in the doorway, his hair mussed from a night of intermittent sleep, his face showing the stress of fitful dreams, his dark eyes blazing with anger. "That will be all, Raskett. Take yourself elsewhere."

"Yes, milord."

Once they were alone, Hilary sat quietly, her hands folded around her coffee mug, the rich fabric of her dressing gown falling about her legs in graceful blue-green folds.

"Madame, I have the reputation of being a moderate man, one not given to fits of temper, but you test my patience to the breaking point."

After what seemed like a long while, but was not, Hilary answered him. "I was merely sharing a cup of coffee and conversation with Raskett. No one else is up and about at this hour and I didn't want to wake you."

"From my drunken oblivion," he said all too calmly.

The time for polite evasion had passed.

Her patience tested until she could no longer refrain from asking the questions that were echoing wildly in her mind, Hilary met her husband's disgruntled gaze. "Why do you lock yourself away in your library and drink? What's in that journal? Why must you persist in keeping me at arm's length? We are husband and wife, bound by vows to spend the rest of our lives together. Is there to be no happiness in that life, no mutual trust?"

"Bloody hell, but you have more balls than most men I know. A wife does not question the actions of her husband when those actions bring harm to no one. Nor does she gossip with the hired help."

There was a decided pause after the fury of his words. Hilary couldn't quite interpret the expression on Fitch's face, but his eyes spoke volumes.

"Raskett is more than hired help—he's your friend."

"What he is, madame, is none of your business!"

Hilary flinched from the bite of his words, but she didn't relent. If she was stubborn, it had to be now—now when so much depended upon getting past her husband's unreasonableness.

"The whys and wherefores of my life are not open for discussion, madame. You are my wife, not my conscience."

"We have had this conversation before, my lord, and I warned you that I would not be a puppet. I am not your conscience, but I am your wife. What disturbs you, disturbs me. What brings you trouble, delivers that trouble to me, as well. Can you not see that? Can you not see that you hold back that which I would have most, your friendship and confidence."

"At the moment, *you* disturb me, madame. Your willfulness to do as you please, whenever you please, disturbs me. Your inability to understand that I have full jurisdiction over you disturbs me. Your insistent questions disturb me. Your stubborn nature disturbs me."

"Your temperament is hardly conducive to a good marriage, my lord," she said, arguing back because his current mood allowed no defusing of the situation. "You are brooding and secretive, and at times such as this, intolerably arrogant."

"What disturbs me the most, madame," he went on, choosing to ignore her remark completely, "is your total lack of common sense, a commodity with which I once thought you well endowed."

Hilary stood up, her temper at a full boil. "Common sense dictates that a man does not take himself away from a warm bed in the middle of the night unless there is something troubling him. Common sense implies that a wife should try to discover the cause of his unrest, and thus a remedy."

"Your vain preoccupation with being the perfect wife is becoming bothersome," Fitch snapped back. "I married you to obtain legal access to my daughter. I did *not* marry you to have you oversee my life. Once and for all, understand that you may not go about doing as you please with no thought to the circumstances or consequences. You make too much of things."

She paused in her fury to study his face—the tension, the shadows around his eyes and in their depths. He looked tired, a weariness of the soul as well as the body. It pained her to push him, but if anger would release what he was keeping bottled up, she'd risk his wrath.

"I am not given to fits of fancy, my lord. And pray tell, what consequences? The stability of our marriage, of our future? I accepted your proposal on the grounds that I did not wish to be maintained as an ornamental wife but respected as an equal partner. You deny me that now."

"Equality be damned! You will take yourself upstairs and remain there until a decent hour. If you awaken on some future night to find me absent from our bed, then you will not come looking for me, prowling about the house in your nightclothes and asking questions of servants."

"So I'm to be banished above stairs like a disobedient child."

Fitch stepped aside, clearing the door. "Now, madame. This very instant."

With her head held high, she resigned herself to endure, and endure she would, but not in the manner her husband demanded. Never that. She cared too much, wanted too much, to give in that easily.

With a swish of her dressing gown, she exited the room and made her way toward the front of the house. She met Raskett along the way.

"I'm sorry, milady," he said.

"It isn't your fault," she told him. "Please return to the kitchen. I believe my husband has need of you."

"His temper erupts from time to time, but he isn't a cruel man. You caught him unprepared, 'tis all."

"Yes. I'm sure you're right."

Just as she knew she was right—her husband was hiding something.

Fitch had helped himself to a cup of coffee by the time Raskett returned to the kitchen. He stood at the small window set into the wall above the sideboard, looking out into a dull gray dawn, knowing he should get himself upstairs and into a hot bath, but he didn't move. His head hurt from too much drink and his stomach felt as if he'd taken a gut punch, and he deserved no less.

"Cook will be here soon," Raskett said, returning the tray that he'd previously delivered to the library. "Shall I have Percy draw your bath?"

"I suppose my wife is in tears," Fitch remarked as he exchanged his empty coffee cup for one Raskett had just filled.

"Her ladyship looked upset, but I saw no tears as I passed her in the hall."

"Damnation! What is it about women that makes them want to meddle in everything?"

"I couldn't say, milord."

"I thought marriage would be beneficial to Lizzie, that having a family would bring me peace of mind. Now I've a wife who thinks me a domineering ogre."

Raskett said nothing.

"A man shouldn't have to divulge his every thought," Fitch went on, talking to himself this time. "He shouldn't have to explain every memory in his head, every action. I've a right to some privacy."

His heart twisted hard in his chest as he pulled out a chair and sat down. What Hilary wanted was for him to talk about the war, but he couldn't. He couldn't push past the anger, past the fear, the despair, the sense that he'd done something terribly wrong even though he'd answered a call to duty—an honorable call, by all standards. And yet there was nothing honorable about the death and destruction he'd seen. There was no explaining the Crimea, no discussing how it had changed his life. And it *had* changed him. Irrefutably and permanently.

It had been foolish of him to think that marriage would be a convenient thing, that he'd be able to go on with his life as he had before, that he could suffer the nightmares and the doubts, keep them hidden from a wife as easily as he kept them hidden from everyone else.

Hilary's accusation held more truth than she knew. He was hiding from her, hiding his feelings, and with them the fear that once exposed, the flood of emotions would overwhelm him, taking him down into their gloomy depths just as they'd pulled James Hutton under, robbing him of his sanity and his life.

No, Fitch decided. It was better to keep them where they were, assigned to the night. At least there he could control them, cage them behind the library door and drown them in liquor if necessary.

Sixteen

After a fitful day, in which she once again had been forced to paint a smile on her face, Hilary paced unhappily about her room. How strange to contemplate that only yesterday she had spent the day with her husband, riding and talking, laughing and making love.

She stopped pacing and looked around the room. She could grow accustomed to the magnificence of Winslow Hall—one could quickly become used to luxury—but adapting herself to a loveless marriage was another matter.

It was nearing the dinner hour and twilight painted the evening sky, changing the treetops to dark silhouettes. Crimson and mauve and shades of blue and gray melted together, providing a picturesque view from the balcony outside her bedroom.

It was a warm evening with only a faint breeze. Feeling restricted by her clothes, Hilary stripped down to her chemise. She was brushing her hair when the door opened and her husband strolled into the room as casually as if he were walking into his London club.

"Am I to have no privacy, my lord?"

She remained seated in front of the vanity, unyielding in her determination not to be wooed by his charm. She'd had enough of pretense. If there was to be a marriage of convenience, then she'd at least have the convenience of being left alone with her broken heart.

However much Fitch had been defeated by his temper that morning, he refused to let it get the best of him now. Despite the distance between them—she sitting across the room, he standing just inside—Fitch was aware of her gaze, eyes so penetrating they missed very little of what went on about her. They were glittering now, not with passion, but with indignation. He could find no wrong in that, even though he'd come upstairs resolved in what must be said—he would be master of his own home. To be anything less with a woman like Hilary was asking for trouble.

"You may have all the privacy you desire, madame. I will be leaving in the morning."

It was the last thing she'd expected him to say. She put down the silver-backed hairbrush and gave him her full attention. "Are you returning to London?"

"No. Cambridgeshire. It seems my steward has had an accident. He's broken his leg and is unable to oversee the summer's work. The message arrived by afternoon post, thus the promptness of my decision. I need to evaluate the fields before appointing a temporary replacement, a trustworthy man whom Fanshawe can supervise while he's hobbling about on crutches."

Hilary wasn't sure how to respond. Part of her

was glad Fitch would be taking himself elsewhere. The other part dreaded him leaving for as much as a day.

"How long will you be gone?"

"A week, ten days at the most." His gaze flickered to where the neck of her chemise revealed the upper swell of her breasts. "Am I presuming too much in thinking I may be missed?"

She stared at him. There was so much she could be angry about, so much that had hurt her, but regardless of the words that had passed between them, she still loved the man. The thought of never having him return that love, never knowing deep in her heart that she meant more to him than anyone else, made her so angry she wanted to throw something—preferably in his direction.

He sat down on the pillowed chaise longue, looking dashingly handsome in a lawn shirt, open at the throat, and a pair of dark brown riding breeches tucked into the top of knee-high Hessians that had managed to retain some of their polish after a full day spent out of doors. "I came to tell you of Mr. Fanshawe's accident and to talk to you."

Talk. If only he would, Hilary thought, knowing full well her husband's definition of the word. He'd come to lay more dictates at her feet, to list all the reasons she should be mutely content with her new life as the Countess Ackerman.

By all appearances, it was not a time for tears or tantrums. She was a newly married woman, a former spinster who should be smiling to find herself a countess.

"What could we possibly have to discuss, my lord? Upon what shall we agree?" She left the vanity table, walking to the clothespress and withdrawing a dressing gown.

Fitch felt an all-too-familiar hunger overtake his body. He wanted to forget words and reasons. He wanted to rid his wife of two layers of blue silk, to take her to bed, to make love to her until she cried out his name, then hold her. To keep her close and warm, to lie sated in the silence. But that wasn't to be. She was angry and he couldn't appease that anger without revealing a part of himself she couldn't understand.

Hilary remained standing, her eyes fixed on her husband. The realization had been seeping into her all day and she had to voice it or go mad. "We have nothing to say to each other, my lord. At least nothing beyond the required conversation of a man and woman living in the same house, two people attempting to be parents to the same child."

"You're being unreasonable."

"Am I? I've had some time to reflect on what you said this morning, and you are right. I married you knowing full well that Lizzie was the object of your affection, not I. I also know that unless you are in the process of satisfying your physical needs, there is nothing between us. I can accept that because it is the truth, and I would have honesty in our relationship."

"Our relationship is a marriage."

"Yes, a marriage of convenience. Your convenience. You have the freedom to do what you will without a troublesome wife hanging about your neck. An ideal arrangement, is it not? You handle your business, enjoy your daughter's company, and seek physical pleasure with your wife whenever it suits you. I, on the other hand, must learn to be content with whatever crumbs you throw my way."

"You think Winslow Hall *crumbs?*"

Hilary spoke over him, deciding it was time to

purge her system of all the things she'd held back for the sake of patience. She moved about the room slowly, aware that her hair was still tumbling down her back and shoulders, knowing it was one of her best features. She'd never thought to deliberately entice a man before, and she wasn't interested in seduction now. She wanted to make Fitch angry, good and angry. Perhaps then he'd say something meaningful, something unguarded.

"I suppose it's frightfully bourgeois of me to be interested in more than Paris fashions and the London Season. A woman should be content with a predictable life, with afternoon teas and social gossip. How remiss of me to think otherwise."

Fitch knew what she was trying to do, and how close she was to succeeding. He should tell her how he felt, that his feelings for her had deepened, that he loved her in a way he'd never loved another woman, but he couldn't bring himself to say the words, knowing she'd think they would change everything.

By admitting his feelings now, under these circumstance, Hilary would think herself the victor in all that she wanted. His headstrong, independent wife would be impossible to control from this day forth.

"You persist in being stubborn," he said instead. "I have given you all I have, madame. The respect and protection of my name, the availability of my fortune, the possibility of children. What more do you require?"

"If you have to ask, then the answer is beyond your comprehension," she snapped, not bothering to mask her temper this time. "I wish you a safe journey to Cambridgeshire, my lord. Now if you'll excuse me, I am tired."

Fitch wasn't in the mood to be dismissed. Nothing of what he'd come upstairs to accomplish had been done, except to tell Hilary that he would be leaving in the morning.

He moved toward her, his gaze unrelenting, letting her know that things were far from finished between them.

"If this is indeed a marriage for my convenience, then remove your clothing and go to the bed."

Hilary stiffened so quickly he thought her spine might snap. The only reason he caught her hand before it made contact with his cheek was because he'd intentionally provoked her.

"Now, now, my sweet, none of that." He pulled her close, binding her arms at her sides with a firm grip. "You're the one who demanded honesty."

"What I want, you are determined to refuse me."

"I can only give what I'm capable of giving," he told her in a quiet voice. He didn't try to kiss her, knowing she'd turn her head. He held her instead. Tight against his body so she could feel the evidence of his desire. "We are married. There's no going back, no undoing our vows. I would have you accept that, accept me for what I am."

"I do," she almost shouted the words at him. "I accept you as Lizzie's father. I accept you as my husband. I accept you into my bed and into my body. It's you who reject me!"

"Never," he whispered.

The small announcement proved to be just the opposite.

Hilary looked down, sure that he could see the flush in her cheeks, knowing her body was betraying her no matter her mood. Why was it always like this? A touch of his hand, the sound of his voice, and she went all soft inside.

Love, she decided, was an unexplainable phenomenon.

"We are man and wife," he said. "I have bound myself to you as I will bind myself to no other person for as long as I live."

Hilary met his gaze and knew there was no resistance left inside her. She couldn't refuse what welled up in her heart, the feelings that had overtaken her life. Little by little, love had worn away her will to deny the man she loved. Now, his hands on her wrists, his body leaning into hers, his mouth only inches away, all contributed to the downfall of her last defenses.

Fitch drew her even closer, and Hilary sank into him. "I want you," he whispered. "I want you more with each passing day. And I do care. Believe me. Believe that I'm giving all I can give."

He lowered his head and inhaled the perfumed scent of the soap she'd used to wash her hair that morning. He gazed down at her and smiled, then stepped back and extended his hand.

Hilary hesitated a moment before placing her hand in his. She shouldn't follow him to the bed, but she did, holding on to the knowledge that he'd finally admitted that he cared. It wasn't the declaration of love she had dreamed of, but it was something. Spoken, finally, and confirmed by the look on his face. An expression as needy as it was passionate.

The soft light of the summer evening danced over the room as he put his hands on her shoulders, gliding them over the contours of her body, pressing her gently down upon the bed.

Her heart pounded, fueled by a mixture of love and fear; he began to undress her, pausing to kiss the skin he revealed.

Hilary lay still, waiting, her eyes open in wonder at the feelings this man—only this man—could arouse within her. He untied the laces of her dressing gown, then gently lifted her and removed it. Next came her chemise. Then, much to her surprise, he guided her hands to his own clothing.

Hilary tugged the shirt from the waistband of his breeches, then over his head. Her hands flowed over the planes of his chest, moving upward to his shoulders, then down again.

"My boots," he said, moving away from her, but only long enough to pull the Hessians off and drop them unceremoniously onto the carpet. His socks followed, leaving only his breeches and whatever he was wearing beneath them.

Hilary didn't hesitate this time. Sitting up, she reached for the buttons on the front of his riding pants. They came loose and she feathered her fingers across his belly, teasingly close to the part of him that was growing hard right before her eyes. She felt his skin quiver beneath her touch, his taut muscles quaking as she slowly pushed the last of his clothing down his hips. He stepped out of his breeches and stood naked before her, his body long and lean and the most beautiful thing she had ever seen.

Fitch released a hissing breath as her hand encircled him, then measured in a caressing stroke. She leaned forward and nibbled at the skin on his hip, then brushed her lips over the same spot. She kept her hand on him, feeling the power of his need, reveling in her ability to make him want her.

Slowly she tasted him, teasing him with the tip of her tongue. Lifting her head, she caught a glimpse of his face through the curtain of her hair. He looked like a man in torment.

Releasing him, she knelt on the bed, her lips parted, her breasts rising and falling with quick, anxious breaths. "Make love to me," she said.

Fitch didn't waste any time in joining her on the bed. He pulled her over him, turning his head so he could take a swollen nipple into his mouth. His hands moved over her, upward to the swell of her breasts, down to her belly and thighs and in between.

When he finally released her, Hilary was desperate for him to finish what he'd started. But Fitch wasn't in any hurry. He slid his hands over her belly again, then lower still.

The contact of his callused touch against her most sensitive skin, the intimate contact of their naked bodies, made Hilary moan with delight.

She watched as Fitch moved to straddle her hips. He gently urged her legs to open, then sought the soft, shrouded center of her body. His caresses were as gentle as a breeze and as powerful as a storm. Another moan escaped her when his fingers began to arouse her in a different way, stoking the heat already burning beyond control.

Fitch watched her face, watched the pleasure and anticipation build into a raging desire. She climaxed against his hand and he saw her teeth catch her bottom lip to keep from calling out. His mouth curled into a smile as he caressed the softness of her inner thighs.

"There is nothing convenient about this, madame wife. You want me, just as I want you. Admit it."

"Must I?" She snaked her hands around his neck and drew him down to her. "Very well, lord husband, I want you. Now."

Driven by a hunger to possess all that she offered him, Fitch put an arm under her, arching her upward as he joined their bodies. Her sheath tightened around him as he drove himself home in a long, deep stroke.

The exquisite pleasure of being inside her was almost more than he could bear. He fought for control, and, by some miracle, found it. Closing his eyes, he began the ancient rhythm. Soon they were both lost in the power of passion, joined in a timeless, intimate dance of bodies and mutual need. He stayed with her, stroking her inside and out, leading her toward another climax, knowing that this time he'd join her.

"I love you," she whispered a moment before her nails dug into the skin of his back, a second before the world exploded for both of them.

The next morning, Hilary stood at one of the many second-floor windows that overlooked the circular drive in front of Winslow Hall and watched as her husband's coach rolled away.

She had seen a spark of something in Fitch's face just before he'd climbed into the coach, a flash of regret that he was forced to leave her, even for a short period of time. She had no way of knowing if he'd heard her whispered confession of love, or if, having heard, he'd chosen to ignore it.

They had gone down to supper late, and had retired earlier than usual, not to separate beds as she'd imagined they would yesterday morning, but to the same bed. There had been a passionate necessity to their lovemaking

It hadn't been a time for words. They had said enough. What had mattered was that they were together, in the same room, in the same bed, bound by the same marriage vows.

Vows that proclaimed the scheme she was about to hatch as unforgivable. There would be no more questions asked of her husband, no more demands that he reveal his innermost secrets to her. It was time to discover those secrets for herself.

Taking a deep breath, Hilary turned her back on the view of Winslow Hall's spacious front lawn and took herself downstairs and into her husband's library. She closed the door, then walked to the desk.

Fitch had cleared away the papers and ledgers, but there was still evidence that he spent a great deal of time in the room: the scent of his cologne, the unique aroma of his cigars, the crystal whiskey decanters that would be filled and waiting upon his arrival home. Everything about the room was as it should be, yet Hilary knew it was shielding a secret.

She studied the drawers, the pale color of their intricate chevron inlay in sharp contrast to the ebonized oak that formed the foundation of the desk. The blotter was stained in several places, the crystal inkwell almost empty. A stick of sealing wax lay in a tiny brass tray next to a humidor filled with cigars.

Hilary pulled on the gold handles of each drawer. Not one of them opened.

Knowing the key was tucked into the pocket of her husband's waistcoat and on its way to Cambridgeshire, she took a pearl-tipped hatpin from her pocket. She'd once employed a similar technique in the opening of her aunt's strongbox, needing to pay the servants and having no idea where Edwina had hidden the key.

Spreading her skirts, she knelt on the floor to better commit her crime. It was a tedious task, taking her twenty minutes. Fortunately, she had chosen the right drawer. Once opened, she saw the journal, lying dormant atop a stack of papers.

Taking a moment to make sure she had left the room precisely as she'd found it—Raskett had a keen eye and would question anything out of place—Hilary exited her husband's private domain and went in search of a solitary place where she wouldn't be disturbed.

Remembering the small parlor where Fitch had taken her their first day at Winslow, Hilary made her way upstairs again. The parlor was just as she remembered it—small and quaintly furnished. Making herself comfortable, she opened the journal and began to read.

The Contemplations of Ensign James Hutton headed the first page; Hilary paused before turning it. James Hutton. She knew the name. Fitch had attended his funeral only a few days after their marriage.

Not wanting to jump to conclusions, she read on. The date revealed that Hutton had started the journal some ten years ago, on a troop ship that had sailed from London Harbor to the shores of a Balkan peninsula in the Black Sea.

As she read, it was easy to conclude that Hutton had been bent on making a name for himself in the military. His choice of words painted the picture of a young, ambitious man, a soldier eager to embrace the thrill of battle.

As the journal progressed, Hilary was able to ascertain the complicated details of the military campaign. Hutton's writing was as vivid as any newspaper account she'd ever read, and much more informative. Within an hour she had a grasp of the fundamental deployment of British troops, and how close several of the battles had come to being disasters instead of victories.

The war had begun as a quarrel between Russian Orthodox monks and French Catholics over who had precedence in Jerusalem. England had gotten involved because Russian dominance of the Black Sea Straits was a deep political concern. Shortly after their initial landing in March of 1854, the Franco-British troops had dispelled the Russians from both Wallachia and Moldavia.

According to James Hutton, the fighting should have ended there, but it was decided by higher military powers that the Russian naval base at Sevastopol was a threat that couldn't be ignored. As a result, September 1854 saw British forces being landed on the Crimean Peninsula. The following winter proved to be as much of an enemy as the Russians.

By the time she finished reading, Hilary was in despair. No wonder her husband had nightmares. Hutton's description of the battles at Alma and Balaclava and the siege of Sevastopol had been vivid accounts of pain and suffering, of violence and disease so severe they seemed inhuman—impossible to endure. To have survived them seemed a miracle.

Yet both Hutton and her husband had survived. It was the one thing they had in common, a twist of fate that had bound them together not only as comrades in arms but as young men who had been robbed of their innocence by the horror of war.

The tone of the writing had changed with each passing entry, becoming less journalistic and more personal. The worst reading had been the last month of entries, Hutton's conversations with himself, his inability to put the war behind him, to forget the shocking events he'd witnessed. Unable to help herself, Hilary opened the journal to the entry made only two days before Hutton had taken his own life.

If only I had chosen to follow my father's vocation, but alas, I did not, thinking the uniform and associated valor so much more than it is.

Another entry followed.

Chetwynd listens more attentively each day. He knows, I think. Knows that my thoughts are no longer my own, but those of a demon who has risen from the past, a demon who will not be retired no matter my determination.

Hilary closed the journal. Remembering the expression on Fitch's face the night she had entered the library, recalling the harshness of his words, she feared that he, too, was facing a demon.

After reading Hutton's diary, she could finally understand his refusal to speak of his time in the Crimea, especially to a woman. What did she know of war? How could she possibly relate to what he had seen and heard and endured?

The offering of customary comfort would ring empty and hollow in his ears, the very arrogance enough to drive him to anger.

Realistically, there was little she could do to comfort her husband. Their marriage was a fragile one, the situation calling for the most subtle handling. But what?

She had thought to discover the cause of her husband's behavior, but having done so, she was now faced with an even greater challenge.

Leaving the upstairs parlor, Hilary returned the journal to the library, to the locked drawer of her husband's desk. Feeling helpless was an uncomfortable experience, one she disliked even more than she disliked invading her husband's privacy.

James Hutton had taken his own life, of that Hilary had no doubt. His writing, at least the entries at the very end of the journal, had been those of a desperate man, a man no longer bound to reality by the present, but lost to memories of the past. And yet he had been a man with a brilliant mind, a man of clarity and aspiration. The facts contradicted each other, but each held their own truth.

She had seen the same contradictions in Fitch. He was an intelligent and caring man, but still a haunted man.

Reading Hutton's account of the battle of Balaclava had brought more than the facts to light. Hundreds had been killed, hundreds more crippled. Their courage and supreme sacrifice had won the battle, adding their names to the annals of history, never to be forgotten.

Never to be forgotten.

The realization of what had molded Fitch to be who and what he was brought tears to Hilary's eyes. Suddenly she missed him, missed him so desperately she couldn't keep more tears from falling. She couldn't forget what she'd read, nor could she greet Fitch upon his arrival as if she had discovered nothing about his past. It would be hypocrisy.

"There must be something I can do," Hilary told herself as she sat down in the wicker rocker in the conservatory. It was a room given to peaceful thoughts and silent meditations, and she needed its beauty. She needed to look through spotless windows at the glory of a summer day.

Glancing toward the portrait of the previous Lady Ackerman, she asked a question as if Lavinia Minstead might actually answer it. "What can I do? I love him. If only he'd talk to me. Sharing his memories might lessen the pain."

The answer came not in a ghostly voice but in simple logic. She would go to London, to Debrow's, and find someone who *would* talk to her.

Seventeen

Seventy-two hours after making her decision, Hilary was in London. The trip had been a grueling one, but the driver hadn't complained of the haste which Hilary had put upon him, nor had Annie, who had accompanied her as a maid and companion. The weather had aided them by remaining clear, the sky a spotless blue until they reached the city and the smoke from countless chimneys dulled the air.

The sun was low now, hanging over the rooftops in a manner witnessed only in summer. A breeze, soft and languorous, carried the scent of the Thames to the hotel on Tooley Street where Hilary had taken rooms. The air was charged with the seductive scent of the sea, not altogether refreshing, considering it was August, but welcomed after an exhausting day.

Hilary stood near the window, looking out over a small park where a group of young boys, furloughed from their daily chores, were playing hide-and-seek among the bushes.

Tomorrow she would visit Debrow's. She had
learned after making several discreet inquiries
that the sanitarium was located across the river in
the St. Luke's District. A boy who ran errands for
the hotel had carried a note for her to Dr. Chetwynd,
who had replied immediately, saying he would receive her at half past one.

Hilary had sent the note under the name of
Miss Hilary Compton, not wanting to take the risk
of arousing any gossip that could attach itself to
her husband.

Her thoughts remained extraordinarily heavy as
she awaited Annie and the supper tray she'd requested from the hotel kitchen. Having nothing
better to do, Hilary took account of the small suite
she'd rented, using her own money. It was spacious,
far less cluttered with furniture than was the norm,
and done in drab colors. The pictures on the walls
were pastoral, smooth and soothing to the eye but
completely devoid of mental stimulation.

Knowing she was going to spend a miserable, ag-
itated evening, Hilary opened the door for Annie,
but only after plastering a feigned smile on her
face. As far as everyone was considered—everyone
but her husband, who had no idea where she was
or what she was doing—she had come to London
to consult with her solicitor, Mr. Oliver Pratt, on the
matter of selling the house in Nottingham. She
would see the business conducted tomorrow, then
depart for Winslow Hall the following morning,
arriving home before Fitch returned from Cambridgeshire.

At least that was the plan. Of course, there were
always unknowns, circumstances one couldn't foresee, but Hilary prayed that a lengthy conversation
with Dr. Chetwynd would offer some clue as to how

she could breach the gap between herself and her husband. If not, she would be no worse off for trying.

"Are you sure you'll not have me go with you?" Annie asked the next morning. She had just buttoned Hilary into a bottle-green traveling suit. "A lady shouldn't be goin' about the city alone."

"I've gone about the city before," Hilary assured her. She reached for her reticule. "Take yourself shopping. There's no need to sit in the room and wait for me. I shan't be more than a few hours. When I return, we will treat ourselves to a fine supper."

"A lady doesn't sit at the same table as her maid," Annie said, having learned a lot during the short time she'd been away from Nottingham. "Mrs. Ellerbeck would have me head on a platter."

"What Mrs. Ellerbeck, or anyone else, doesn't know won't hurt either one of us," Hilary replied. "Buy something pretty, something you can wear this evening. There's a nice public house on the corner. We shall try the food there, then perhaps take a walk in the park. It's only across the way and well lit. I saw a constable walking there last evening."

Annie's eyes went wide at the sum Hilary forced into her hand. A scant second later, her face brightened with a smile. "I'll buy a dress and a pair of shoes. Fancy shoes, the kind they wear for dancing and such."

Hilary didn't ask with whom Annie hoped to dance. Her mind was preoccupied with the business of the day. Reassuring Annie one last time that she could manage her meeting with Mr. Pratt without anyone's aid, Hilary went downstairs. She did not

request her driver or the footman, wanting to keep
her business private, but instead exited the hotel
and walked the few blocks to Southwark Cathedral.
There, near London Bridge, she hired a hansom
to take her across the river.

It was another bright morning, and it would
have been good to be in the country rather than
here in the city under clandestine circumstances,
but Hilary refused to dwell on the negative aspects
of her trip. She had had more than adequate time
to think of all the reasons why she was justified to
stick her nose into what her husband would say
was none of her business.

The hansom rolled through the streets, following a route that took it past the Bank of England
and the Exchange, before turning northeast toward
Guildhall. Upon reaching the St. Luke's District,
the driver turned onto a street that displayed a
mixture of older homes and modest businesses.

To Hilary's surprise, Debrow's Sanitarium looked
very much like a bland hotel. It was a building of
four stories in need of a good whitewashing.

She flinched at the squeal of hinges when she
opened the gate that separated the minuscule front
lawn from the street. A dark-stained strip of wood,
attached to the fencing, gave the establishment's
name, but no indication of the services it provided.

Upon reaching the main entry door, its wood
gone gray with age and stained by weather, she
pulled on the bell chain and waited. When no one
answered, she pulled again. After several long seconds, each increasing her anxiety tenfold, the door
was opened by a footman who made no inquiry as
to her business but showed her straightaway into a
front parlor.

"Dr. Chetwynd said to make yourself comfortable. I'll be bringing tea."

"Thank you."

Being left to her own devices until such time as Dr. Chetwynd made himself known, Hilary looked around the room. It was a combination parlor and office. Books were piled high on several shelves, their titles those of history and philosophy. The colors of the room were pleasant enough, though a little dark for her taste. The few paintings on the walls had been chosen with discrimination and a flair for color and character.

"Miss Compton."

The sound of her name, or rather her former name, brought Hilary around.

"I'm Dr. Chetwynd." The man held out his hand to capture hers in an ordinary, businesslike grasp. "How may I be of service?"

Dr. Chetwynd was in his late forties, with an average face and unremarkable coloring, the sort of man who would be easily lost in a crowd were one to seek him by description alone. His face was captivating by reason of a certain frankness in his eyes and an honesty of features that said there was very little in life that could surprise him. Hilary found him a man of quiet charm with a soft, mellow voice.

"I'm not sure you can help me, sir."

"Then all I can do is try," he replied, silently indicating a chair. He moved to sit opposite her. "Since it was you who requested the appointment, I will let you explain it. What I will say is that anything you tell me will be held in the strictest of confidence."

Taking a few moments to compose her thoughts, their presentation being so important, Hilary wasn't sure where to begin. Deciding she might as well be honest, she began with the most elemental of the facts. "My husband was acquainted with one of your former residents. He does not know I am here, nor would he be happy to discover that I've been so bold as to visit you."

"Then you are not *Miss* Compton."

"No, but the name suits my purposes today."

"I see." He put his fingertips together as if to hold up his chin, then smiled. "I assume that you are aware of the services we provide here."

"Somewhat," she said. "I know that you house people, mostly soldiers, who find being among others a difficult chore, that you offer them a place of refuge and solace. That you listen when they have something to say."

"I do my best."

"I think my husband needs someone to listen. I would gladly be that person, but he refuses to speak of anything that happened to him in the war. It's as though he wants to ignore a portion of his life, to act as if it never happened."

Another smile, this one more sympathetic. "It is not easy to discuss that which you fear no one will understand, especially if you don't understand it yourself."

"I want to understand," Hilary replied, her voice revealing her desperation. "I want to help him, but I don't know how. I need your guidance."

"You said your husband knew a former resident. Who?"

"James Hutton."

His gaze became very direct. "If I am to guide you, Miss Compton, then I must know more than generalities. James took his own life. I foresaw his actions, but there was little I could do to prevent them. There are no bars on the windows here, no locks on the doors. It is not a prison."

Realizing that he was on the path of misunderstanding, Hilary shook her head. "I am not seeking a place for my husband. I am seeking guidance in how to deal with him. He has nightmares, and broods more than is good for a normal man. But he is not despondent."

"He served in the military?"

"In the 8th Hussars."

"I served in the cavalry under Lord Lucan as a divisional surgeon."

Hilary smiled, beginning to understand. "And you continue to serve, but in a different way."

Dr. Chetwynd stood up and began to move about the room, finally letting out a breath in a frustrated sigh. "This is not a conversation I normally have with a woman." He held up his hand when Hilary would have protested. "That does not lessen your reasons for coming here—it simply makes my task more difficult."

"In what way, sir?"

"War is not a matter easily discussed, even among those who have seen the battlefield. The experience is unique to each man, something private and oftentimes tragic."

"I read James Hutton's journal," she said, thinking to eliminate the preliminaries and to let him know that she did have some concept of what he was trying to say. "It came into my husband's hands shortly after Mr. Hutton's death."

As expected, her confession put a new light on the subject.

"I was told that he requested it be delivered to a friend." Although he didn't say it, Hilary knew he had just identified her. It went without saying that Mr. Hart would have told his employer about giving the journal to the Earl of Ackerman.

"It is locked away in my husband's desk drawer," Hilary told him. "He does not know that I have read it, but sensing that the book and my husband's recent actions were somehow connected, I did what I felt was right. How can I solve a problem if I don't know what it is?"

"Indeed," he said, pausing in his inspection of the room. "What did you think after reading it?"

"That James Hutton was a brave man. That his death was tragic and unnecessary."

"You are a woman of extreme perception, Miss Compton. Do you fear that your husband may do as James did, that he may one day find his memories so unbearable he puts a pistol to his head?"

"No. Fitch won't kill himself, but I do fear that he will continue to keep his feelings walled up, that he will continue to carry the burden alone."

"He never speaks of the war?"

"Not to me, nor to anyone, I think. We do have a man in service, a butler, who served with him in the Crimean. When my husband drinks himself to sleep, Raskett is there in the morning with hot coffee and whatever else he needs to regain his composure."

"A friendship gained on the field is one that often lasts a lifetime. I have seen men from varying walks of life become as close as brothers. Again, it is difficult to explain to anyone, man or woman, who has not experienced what a war is really like."

"I recall a line from Hutton's journal," Hilary said. "He wrote that heroism isn't difficult when one expects to die."

"It is not," Dr. Chetwynd replied. "People so often

think of soldiers as gallant and fearless, but I assure you, we are no less human than anyone else. It is duty that calls us forward, and duty that binds us together."

"I have witnessed that between my husband and Raskett," she said with a sharp sadness. "Is it wrong of me to want the same thing for myself and my husband? Oh, I know I can never fully understand what he experienced, but I do so want him to know that he can share his memories with me. Without them, he is incomplete to me and to himself."

"Your husband is a very fortunate man. Most women would draw away from such a thing. It is natural, I suppose. Men are civilization's protectors. We are taught from the beginning that it is our responsibility to defend those we love, to provide for them. Tears are discouraged, even in the smallest of boys. We are told to keep our chins up and our complaints to ourselves. The genius of our male society is not to exclude emotion or suffering, but to bear it bravely."

"I do not know what my husband suffered in the war that so haunts him," Hilary replied, "but I do know that he is a fine man. Strong and generous of heart. I would not think of him as weak or cowardly were he to weep like a child."

"Ahhh, but silence is part of the code," Chetwynd said. "We return from the war, heroes to most but failures to ourselves, the memory of our fallen comrades ever present in our minds. We brood over what we cannot say without burdening others with our sorrows and regrets. In that way, we are all casualties of the war."

His words frightened Hilary because she couldn't deny there was truth in them. "How can I help him?

How can I bring him to understand that whatever causes his nightmares is best exposed to the light of day, to be shared—and, hopefully, healed?"

"Were you not already claimed by another man, Miss Compton, I would drop to one knee and propose this very moment. If only more wives and mothers and daughters and sisters could open their hearts so readily, be willing to hear the unpleasant. You come to me for guidance, but I have little to give you. Love is the greatest healer, and it is impossible not to see that you love your husband very much."

"Yes, I love my husband. But I'm no closer to helping him now than I was when I walked through the door."

Chetwynd returned to his seat. He remained silent for a short while, which was just as well because tea was served. Hilary wondered if the unnamed, silent footman was one of Dr. Chetwynd's residents. He was of the age to have served in the war, but it was impossible to tell. The sanitarium did not serve visible injuries, but invisible ones.

Once she was balancing a cup and saucer in her hand, Hilary waited, hoping for some grain of insight, something she could take back to Winslow with her.

"Tell me about him," Chetwynd said once he had added sugar and cream to his own tea. "How long have you been married? Do you have children? It is difficult to evaluate that which I have no knowledge of, and I would seek to help you."

Knowing the truth would serve her best, Hilary let down her defenses and told Chetwynd the entire story, how she had met Fitch, his proposal and the reasons behind it, how she had come to love him, the arguments they had had, and why she felt compelled to do something before their marriage became an impossible situation for all considered. She ended the convoluted story with a lame smile. "What you see before you, sir, is a pathetic woman who has nary an answer to anything."

"On the contrary," he said, smiling. "What I see is a woman of great courage and devotion. Your story is not unlike others I have heard, though the circumstances of a child make it a bit unusual. You are right in thinking that your husband's devotion to Lizzie proves his capability to love. We know very little about the human mind or the human heart. There are physicians, such as myself, who are striving to understand more. There is a clean finality to death, but war does more than claim lives. It claims hearts and minds. The experience can paralyze a man sometimes, making him feel as if he's stuck in time. Most find their way back to the present, and on into the future."

"My husband has, for the most part," Hilary admitted, knowing Fitch would not be able to function in Parliament or on his estates were he as lost as James Hutton had been.

"Then perhaps the question to ask is not whether his behavior is justified, but what is revealed by it."

He stood then, looking at her, not smiling but saying with his gaze that he understood her heartache and wished her well.

She took her leave, thanking him for his time. Despite his kindness, Hilary climbed back into the hansom with a vague feeling of defeat. Still, she had learned something—that men such as her husband were not uncommon, that they longed to be understood, to feel acceptance, to be loved.

Her next stop was the office of Oliver Pratt on York Road. She could see the tower of Big Ben and the spires of Westminster when she alighted from the hansom a second time. The afternoon had begun to fade into evening, the sun low in the sky, the heat stifling because there was no breeze.

Mr. Pratt greeted her with his customary smile, having considered her aunt, Edwina Hoblyn, a remarkable woman and one of his favorite clients. He was an elderly man, close to his seventieth birthday, but still spry and well able to conduct business with a limited number of clients. His hair was a dull gray, matching thick, bushy brows that framed the palest of blue eyes. His face was serious and lined with wrinkles, but there was no mistaking his intelligence. He would continue to practice his profession until the day he died.

They discussed the house in Nottingham and another parcel of property that had come with Hilary's inheritance. He showed no surprise when she told him that she'd decided to sell the house and all its furnishings, except the piano.

"I would have the proceeds go to Debrow's Sanitarium in the St. Luke District," she said. "Along with the parcel of land. Dr. Chetwynd may find a use for the site—another sanitarium, perhaps. The contribution should be given anonymously."

"Very well, I will make the necessary arrangements."

They spoke of casual things after that. Polite conversation, but Hilary enjoyed it, needing something normal to balance out the day.

Upon leaving, she directed the cabbie to take her back to Tooley Street and the hotel where Annie was waiting to show off her new dancing shoes.

Hilary behaved as she was expected to behave for the balance of the evening, admiring Annie's dress and shoes and the lace handkerchief she'd purchased, using every last coin but enjoying it so much Hilary had to laugh along with her.

"Whom do you intend to impress?" she asked as they sat down to a dinner of broiled beef and summer vegetables.

"Raskett."

Hilary remembered they were in a public house and closed her mouth before anyone noticed. "Raskett!"

"He's a very nice man," Annie said, defending her choice. "He isn't married, but he's lonely. I can see it in his eyes the same way I saw it in the earl's when he first came to Nottingham. I think he likes me. He smiles whenever I pass him on the stairs, and he calls me Miss Annie. It's a politeness, don't you think?"

"Yes," she agreed. It was pleasant to talk to Annie. She was a young woman without pretense or false expectations. "I suppose I've been too selfishly preoccupied with my own life to take notice of anyone else's. Are you sure? He is a good deal older than you."

"He's not *that* old," Annie protested, then blushed to the roots of her red hair.

At the end of the day, it was Hilary's fundamental optimism that saved her from pacing the floor, fretful and unable to sleep. She had learned the value of keeping one's mind busy, of getting through each day, and of finding pleasure in what she could. Her aunt had taught her that, and she drew on those lessons as darkness blanketed the city and the sound of foghorns drifted from the nearby harbor.

She would return to Winslow Hall tomorrow

with not one whit more of an idea how to make her husband happy than she'd had before leaving the country. Still, Dr. Chetwynd had eased her mind, and she refused to go through life miserable. Time was on her side, and if nothing else, she would out-stubborn her husband before all was said and done. That decided, she bundled up her problems and put them aside for the night.

Eighteen

When the carriage drew up in front of Winslow Hall, the afternoon sun was slanting off its tall windows. A footman, busy polishing the front-door brass, quickly tucked his cloth away and came running down the steps to offer his hand to Hilary.

Glad to be home, and eager for a hot bath and a cup of tea, she had no sooner shaken the wrinkles from her skirt when the front door opened and Raskett showed himself.

"Welcome home, milady."

Something in his tone gave Hilary pause. "Is everything all right?"

"There's been an accident."

Hilary's heart lodged in her throat.

"Lizzie was riding in her pony cart when it overturned," Raskett explained, his tone calm but sympathetic.

Hilary swept past him, intent on getting upstairs as quickly as possible. She tugged impatiently at her gloves, tossing them on the foyer table before unpinning her pancake-brimmed hat. "When?"

"The day after you left for London," Raskett replied. "Mrs. Ellerbeck sent for Dr. Taunton immediately." He made his way in front of her—not rudely, but enough to bring her to a standstill. "No broken bones, but she does have a nasty cut. His lordship is with her."

Hilary's heart dropped from her throat to the pit of her stomach. "Fitch is home!"

"He arrived yesterday morning. Dashed upstairs the moment Mrs. Ellerbeck told him that Lizzie had been hurt and hasn't come down since. He spent the night in the nursery."

She hurried upstairs, not stopping until she reached the third floor where the nursery was located. Lizzie's fondness for the outside world and animals could turn dangerous without proper supervision. Even when Fitch was riding alongside the pony cart, patiently guiding her movements, he often had to remind her that ponies weren't born with wings.

Hilary knew she should have left specific orders that the pony cart not leave the stables while she was gone, but her mind had been occupied with getting to and returning from London without the purpose of her visit being detected by Fitch.

Now, instead of one problem, she had two—Lizzie's injuries and her husband's forthcoming wrath.

The corridor was empty as Hilary made her way to the nursery. In fact, the entire house seemed unusually quiet, as if there had been a death instead of an accident. Her husband's mood was dominating the house.

She was almost to the nursery's closed door when Mrs. Crombie appeared, stepping out of the room she occupied directly across the hall from Lizzie's.

"Oh, your ladyship, you're home," she said. She looked tired and fretful, and Hilary knew she was concerned that she'd be dismissed without reference. Lizzie had, after all, been left in her care.

"Tell me what happened?"

"It was the pony cart," Mrs. Crombie said solemnly. "Lizzie insisted on having an afternoon ride. I allowed it because she'd done so well with her lessons. Gilleon was walking alongside, but Lizzie would have none of it unless she could make the pony trot. Gilleon tried to stop her, to grab hold of the bridle, but she's a quick one, and the cart went rolling off faster than the poor old man could run. There was a branch or a stone on the ground, I'm not sure which. The cart turned over and Lizzie was pinned underneath it. Gilleon got her free and carried her to the house."

She started to cry, dabbing her eyes with a handkerchief.

"Calm yourself," Hilary said, wishing it were as easily done as said. Her legs were shaking and her stomach had turned sour. "How badly is she hurt?"

"Her right leg is badly cut. Dr. Taunton had to stitch it. She cried something fierce, even with the laudanum. I felt so helpless. She wanted you, of course. Mrs. Ellerbeck and I took turns sitting with her until his lordship came home. I should have kept her inside."

Hilary gently squeezed the trembling hand of the older woman. "Keeping Lizzie inside is next to impossible when the sun is shining. Accidents happen, Mrs. Crombie, especially to children. You weren't at fault. I should have instructed Gilleon to keep the pony and the cart in the stables until either myself or his lordship returned. It was my negligence, not yours."

The governess looked somewhat relieved. "His lordship hasn't left her bedside since he got back. He slept in the nursery last night, in a chair. Mrs. Ellerbeck tried to get him to take breakfast downstairs or in his room and to get some sleep, but he refused."

Hilary could well imagine Fitch's reaction. He had returned from Cambridgeshire to find his wife missing and Lizzie bandaged from an accident that could have proven fatal.

Riddled with guilt, Hilary opened the nursery door and stepped inside. The room was in shadows, the drapes drawn to keep out the afternoon sun. Lizzie was napping, her leg propped up on a large feather pillow. She wasn't alone. Two kittens lay sleeping next to her. Sylvester had been sprawled on the rug at the foot of the bed, but was standing now, his tail fanning the air. Hilary patted her skirt and the spaniel padded over to her. She gave the dog a good petting and a few whispered words of praise.

Fitch was sleeping in a chair that had been pulled up next to the bed. Her husband was wrinkled and rumpled and badly in need of a shave, but Hilary thought him as handsome as ever.

Walking quietly to the bed, she stared down at Lizzie. "I'm so sorry," she whispered. "I shouldn't have left you."

Lizzie stirred, but she didn't wake up. The faint scent of vinegar was in the air, and Hilary knew it had been used to wash the scrapes on Lizzie's hands and knees before salve had been applied. From the location of the bandage, she could see that the cut Dr. Taunton had stitched was in the fleshy part of Lizzie's left calf.

Hilary glanced from Lizzie's curly head to her husband's face, suppressing the need to wake them both, to enfold them in her arms, to comfort them, and be comforted in return.

"Ahhh, I awaken to find the prodigal wife returned," Fitch said in a low voice. He leaned forward in his chair, then rubbed his hand over the stubble on his face. "Excuse me, madame, if I do not offer you a welcoming kiss. I've been home nearly two days and have yet to see my valet."

"I'm sorry." It was all she could say.

"Hilary," Lizzie mumbled as she came awake. She held out her hand, wiggling her fingers. Her face was pale except for a small bruise on her cheek. "You're home."

"Yes, darling, I'm home." She sat down on the bed, then pulled her close, wrapping her arms around her. "And I shan't leave you again. I promise."

Lizzie wrapped her arms around Hilary's neck and squeezed tight. "My leg's hurt. Papa said I will have a scar, but I shouldn't worry because no one will be able to see it. Don't let him sell Mr. Pony to the sausage vendor, please. I promise to drive my cart very, very slow from now on."

Hilary drew back and looked at her. "I don't think Mr. Pony would make very good sausage, do you?"

Lizzie shook her head.

"Then, you must be sure to be very, very careful the next time. No more trotting and no more ignoring Gilleon when he tells you to do something."

"I promise." She picked at the embroidered edge of her blanket. "I'm glad you're home."

"Oh, so am I, darling."

They clung to each other for several minutes. Hilary stroked the dark curls she loved so much. "Is your leg hurting?"

"Just a little bit," Lizzie conceded. "Papa said I can't get out of bed."

"Not until Dr. Taunton says you can," Fitch confirmed the prognosis.

He was standing beside the bed, holding on to Lizzie's other hand. Hilary could see him from the corner of her eye, but she didn't turn her head to meet his gaze. He'd be smiling for Lizzie's sake, but only for Lizzie's.

She wished passionately that they could set aside their differences, just for a few moments, so he could put his arms around her and let her weep the needed tears. But alas, that was not the case. There was nothing she could do at this moment, no miraculous words she could speak.

Hilary closed her eyes. She wasn't going to cry. Her husband would think it only a ploy to gain sympathy. She had come home hoping to find some way to reach him, to gain more than a surface normalcy to their marriage. But now? God only knew what he was thinking.

A light knock on the door brought Hilary's head around. It opened to reveal Mrs. Ellerbeck. Like Mrs. Crombie, her face showed the strain of the last few days.

"Dr. Taunton is here, your lordship," she said.

"Show him in," Fitch replied. He gave Lizzie's hand a quick squeeze. "Clean bandages, pumpkin. That's all."

Dr. Taunton was a small man, trim at shoulder and hip, with thin white hair and finely veined hands. He looked to be in his late sixties and Hilary wondered if he'd doctored Fitch and his brother,

Christian, through childhood bumps and bruises. His name had been on the list of local dignitaries whom she'd invited to attend Fitch's birthday ball, though she'd yet to meet anyone in the village.

"Lady Ackerman," he said formally. "I regret that our first meeting is under such circumstances. Whatever the reason, may I take this opportunity to welcome you to Winslow."

"Thank you for taking such good care of Lizzie," Hilary replied. "She is very precious to me."

Fitch shooed the kittens off the bed, then helped Lizzie to lean forward so he could fluff her pillows. Mrs. Ellerbeck stood near the door in case she was needed.

Dr. Taunton deposited his leather bag on the bench at the foot of the bed. "And how are you, young lady?"

"I'm feeling much better," Lizzie said, wiggling back against the pillows until she was comfortable. She folded her hands in her lap. "Papa has been taking care of me."

"Excellent," Dr. Taunton told her. "Any signs of fever?"

"None," Fitch answered.

Hilary heard the relief in his voice and knew why he'd spent the night in the nursery. Not because Lizzie's injury was life-threatening, but because wounds bred infection, and infection bred fever. He'd been worried that he'd lose Lizzie the same way he'd lost men under his command in the Crimean—to infectious fevers brought on by their wounds.

Hutton had described the hospital tents in his journal—filled to capacity and reeking with the stench of sweat and vomit and blood. The English army had lost as many men to fever as it had to

Russian guns. They would have lost even more if it hadn't been for Florence Nightingale and her courageous nurses.

"Well, now, miss, let's have a look at you." Giving Lizzie a hearty smile, Dr. Taunton removed his jacket and rolled up the sleeves of a spotless white shirt.

Once the bandage was removed, the wound proved to be small and round—a puncture from some part of the cart's railing. Sealed now by three very small, very neat stitches, it showed no signs of infection.

"I'm going to wash it off," Dr. Taunton told her. "You'll feel something wet and cold, but it won't hurt."

Lizzie nodded. "I shan't cry this time."

Guilt ripped at Hilary's heart. It crushed her to know that Lizzie had been hurt and crying out for her and that there'd been no one but a governess and a housekeeper to answer. Fitch had every right to be furious with her. He couldn't blame her more than she blamed herself.

After the wound had been washed and patted dry with a gauze square, Dr. Taunton applied a thin layer of yellowish ointment. A new bandage followed. When he was done he looked at Hilary. "I will leave a tin of salve with Mrs. Ellerbeck. The dressing should be changed morning and night, and in between, should it start to drain. I'll call again tomorrow afternoon."

Lizzie's mouth lifted into a quick smile. "I promised Papa I wouldn't try to walk." She pointed to a pewter bell on the table next to the bed. "I'm to ring the bell and he'll come running."

"Your papa needs to get some sleep," Dr. Taunton said. He put on his jacket. "She is doing very well, my lord. Children are extremely resilient. I recall a time not so long ago when you were confined to the nursery with a broken arm. A fall from one of the trees in the orchard, wasn't it?"

"It was Christian who fell out of the tree," Fitch said, correcting the memory. "My confinement was the result of a wrestling match with Samuel Edgerton."

"Yes, well, as I recall you mended fast enough. And so will Lizzie. No need to worry."

Once Dr. Taunton had left the room, insisting that he needed no one to show him the way out, Fitch directed his first words to Mrs. Ellerbeck, requesting that she summon Mrs. Crombie so the governess could sit with Lizzie. After that, he turned a cold glare toward Hilary. "You, madame, will come with me."

The library was the appointed room. Situated in the eastern half of the house, its windows were spared the blaze of the afternoon sun. Hilary followed her husband inside, hearing the click of the latch as heavily as the tolling of a funeral bell. The time had come to pay the piper.

Nothing was said until her husband had poured himself a drink.

"Sit," he said to her. He stood behind the desk, a figure of stern immobility, like the soldier he had once been.

"Thank you, my lord, but I'm comfortable standing." Her hands were at her sides. One held a lace handkerchief, which she had pulled from her pocket when she'd thought she might burst into tears. It remained dry, but ready should she need it.

He looked at her, his gaze tense, dark, and concentrated with anger. "Then stand, madame. I care not what pose you take as long as you explain yourself."

"Will you listen?" she asked, her voice faltering with the extremity of her emotions, her thoughts settling upon the stark possibility that her hopes of a real marriage might never be more than a wishful fantasy. "Will you hear what I have to say or only what you choose to hear?"

"Do not play coy with me, madame. I am in no mood for witty dialogue. I did not request your company to engage in a debate, but to hear the reason that sent you dashing off to London the moment my back was turned. What business took you away from your home? Away from Lizzie? Nothing which you discussed with me—your husband," he finished with bitter mockery.

Hilary said nothing for several moments. There was no sound but the steady ticking of the mantelclock and the song of a bird perched in a tree outside the open window.

What could she say? No matter the words, they would bring a verdict of guilty. She had broken into her husband's desk, pried into his most private, most personal business, gone behind his back. Would he believe that she had done it for the sake of love? Did he even want her love? It was a question she feared she should have asked herself long before now.

"If you wish to blame me for Lizzie's injuries, then do so," she said in a tone that lacked her normal confidence. "You are right. Had I been here, the accident might not have happened. Then again, there is no guarantee things would not have taken place exactly as they did. My strongest regret is that

I was not here when Lizzie needed me most. That my being away prevented me from holding her in my arms, from saying the soothing words children need when they are hurt, no matter the degree of the injury. To know that she is loved."

"You confuse the issue," Fitch retorted impatiently. "The question is not one of Lizzie being loved. Nor how much. The question is what the bloody hell were you doing in London? If you tell me that you felt the need for more dancing lessons, I warn you my response will not be a pleasant one."

"My business had nothing to do with dancing."

"Then what? Blast and damn, woman, you are testing my patience."

Hilary braced herself against a wave of dizziness—mental, not physical. She was tired of the circling patterns her life had taken: hiding her feelings, trying to discern those of her husband; guessing, assuming, fearing the past while she looked toward the future.

Emboldened by her love, she raised her head a fraction of an inch and met Fitch's unwavering gaze. "I called upon Mr. Pratt, my aunt's solicitor. My solicitor," she said. "He is arranging for the house in Nottingham to be sold and the proceeds donated to charity."

"The house sold? I don't recall mention of the house," he said much too conversationally for Hilary to think that he believed one word she'd said. "I commend the charitable contribution, of course. 'Tis the haste in which the decision was made that gives me pause. Could not such business be conducted by post? Or when we are next in London?"

Hilary braced herself for an explosion—there was no way around it. "I saw Mr. Pratt before leav-

ing London," she told him. "After I called upon
Dr. Chetwynd at Debrow House."

"What!"

She took the time for one quick, deep breath.
"Dr. Michael Chetwynd of Debrow House. I went
to London to speak with him."

The drink in Fitch's hand found its way to the
desk with restrained force, his hand so tightly
clenched around the glass, he came close to shat-
tering it. "You went to London to speak with Dr.
Chetwynd?"

"Yes."

"May I ask how you learned of him?"

Hilary instinctively stepped back as Fitch leaned
over his desk, his hands braced palms down on the
blotter. His expression turned cold, his eyes hard.
Suddenly she was conscious of the real power he
possessed: the power of an angry man, the power
to do her harm if he so desired, and the legal right
to do it. For a moment she questioned the wisdom
of telling him the truth, but only for a moment.
She refused to believe that their marriage meant
nothing to him, that he held no real affection for
her.

Despite his current state of mind, this was Fitch,
the man who had carried a hedgehog in his hat, the
man who had taken Lizzie up in a balloon, the man
who had spent the entire night by that same child's
bedside. This was the man she loved, the man to
whom she had pledged her body and her heart.

Acutely aware of the thin ice upon which she
stood, Hilary met his gaze again. "I found Dr.
Chetwynd's name in James Hutton's journal."

His gaze flickered down to the locked drawer,
then back to her. "You broke into my desk!"

"I picked the lock with a hairpin," she admitted. "I had to know."

A moment passed, one in which her husband's anger grew. "Know what?"

"About you. Why you lock yourself away in this room or one like it. Why you refuse to talk to me about your deepest feelings. What happened to you. What's still happening. I wasn't sure it was the war until I read the journal."

Fitch closed his eyes and tried to control his temper, but two nights with little sleep, two nights in which he'd done nothing but worry about Lizzie and his wife, had exhausted his reserves. He had no patience left, nothing with which to fight the anger that flooded him.

He came around the desk so suddenly, Hilary backed away from him in surprise. "You know nothing, madame! I return home to find my daughter hurt and my wife missing. And now I'm told you *had* to know things about me, things that are no one's business. Things that have nothing to do with you, that happened years ago. What is this obsession you have? You pry and poke and meddle and scheme behind my back like some sort of spy. You think me incapable of handling my own affairs, of dealing with memories of a war that ended years ago."

"That's just it. The war hasn't ended. Not for you," Hilary said as calmly as the situation would allow. "You have nightmares. It's still in your mind."

"Of course it's in my mind. You don't forget fighting for your life." He turned away from her then, back to his desk and the unfinished drink which he downed in one swallow.

His words bit into Hilary's heart, gnawing at her

resolve until she wasn't sure she'd done the right thing after all. But having done it, there was no path to follow but the one she had chosen.

"Reading Hutton's journal broke my heart," she said in a whispering voice that was still strong enough to be heard from where her husband stood with his back to the room. *"You're* breaking my heart."

Instead of responding to her, Fitch poured himself another drink. Hilary waited, hoping that he might begin to understand, praying that she hadn't slammed the door in her own face. They stood apart for long minutes—she waiting, her husband staring out the window toward the fields planted with rye and barley. The land was ripening, preparing itself for harvest.

Hilary's heart quickened at the thought. She was certain she was pregnant. She longed to tell Fitch that his dream of having another child would soon be fulfilled, but she continued to stand perfectly still—waiting and watching as he drank from a second glass of claret.

Somewhere in the house, doors opened and closed as servants went about their work. Beyond the open windows, the afternoon sunlight danced over summer leaves and set the water in the garden fountain to sparkling, and still Hilary waited.

The rage inside Fitch died away, the anger so forceful only a moment ago consuming the last of its fuel, leaving only a painful ache. A dozen replies to Hilary's remark flashed through his mind, all of them sarcastic or critical, but he refrained from saying them. He would not allow her to dictate what would be said next. He had every right to be furious with her.

He held his glass of claret up to the light and looked into its ruddy glow before putting it to his lips. He hadn't eaten for hours; he shouldn't be drinking. But damn it all, it was either wrap his hands around a glass or put them around his wife's lovely throat.

After a mere taste, he put down the drink. He couldn't make a decision now, not one this important, and he refused to be forced into one when he was being pulled in so many directions. Still, the matter demanded some settlement.

There were no secrets now; Hutton's journal had been eloquently descriptive in its details, especially toward the end. The words hadn't been the rantings of a madman, but the painful confessions of a tortured soul. Did Hilary see him that way—a man unable to control his emotions, a man lost to all but the past? Surely not. And yet, he often felt as if life were spinning away from him, beyond his grasp.

Determined to keep control, at least for now, Fitch turned to face his wife. Her expression was solemn, but it took nothing away from the intensity of her eyes or the sensual curve of her mouth. As always, there was nothing self-indulgent about her—no unnecessary ribbons or flounces, no over-indulgence of jewelry, but rather the opposite. She was wearing a dark lavender traveling dress underneath a short bordello jacket with black piping at the collar and cuffs.

The sight of her made Fitch's heart falter a beat. How vulnerable she looked. More vulnerable than he'd ever seen her. Then he realized that her eyes were damp with unshed tears. He caught himself on the verge of opening his arms.

He closed his eyes for a brief moment, giving in to the stress of the last forty-eight hours, letting the anger win because his mind felt splintered. His wife had gone to London to discuss him with a stranger, a man who knew nothing about him, the very man who had been unable to keep a gun from finding its way into James Hutton's hand.

A rage of conflicting emotions raced through him, the least of them forgiving. "I am breaking *your* heart, madame? And what, pray tell, do you think you are doing to mine? I married you thinking that a woman who requested personal privacy in matters that would normally fall under a husband's domain would in return respect *my* privacy. And yet, the opposite is true. By your own confession, you have delved into matters that do not concern you. You have betrayed my trust."

It took all Fitch's energy to keep the world he'd created since the war—a world he kept balanced only as long as he was in control—from spinning away from him.

Is that what Hilary thought? That he was losing control the way James had lost it, that he was no longer capable of differentiating between dreams and reality? Did she fear that he'd do harm to himself? Did she think him weak and unreliable?

"I'm sorry," she said again, seeing how weary and grievously hurt he looked. Realizing that she had failed him, and herself, she finished the last of what she had to say. "It seems I have totally misunderstood everything, my lord. Your need for Lizzie, your proposal of marriage. I thought that perhaps you might actually want a real wife, someone who could put her arms around you when life becomes too harsh. Someone to hold you in the dark when you wake up tormented by memories of the war. Someone to share your entire life, not just a small portion of it."

"I told you what I wanted from this marriage,"

he said, his voice sharpened by the pain of her betrayal. "Why do you insist on making trouble where there should be none? Can you not be content with what I *can* give you?"

He stood in front of her, dressed in dark breeches that outlined the lean form of his hips and legs, and an open-necked shirt wrinkled from two days of wear. Despite his appearance, he was every bit the gentleman she had married, a man who exerted an aura of power and grace that made Hilary's breath catch in her throat. She trembled with her love for him, a love he was now rejecting.

"No," Hilary replied honestly. "I have tried, but it is not in me to be content with house parties and balls, with aristocratic companions, luxurious homes, and fashionable clothes. I admit my selfishness. I want to be judged not by my ranking in Society, but for myself. I want a marriage that is stronger than passion, more enduring. A love that sustains itself because it is built on friendship."

Fitch continued to stare at her. She had put his back against a wall. If he accepted what she said, then he was giving free rein for her to meddle for the rest of their lives. It was the principle of the thing that kept him silent a moment longer. She had overstepped her bounds.

He set his mouth in a hard, grim line. "Friendship demands respect, madame. What respect did you show me by breaking into my desk, by reading a journal that was never intended for your eyes, by sneaking off to London behind my back?"

"I can offer no defense for my actions other than the truth. I have loved you," she said, looking him square in the eye. "I have loved you with my body and my heart. I thought to strengthen that love, to understand what you would not tell me, but I know

now I was wrong to believe what I want can be gained without your cooperation. You are right—I betrayed your trust. For that I ask your forgiveness. As for loving you, I fear nothing short of death will serve as a remedy."

Unable to stand before him another moment with her soul stripped bare, Hilary turned and walked out of the library.

. She made her way upstairs, not stopping until she was in her room, behind closed doors. The house was still unusually quiet. There was no sound abroad except the chattering of birds, and the soft murmur of the breeze that drifted through open windows, singing a soft lullaby to the setting sun.

Hilary drew a shaky breath, then began to cry. There was no consolation to her tears, no healing to be found, but they fell nevertheless. They came fast and hard, wetting her cheeks before falling onto the bodice of her jacket. Throwing herself on the bed, she put her face into the bend of her arm and went on crying, not caring any longer if anyone heard her. Life had never weighed this heavily on her shoulders before.

An indescribable depression generated in the very heart of her, filling her whole being with anguish. It was like a shadow over the sun of a summer day, a thickening mist that refused to lift and evaporate.

She cried, not lamenting fate, or its twists and turns, but surrendering to them, unable to fight any longer.

When there were no more tears, she left the bed and walked to the vanity table. Without looking into the mirror, she poured water from a delicately made French ewer into a matching basin and bathed her face. Then, in a fit of sweeping passion, she threw the basin, water and all, at the wall, breaking it into shreds that littered the carpet.

The anger appeased the pain, but only for a moment.

Annie found her a few minutes later, kneeling on the floor, gathering up the broken pieces.

"Oh, no, mum. I'll do that. You might cut yourself."

"I broke it," Hilary said wearily, "and I fear it's beyond repair."

" 'Tis only a vase," Annie replied patiently. She had met Raskett in the hall and been warned that the balance of the day could prove awkward. Whatever had happened between the earl and Hilary had taken its toll. Her mistress looked ready to faint. "Get yourself a nap, mum. I'll finish here, then go down to the kitchen and bring up a tray. A nice cup of tea and a slice of Cook's ginger cake will set you right until supper."

Hilary relented, but only because there was nothing else she could do.

Fitch took a moment to organize his thoughts. How foolish of him to think that he could take a wife and continue on with his life in civil convenience, that he could, as Hilary had so aptly put it, keep a portion of himself in reserve.

It seemed as if all the tension, all the questions, all the guilt and tangled feelings of the past few years were piled on his shoulders. He had done what he thought to be right, but instead of giving Hilary a secure and contented future, he'd given her pain. And she had given him a challenge—could he forget what was so deeply embedded in his mind?

Could he separate the soldier he had been from the man he was?

Fitch sat at his desk with Hutton's journal in front of him. He didn't have to open it, didn't have to read a single word, for the memories to come flooding into his mind like stormy water over the brim of a dam. His mind jumped from one to another, from that first day in Calamita Bay to the Battle of Alma, then to Inkermann and Balaclava—he hated them all.

Had he a pistol at hand, he would shoot at them like targets on a firing range, one after the other, and count corpses as he'd done for real during the war. But it wasn't the nature of ghosts to be easily laid to rest.

Nineteen

Winslow Hall was a hubbub of activity. Cook was at her work, basting the wild ducks bagged that morning and delivered to the kitchen. Raskett was supervising the footmen as they set the formal dining room to rights. Valets and maids were rushing up and down the back stairs, making sure that the needs of their respective lords and ladies were met. There were gowns to be pressed and feathered fans to be fluffed, shoes to be polished and jackets to be brushed. It was Lord Ackerman's birthday and the event was to be celebrated in grand style.

Hilary turned away from the balcony railing where she had been staring out at the gardens. The air was warm and clear and twilight was encompassing the open slopes of the neighboring fields. The cheerful afternoon sun had vanished, and with it, the smile she'd painted on for her guests. It had been ten days since she'd returned from London—ten long, wretched days.

After the first day she had struggled with anger and frustration, swearing that she would find some

way to exist without the love she needed, vowing to
endure the circumstances of her marriage, thinking that life would eventually become bearable
again. But the opposite was proving true.

She loved Fitch as much today as she had yesterday and the day before, and she was miserable.

Her gown was lying on the bed. A beautiful rus-
set red taffeta with a black underskirt and a lacy
front panel, it represented just how far she'd come
since the evening she'd knocked on the door of
Fitch's London residence.

Hilary frowned at the sight of it. She was obliged
to put it on and to appear as she had earlier in the
day—as if she had everything her heart desired.
Yet, for all that she had gained by marrying the
Earl of Ackerman, she felt as if she had nothing.
Certainly not her husband's love and respect. Fitch
would never be hers, despite his obvious affection
for Lizzie and his desire for other children.

Since their last confrontation, life had taken on
the attributes of a theatrical production—feigned
smiles and polite conversation for appearances'
sake. Fitch had not entered her bedroom, nor had
she dared to breach the threshold of his room.
Once, during the course of an evening meal, she
had tried sharing his interest in the estate, partly
because she, too, loved the land as he did, and
partly because it was something she could speak of
that had no connection to her ill-fated trip to London. He had returned her remarks, but his tone
had implied an impatience to say as little as necessary.

Lizzie consumed his attention; he was devoted
to her since the accident, spending each afternoon
in the nursery. Behind the closed doors of Hilary's
private thoughts, jealousy was beginning to reign.

She wanted a portion of the affection Fitch was showering on his daughter. Even in the midst of her current misery, she could feel his child growing inside her.

She longed to share the news with him. Even more, she longed to be held in his arms, to feel the warmth of his body beside her during the night. She mourned the lack of his company, but Fitch was far from ready to share anything with her, least of all his affection.

Annie came into the room, her smile reflecting the festive atmosphere assigned to the evening. "Oh, mum, we've got to get you dressed."

"Yes, I suppose we must."

It took longer than usual to dress Hilary's hair, which was obeying its natural stubborn nature, but once Annie had the last pearl-tipped pin in place, she announced that Lady Ackerman was truly beautiful.

Hilary walked to the mirror and assessed her appearance. "I don't feel very beautiful," she confessed. "Truth be told, I'd rather sleep than spend the evening entertaining."

"It's the babe," Annie told her. "Makes a lady want to sleep the day away."

"So you know."

"I'm yer maid," she replied simply. "Is that what you're givin' his lordship for a birthday present? The news that he's goin' to be a father."

Hilary shook her head. "I'm not sure when I'm going to tell my husband, though it's inevitable that I do tell him. He's certain to notice sooner or later."

"*Sooner* would be my guess," Annie said. "He's not a man who misses much."

Then how can he not know that my heart is breaking?

Hilary thought. During the tumultuous days since she'd returned from London, she'd gotten dressed each day, sat calmly during their shared meals, spoken softly when she wanted to scream, and cried herself to sleep at night. Nothing in her life had prepared her for the invisible, slashing pain that was tearing her life apart. She took a moment to reminisce on how the evening might be spent, then shook off the regret before it could weigh her down.

"I'm going to look in on Lizzie," she told Annie. "She's certain to be giving Mrs. Crombie fits this evening. It will be no easy task to get her settled down for the night."

Leaving the room, she made her way to the third floor and the nursery without encountering anyone. Hilary opened the nursery door, hoping to find Lizzie asleep. What she found was Fitch tucking his daughter into bed. He was dressed in elegant black and looking very handsome. Despite the hurt and frustration that had dominated her feelings for the last ten days, she felt her heart gripped by love.

Realizing that she hadn't as yet been seen or heard, Hilary remained where she was, standing in the shadows near the door.

"Now, not another word out of you, young lady. And I do not want to find you peering over the railing again. It's very dangerous, and I shan't want to call Dr. Taunton away from his dinner to bandage your broken head should you topple over."

"Yes, Papa," Lizzie said. "Can I go outside tomorrow? I haven't seen Hattie, and Mr. Pony is missing me something dreadful, I'm sure."

"I'm sure," Fitch chuckled. "As for tomorrow, I

will allow you a short visit to the stables, but only if you promise to stay tucked in this bed tonight."

"I promise." She hugged him around the neck. "I love you, Papa."

"I love you, too."

Lizzie gave his neck another tight squeeze, then leaned back against the pillows. "Will you love me after Aunt Hilary has her baby?"

Hilary's breath caught in her throat. Fitch had his back to her so she couldn't see his reaction. He voiced it a second later.

"What baby?" he asked suspiciously.

"The one Annie told Mr. Raskett that Aunt Hilary was going to have. I heard them talking about it this afternoon. I was supposed to be napping, but I wasn't. I closed my eyes and pretended to be sleeping to keep Mrs. Crombie from scolding me. Annie told Mr. Raskett that you were sure to love the baby."

"I'm sure I will," Fitch said. "I'm also very certain that I will continue to love you. Satisfied?"

Lizzie's curls set to bobbing. "I hope the baby comes soon. It's dreadfully lonely here in the nursery."

"Yes, well, I shall have to consult with your Aunt Hilary as to the expected date of arrival," Fitch said. He gave one of Lizzie's curls a gentle tug, then kissed her on the forehead. "Sleep well, pumpkin."

He turned away from the bed, took one step, and came to an abrupt halt when he saw Hilary standing just inside the door. "Madame," he said, his voice purposefully formal.

"My lord," she replied, just as politely. "I thought to say good night to Lizzie."

"Of course." He stood aside as she approached the bed where Lizzie was once again sitting up.

"How are you feeling, sweetheart?" Hilary asked, intentionally avoiding eye contact with her husband, who had decided to remain in the room. "Does your leg hurt?"

"It's itching," Lizzie told her. "Mrs. Crombie said that's because it's healing. I'm not suppose to scratch it. Papa's going to let me visit the stables tomorrow. I miss Hattie."

"I saw her this morning. Gilleon had her perched on his shoulder like a parrot."

Lizzie laughed before getting a very serious look on her face. "Are you really going to have a baby?"

"Yes."

"Will it be a boy or a girl?"

"There's no way of knowing," Hilary told her. "It will be a surprise for all of us. You like surprises, don't you?"

"Oh, yes, but I don't like waiting for them. When will the baby get here?"

"Early spring, I should think," Hilary replied. "Right about the time the Easter lilies are in bloom."

"We have guests waiting," Fitch reminded them. He offered his arm, and Hilary took it. The next few moments felt like a century. Once they were beyond hearing of the nursery, on the landing between the third and second floors, Fitch stopped.

"You are well?" he inquired.

His gaze was a poignant reminder of the intimacy that had created the child she was carrying. Despite the riot of emotions that threatened to erupt within her, Hilary managed to remain outwardly docile. "Yes, I am well."

She wasn't in the mood to discuss her pregnancy. She should feel some sort of happiness at this moment, but she didn't. All she felt was an urgent need to be alone, to find someplace where she could cry out her misery.

Fitch set his fingers beneath her chin and forced her to meet his gaze. "When were you going to tell me?"

"Later this evening. The news was to be an additional birthday present."

"It's a wonderful present." He reached for her hand and brought it to his lips. "I am *very* pleased."

Hilary closed her eyes, fighting the urge to throw herself into his arms. At some previous time she might have foolishly mistaken the emotion in his voice for love, but she knew better now. She'd not be fooled again.

"I hadn't expected otherwise," she replied stiffly. "An heir was one of the reasons you married, was it not? Let us hope the child is a son."

"I would be pleased with another daughter," he said, his voice low and soft. "There is still time to gain the son I require."

Hilary didn't comment. Suddenly she was angry, good and angry. Her husband was an intelligent man, but he had yet to learn that loving and being loved were more than physical satisfaction. True love was no fit of passion—it ran deep, to the very center of a person's heart.

"We have guests waiting," she said, turning her gaze away from him.

Fitch hid his disappointment. He remembered the closeness they had shared during the first weeks of their marriage, the walks in the garden, the long hours of conversation, and the nights filled with passion. And yet at the back of his mind there had always been other thoughts and memories intruding into the contentment.

He wasn't surprised that Hilary was turning away from him now. She was a remarkable woman, possessed of an honesty which he greatly respected. These past weeks had wrought a change in her, and Fitch blamed himself. The hurt in her voice, the pain in her eyes, burned through him as hotly as a brand. The news of their child washed away every reason he had given himself for holding on to his pride, and yet he couldn't find the words to renew their relationship, to undo the damage.

A house full of guests didn't help matters. He couldn't invite her to take a walk in the garden, or better yet, sweep her into his arms and carry her into the master bedroom, bolting the door against any intrusion. Social obligation demanded they walk down the stairs arm in arm and attend those who had traveled to celebrate his birthday.

"You are right, madame, we have guests waiting." He offered his arm again. "But the evening will not be so occupied with conversation and music that we cannot find time for ourselves."

Hilary looked at him for a brief moment, raising one eyebrow. "My lord?"

"It is my birthday," Fitch replied. "I will have the first and last waltz of the evening with my wife."

For a moment the joy that he might actually regret the things he had said to her gave Hilary hope, but she forced herself to suppress it. She'd not cry herself to sleep again tonight. She would not.

The ballroom was illuminated by massive chandeliers that hung from the domed ceiling, their crystal prisms twinkling and sparkling. Classical columns supported the musicians' gallery.

It was a crush. People pressed together, men and

women, some moving about the room greeting their friends, others seated along the perimeter of the dance floor.

The entrance of Lord and Lady Ackerman began the party, and within minutes, Hilary was surrounded by people. Lord and Lady Granby had chosen not to attend, since Catherine was within days of delivering their first child. But Lady Waltham was there, as was Rebecca, Lord Sterling's wife, and, of course, Lady Felicity Forbes-Hammond.

Dressed in her customary dark gown, Felicity breezed across the room to offer Hilary her hands. "I say, my dear, but you've done wonders tonight. It's been years since I've attended a party at Winslow Hall, but the servants appear as well practiced as if they do this sort of thing on a weekly basis."

"It's Mrs. Ellerbeck and Raskett to whom you must give the credit," Hilary insisted. "I did little more than compose the guest list, and even that required their help. I know few people in Buckinghamshire."

Fitch was still at her side, though his attention had been drawn away by his friends and more manly conversation. Evelyn joined Felicity in congratulating her on such a fine turnout. She complimented Hilary on her gown, then smiled sympathetically. "It's a bit overwhelming, isn't it? Finding oneself an aristocratic lady."

"Yes," Hilary replied, knowing she couldn't keep her comments limited to solitary words all evening. She did her best to keep at least a thread of conversation going until the musicians took their place.

"The first waltz," Fitch said, turning toward her. "If you will excuse us," he said to the others, "I will begin the evening with my wife in my arms."

The intimacy of the remark brought a flush of

color to Hilary's face and an understanding chuckle from Lord Sterling. Rathbone laughed brusquely. Everyone thought Fitch besotted with his wife— only his wife knew better.

Her husband's arm snaked around her waist and Hilary was led onto the floor. The feel of Fitch's body in close proximity to her own brought back a flash of memories—the way they had made love, the hours spent sleeping in each other's arms. Dear God, Hilary thought, how can I go on when his slightest touch arouses such feelings in me?

"The Duke of Morland has requested the honor of giving your birthday toast," she said as they moved about the floor.

"I'm sure it will be something profoundly wise," Fitch replied. The hand holding hers tightened for a moment. "Tell me, madame, if you were to give the toast, what would you say to me?"

Hilary glanced around her, noting that many of the guests were watching them with keen interest. Nervously, she wondered at her husband's question.

Her hesitation in answering him brought another question.

"Is there nothing upon which I can use advice?"

"Upon what should I advise you, my lord?" she retorted, becoming irritated by his shifting moods. "You are a successful man, celebrating his birthday among his friends. You have just been informed that the child you want has been conceived. What more could I add?"

"Surely there is something?" he asked in a soft, teasing voice that confused her even more. His arm wrapped possessively around her as he negotiated a graceful turn. Hilary followed instinctively.

Taking up the verbal gauntlet, she leaned her

head back so she could look into his eyes. She was startled by the emotion she saw swimming in their dark depths. "I have no advice to give you, other than to say that for a successful, intelligent man, you can't see the forest for the trees."

He laughed, causing even more heads to turn their way. "In need of spectacles, am I?"

"I fear so." She rendered the verdict with stolid British seriousness. "I also fear that I will never be the wife you expect me to be."

The music ended, but Fitch continued to hold her. Applause went up around them when he drew her to him and kissed her. "That, madame, is a fact that I have finally accepted."

Hilary didn't know whether she should be embarrassed or insulted, so she decided to be both. "Really, my lord," she hissed under her breath. "Married couples do not make a show of themselves."

The corners of his mouth curved up in the familiar, cocky smile that she loved so well. "'Tis my birthday. I shall do as I please this evening."

She gave him a gentle push before turning to face their guests. Rathbone, the rascal, was grinning from ear to ear. Felicity was smiling, as was the Duke of Morland. Hilary suspected Fitch was very proud of himself, and why shouldn't he be? He had exactly what he wanted.

Keeping her promise to herself that she would not allow the night to end in tears, Hilary spent the next hour mingling among the guests, greeting acquaintances from London, and making new friends among the gentry of Buckinghamshire. Mrs. Taunton, the doctor's wife, was a small, birdlike woman with a timid voice who seemed surprised that the Countess Ackerman found her company enjoyable. They sat on a small settee near the doors that opened onto the terrace. Hilary was conscious that her husband kept sneaking surreptitious glances in her direction and she wondered what he was thinking.

As she went about playing the role of hostess, Hilary couldn't set aside the emotions constantly changing inside her: anger, confusion, frustration, doubt, respect, love. They plagued her endlessly, even after the orchestra put away its instruments for supper, a lavish collation served in the formal dining room.

Being escorted to the table by the Duke of Morland, Hilary managed the spontaneous conversation required of her, but she knew her husband was watching and that her agitation did not escape him. She managed a weak imitation of a smile when their gazes met, while inside, her stomach churned and she prayed she'd not embarrass herself by getting sick.

Fortunately, she managed the meal with the poise and artful conversation that had carried her through the first half of the day. Only a few more hours and she could retire to her room.

But the evening wasn't over yet. After dinner the ladies retired to the parlor for a brief respite while the men sought out the conservatory, which had been opened for the night. The library was much too small to house all the male guests; with its windows opened wide, the conservatory served for brandy and cigars just as nicely.

It opened onto a covered terrace at one end, with steps leading down to the main gardens at the other. At another time, and with his wife as his sole companion, Fitch would have enjoyed strolling among the shrubbery and flower beds, but on this occasion he was forced to be patient.

The men took the glasses of brandy Raskett presented to them and sat down. The duke, who claimed a chair that had once been favored by Fitch's father, fixed his gaze on the man he had just toasted in the dining room. "You seem to have settled into marriage well enough," he said. "The kiss you gave your wife hints at it."

"I haven't settled nearly as well as I should," Fitch admitted. "But I will. Hilary's going to have a child."

"Heirs!" Rathbone remarked, shaking his head. "They're popping up everywhere these days." He raised his glass, regardless of his personal sentiments. "Congratulations."

"Thank you." Fitch began to relax. He was among friends. "Tell me, Your Grace, how does a man go about admitting that he's been a bloody fool?"

The remark gained the prompt attention of Sterling and Waltham, who had been conversing about some political matter.

"Just how bloody a fool have you been?" Sterling asked.

"A real horse's ass," Fitch confessed. "I didn't realize it until tonight." He looked at his closest friends. "Thought perhaps I might draw on your expertise in the matter."

"So it's the little wife," Rathbone chuckled. "Can't help you there."

"The last time Evelyn was upset with me, I . . ." Waltham smiled at the memory. "I used my imagination, so to speak. By the way, she's pregnant. I'm hoping for a daughter this time."

"Egads! I hope it's not contagious." Rathbone downed his brandy, then waved for Raskett to bring him another. "Marriage and babies. It's all so predictable."

"Not nearly as predictable as one might think," Fitch corrected him with a devilish smile. "On the contrary, I'm discovering that marriage makes a man's life impossibly unpredictable."

Twenty

"You have the look of an impatient man," Waltham said to Fitch later in the evening.

"Do I?" He sipped his champagne, but he couldn't keep the gleam from his eyes.

"What has you looking so blasted pleased with yourself?" his friend prompted. "An hour ago you were seeking advice. Now, you're looking as if you've found every possible answer to every possible question."

His friend was very close to the truth. It was remarkable how clear things could become when a man opened his eyes—and his heart. Since the day Hilary had returned from London and confessed that she'd meddled in his private affairs, Fitch had spent most of the time being furious.

But tonight, he was watching from the sidelines, using the time to look back across his life, searching for some meaning, only to find very little. His life had changed since the war, but it had changed even more dramatically since meeting his daugh-

ter and Hilary. He had finally found the one thing
that mattered. He had found love.

Or, more precisely, it had found him.

To have Hilary at his side was to have vigor and
determination mingled with tenderness and love.
To have her as his wife was to have passion and
laughter and contentment unlike any he'd ever
known. She was his future. She and Lizzie and the
children that would soon begin to populate Winslow
Hall. His past meant nothing compared to the possibilities of his future.

"I've never told her that I love her."

Waltham blinked, then looked down at his own
glass of champagne as if to blame the bubbling
liquor for his lack of hearing. "What did you say?"

"I've never told Hilary that I love her."

"No wonder you referred to yourself as a bloody
fool," Waltham mumbled, then added more co-
herently, "I found myself caught in the same trap.
Damn near did me in. Not a course of action I recommend."

"I intend to remedy the situation," Fitch said.
"Just as soon as I can get her out of this bloody
ballroom."

"Excellent idea. Shall I tell the orchestra to play
a final waltz?"

Being a true friend, the marquis did just that.
Fitch handed his empty glass to one of the dozen
footmen circling the ballroom, then went in
search of his wife.

He found her, chatting with Felicity. Fitch knew
Hilary would resent his solicitousness should he
suggest that they retire upstairs, leaving their guests
to spend the remainder of the evening as they
pleased.

"My lady," he said, after excusing the interruption to Lady Forbes-Hammond, "the last waltz is upon us. I would dance it with you."

Hilary accepted his outstretched hand. From that moment on, having won her concession, Fitch plotted his next move.

His wife looked at him with intense surprise when he remarked that she looked tired and inquired if she'd been sleeping well. "I have not," he said, giving her no time to answer. "The master bedroom has been lonely without you. I would ask that you join me there tonight."

Hilary took a moment to reply. She had been privately congratulating herself for enduring the evening when Fitch had sought her out and claimed the last dance. Having no idea that he'd come to his senses, she replied somewhat bitterly, "Am I to be rewarded with the pleasure of your bed, my lord? A token night of passion in exchange for a fruitful womb?"

Fitch felt the intended sting of her words, knowing they were well deserved. A babble of voices surrounded them, but he kept his own tone low, so as not to draw any undue attention. "I cannot be anything but pleased by the news of our child," he told her. "As for seeking your company, it is not out of reward but out of necessity. I find myself at odds without you. A ship lost at sea."

Hilary's face remained carefully expressionless, but the color in her cheeks increased. He pressed his cause by drawing her indecently close. They continued to dance through the mute interval, Fitch's body responding as he pressed himself closer, Hilary's breathing coming in quickened gasps as he swirled her around the floor.

"I love you," he announced a moment later. "I love your body and your mind, your laughter and your wit. I love your spirit and your soul. Forgive me for not saying it when I should have."

Hilary stumbled, forcing him to come to a halt. She looked up at him, into eyes bright with what could only be the truth. She smiled, then fainted dead away.

"Bloody hell!" Fitch swept her up and into his arms. Raskett appeared out of nowhere. "Find Dr. Taunton," he was told.

The crowd parted as Fitch walked from the room with Hilary in his arms. Waltham met up with him in the foyer. "I say, shocked the lady into a swoon, did you?"

"The devil take you, Waltham."

His friend only laughed.

Dr. Taunton came hurrying their way, his medical bag at the ready. "Has her ladyship been ill?"

"She is with child," Fitch told him.

"Congratulations. Let's get her upstairs. I'm sure there's nothing to worry about, your lordship. Just the strain of the evening. Lots of guests, stuffy rooms, and all that."

Fitch marched up the stairs, past a shocked Annie, and into the master bedroom. He placed Hilary in the center of the bed he was determined she'd sleep in from this night on, then went to the windows and pushed them open.

"Fresh air is always an excellent idea," Dr. Taunton said, before turning to Annie, who had followed them into the room. "Pour some water into a basin, then request some tea from the kitchen."

"Will tea help?" Fitch asked after Annie went scurrying from the room.

"It can't hurt," the physician told him. "And the maid looked as if she needed something to keep her busy."

Fitch laughed. "I'm the one in need of an occupation, sir. What can I do?"

"Cool her forehead with a damp cloth and wait," he was told. "She'll come to in a few minutes."

"Then what?"

"Make her comfortable and see that she gets a restful night's sleep."

When Hilary finally began to stir, Fitch breathed a sigh of relief and a quick prayer. He stood by while Dr. Taunton asked a few personal questions, then instructed her ladyship that she needed to sleep when she was tired, eat when she was hungry, and cry when the need came upon her. All were as natural as breathing in her condition. "From what you have told me, the babe should be born before Easter. A brisk walk each morning is advised, as long as it causes you no distress."

"I'm feeling much better," Hilary said sheepishly, which wasn't at all like her; but then, fainting dead away in the middle of a ballroom wasn't her usual fashion, either.

Had the champagne punch caused her to hallucinate? Had Fitch really said that he loved her?

Annie delivered a tray of tea, then hovered until Fitch assured her that he could see his wife put to bed without assistance. Dr. Taunton took his leave as well, saying that he would call again in a few days.

"I shall put you to bed properly," Fitch said once they were alone. He made it sound very casual, as if they hadn't been sleeping in separate rooms for the last ten nights.

Hilary watched as he shed his jacket and waistcoat, then untied his cravat. He tugged the length of white silk from around his neck, then tossed it aside. It missed the chair he'd aimed for and fell unheeded to the floor.

"Would you like a cup of tea now?"

"No." She sat up, intending to make her way to her own room, but he pressed her gently back onto the bed.

"You will remain where you are," he said. "And I shall play the lady's maid."

His hands were gentle as he unhooked her gown, then helped her out of it. When she was down to a silky chemise and her stockings, Hilary reached for the coverlet.

"No," Fitch said, his voice thick with emotion. "I want to see."

"There's nothing to see." Hilary slapped at his hands. "We have guests. You should go downstairs and attend to them. Please pass on my apologies."

"A wife does not have to apologize for her pregnancy."

"They must be thinking—"

"They will think that I am a concerned husband looking to the comfort of his wife. And I will see what my child is doing to you," he said more firmly, then smiled. "It isn't as if I haven't had you naked and in my bed before, madame wife."

"I do *not* wish to be naked and in your bed."

Hilary soon realized that she might as well be talking to the teapot Annie had fetched from the kitchen. There was no deterring Fitch's hands. Nor the pounding of her heart once he was looking down at her. His gaze was as gentle as moonlight, his hands just as tender as they settled on her body. He smiled at her then, and Hilary couldn't stop the love that flowed from her heart.

"What you said . . . It wasn't just because of the babe?"

He lowered his head and placed a kiss on her abdomen. The feeling of his mouth on her skin caused Hilary to hold her breath. She was smiling and tearful and altogether confused by everything. Did the man love her or not?

"Your breasts look larger," he said, examining them with delicate caresses that made her nipples harden. "Can you feel the babe?"

"Not yet." She had vowed to stop hoping, and yet, he was being kind and charming and looking at her as if the words he had spoken in the ballroom might indeed be true.

Oh, please God, let them be true, she thought, then flinched as he rubbed his thumbs over the crowns of her breasts. They had become overly sensitive these last few weeks.

"I will find you a comfortable rocker," he said, speaking as if she lay naked beneath his hands every day and it was nothing out of the ordinary for him to be scrutinizing her body as if he'd never seen it before. "Perhaps two rockers. You will sit in one, nursing our child, and I shall sit in the other, watching you. Then again, it might be best to employ a cabinetmaker to make one very large rocker. I will hold you on my lap while you suckle my son."

He spoke with a tenderness so profound it tugged at Hilary's heart. She began to weep, silent tears that couldn't be stopped.

"None of that," Fitch said, drawing her into his arms. He held her while she cried, her cheek resting against his shirt. Soon she was sobbing, helplessly emotional as he whispered that he loved her, had loved her for quite some time, and had been too stubborn to admit it.

"But no more," he said as he pulled the pins from her hair. Seeing it fall to cover her naked shoulders was a sight Fitch vowed he'd not soon forget.

Then he began to talk, to speak to her in a soft,

low voice. The memories weren't pleasant ones, but their telling removed the last barrier, the last secret between them.

"I was twenty-three when I went to war. As young and cocky as they come," he said. "It's difficult for a woman to imagine the power and status that comes to a brash young man the first time he puts on an officer's uniform. I thought myself quite the fellow."

"Beth told me you were the most handsome man she'd ever seen."

"Yes, well, I didn't prove the officer and gentleman I should have with her," Fitch admitted sadly. "But that was then, and this is now, and I will say what needs to be said so that we can go on with our lives. I would have you happy, madame, if you will allow it."

"I want both of us to be happy."

"No man could be happier than I am at this moment." He combed his fingers through her hair. "Let me remove some of my clothing, then I shall join you in bed. We will talk, and then, if you aren't too tired, I would like to make love to you."

Hilary watched as he undressed, realizing that pregnancy hadn't quenched her desire for her husband. Her blood was humming with anticipation when he finally pulled back the coverlet and settled them both beneath it. Tucked into the curve of his arm, she smiled up at him.

"Say it again."

"What?" he teased, his dark eyes glittering with mischief. "That I realize you will never be a docile, biddable wife? That the rest of my life will be consumed by keeping you in line? And our children. I can tell from Lizzie's current shenanigans with a certain pony cart that my offspring are going to be strong-willed and totally unmanageable."

"Say it."

"What? Oh, yes. I love you."

She laced her hands around his neck and pulled him down for a long, delicious kiss. "Do you know how long I've waited to hear those words? There were days when I contemplated shouting my love for you from the rooftop on the chance that you might hear and echo the words back to me."

"As I said, our children are going to be a stubborn lot. You may blame their father."

They kissed again, long and slow, as if for the first time. A few minutes later, Hilary laid her cheek against his chest so she could hear his heart beating. "You don't have to tell me about the war if you don't want to," she said. "It's enough that you're willing to speak of it."

"There are some things that I shall never speak of to you, but you were right when you said that I'm holding on to the past. Perhaps talking will free me from the burden. If not, then I ask that you understand and not take offense when I seek time alone."

"As long as you love me, I won't be jealous of memories."

"Were you? Did you think I'd rather spend my time in the library drinking myself into oblivion than be with you? If so, then you are the one who couldn't see the forest for the trees, madame. No man in his right mind, and I am in my right mind regardless of what you may have thought after reading Hutton's journal, would prefer drink to the warm, willing arms of his wife."

Another kiss was required. It was several minutes later before Fitch spoke again. Hilary quickly realized that she had not understood the situation as fully as she'd first thought. Settled into the warmth of her husband's arms, it was difficult to imagine what he could picture so clearly in his mind: the cold of a Balkan winter, the noise of the battlefield, voices thick with pain, burial pits overflowing with bodies.

"All the able-bodied men, enlisted and officers alike, helped to dig graves," Fitch told her. "I remember standing with my shoulders hunched against the wind. The ground was frozen and we had to use picks before we could use shovels. I hated digging the graves. I felt as if I were deserting my men. They were English. They deserved to be buried in England's soil, in proper cemeteries where their families could visit and mourn and leave flowers."

Hilary hugged him close. "You did what you had to do."

"After the battle at Alma, I realized that war has a way of twisting a man's mind into thinking, even if only for a short while, that suffering and death are acceptable, even admirable. But they aren't. No matter the cause, war should be the last resort. There is no glory in dying, no courage in causing the death of others. There is only the emptiness that is left behind, the graves of your comrades, the cries of their widows and their children. And yet, fool that I was, I was proud to wear a uniform."

He sighed deeply. Even now, like a learned response, the anger came back to him—the fury and frustration of it all. "Balaclava was the worst for me."

Hilary held him close as he forced the words out. Words that choked and stumbled because they'd never been spoken aloud before.

"I told Dr. Chetwynd that I thought James Hutton a brave man," she whispered. "So are you, my love. Brave and gentle and kind."

Fitch looked down into eyes filled by tears. He put his chin into the curve of her shoulder and his cheek against the softness of her unbound hair. He gave himself over to her loving arms and smiled. "I realize now that we can look deeply into our hearts and never understand why we feel what we feel. If I could, I might have realized that it was foolish to be afraid to admit that I loved you. I thought instead that I could make a place for you in my life, and I in yours. A space where we could fit together and still remain apart."

"You're right, it was a foolish notion," Hilary said. She held his face between her hands, then kissed him—a soft, delicate kiss. "All I ask is that whatever happens in our lives, we share it. The good and the bad. The sunshine and the storms."

"You turned my life upside down, then set it to rights again," he told her. "I love you. This evening on the staircase when you told me that you were going to have my child, I wanted to weep with joy. I can't imagine my life without you. Nothing I do means a damn if you aren't with me—if I can't go to sleep at night with you in my arms, if I can't open my eyes in the morning to find you beside me. My heart is worthless without you."

"Not worthless, my love, never that."

He made love to her then, his hands as gentle as moonlight on her body, his voice a sultry whisper as he told her how much he'd missed having her beside him.

"I won't break or bruise," she told him when the pace was too slow for her liking.

"You will be bruised," Fitch said, laughing as she

tried to push him over so she could ride him the way he liked. "I am too hungry to lose control. You will lie under me and I will be gentle."

"Not too gentle," Hilary coaxed with a smile.

He wasn't. Soon they lay exhausted, their bodies satisfied, their hearts content.

Fitch talked again, not of the war this time, but of the feelings of inadequacy that had returned with him from the Crimean, and of the awful day when he'd sat by his brother's bedside and watched Christian's life slip away.

"I'd lost men in battle, but losing Christian was like losing a part of myself. We were brothers in the best sense of the word. And to find myself the earl—it was the strangest thing. At times, it still feels strange."

The windows were open, the night warm. A distant flash of lightning told of an approaching storm, but her husband didn't seem to notice. He was holding her close, and it felt wonderful.

"You are a good man," Hilary insisted. "A decent man. I know it, as do your friends. James Hutton knew it. It was the reason he had the journal delivered to you. He knew you would understand where others might scorn him or call him a coward."

Fitch realized in that moment how little he had told Hilary about himself, and how much of her love had been built on instinct and faith. "I had been thinking about going to London myself, but you, my conniving little wife, beat me to it."

"You should go, when the time is right. I think Hutton's journal might be helpful to Dr. Chetwynd. He's a compassionate man. A caring man. I will tell you now that I requested Mr. Pratt to sell the house in Nottingham and donate the money to Debrow House."

"You are the most remarkable woman," he said, smiling down at her. "I knew it that night in London when you demanded that Raskett stop dallying and let you inside. By the time you had left, I was plotting to marry you. Oh, I know, Lizzie was supposed to be the real reason, but there was more to my scheme than even I wanted to admit."

"We are both stubborn, are we not?"

He kissed her, then rolled over and drew her across his chest so they could sleep heartbeat to heartbeat. "Ah, we are both stubborn, madame. Our children are sure to be hellions."

"They will be *our* hellions," Hilary said. "And we shall love them all the more for it."

"And each other," Fitch assured her. "We shall grow old and crotchety together."

"Old, yes, but not before I've seen Paris and the Great Pyramids and Athens and Rome and—"

Fitch hushed her with a kiss, which led to another kiss and another kiss and . . . Finally, they slept, their dreams sweet and undisturbed by the stormy night.

Author's Note

The Crimean War was fought between Russia and the allied powers of England, France, Turkey, and Sardinia. Its cause was inherent in the Eastern question; the pretext was a quarrel between Russia and France over guardianship of the holy places in Palestine.

The fighting centered around the port city of Sevastopol, which was heavily fortified by the Russian fleet. After a long and bloody siege, the city fell and the war ended.

Though short, lasting from 1854 to 1856, the Crimean War had an impact on the English citizenry that was not to be forgotten.

It was the first war to be photographed. Newspaper photos of the battlefield brought the misery of the harsh winters and bloody fighting into the homes of the English people in much the same way that television brought the atrocities of Vietnam to those of us in America.

The only bright light to be shed on this conflict was cast by Florence Nightingale, whose work drastically cut the mortality rate of the British soldiers who fought for Queen and country.